a corrupt land.
an intolerant people.
an unnatural gift.

"Your magic recognizes you," Gersalius said.

Elaine stared at the glowing shield. It recognized her? She tried to be afraid but wasn't. In fact, she wanted to touch it, to run her fingers along its gleaming surface. It was akin to the desire she'd had to touch the wizard's hands in the kitchen. Magic called to magic. Her own magic called most strongly.

"Touch it," he said softly.

Elaine reached out to it. Her hands tingled with its nearness. Her skin was stained violet, as unnatural-looking as the elf's, but she didn't care. Her hands sunk into the glow with a gush of sparks that flared and blinded her. She took a sharp breath, and as the air went into her lungs the spell went into her skin. She felt it being absorbed, like a tingling lotion. Then it was gone.

From *The New York Times* best-selling author of the Anita Blake Vampire Hunter novels comes *Death of a Darklord*, the story of a girl struggling to realize her gift for magic without compromising the love and lives of those around her.

Ravenloft™

The Covenant

Death of a Darklord
Laurell K. Hamilton

Vampire of the Mists
Christie Golden

I, Strahd: The Memoirs of a Vampire
P. N. Elrod

To Sleep with Evil
Andria Cardarelle

Tapestry of Dark Souls
Elaine Bergstrom

Scholar of Decay
Tanya Huff
(October 2007)

Laurell K. Hamilton

Death of a Darklord

Ravenloft™
The Covenant

Ravenloft™
The Covenant
DEATH OF A DARKLORD

Published by Wizards of the Coast, Inc. RAVENLOFT, WIZARDS OF THE COAST, and their respective logos are trademarks of Wizards of the Coast, Inc., in the U.S.A. and other countries.

Printed in the U.S.A.

Cover art by: Jon Foster and Matt Adelsperger
This Edition First Printing: September 2007
First Trade Paperback Printing : July 2006
Original Paperback First Printing: June 1995

9 8 7 6 5 4 3 2 1

ISBN: 978-0-7869-4734-8
620-21577740-001-EN

U.S., CANADA,
ASIA, PACIFIC, & LATIN AMERICA
Wizards of the Coast, Inc.
P.O. Box 707
Renton, WA 98057-0707
+1-800-324-6496

EUROPEAN HEADQUARTERS
Hasbro UK Ltd
Caswell Way
Newport, Gwent NP9 0YH
GREAT BRITAIN
Save this address for your records.

Visit our web site at www.wizards.com

Dedication

To Baby Bird,
who died during the writing of this book.
This was the first book written without her
sitting on my shoulder.
A bit of magic has gone out of my life.

ONE

THE SKULL LAY ON THE DESK, GLEAMING IN THE THIN daylight. It was an old piece of bone, clean and dry. It looked human until held in one's hands and studied. The eye sockets were huge, almost as large as the empty sockets of a bird of prey. The strong yellowish teeth had sharp edges; the front teeth were fangs, made for piercing flesh, spilling blood.

Calum Songmaster remembered what the thing had looked like when alive. Something between a hawk and a wolf . . . and what was left of the human the creature had once been. The man had been Gordin Smey, a friend, a comrade in battling evil. With the remnant of his mind, his decency, he had begged Calum to kill him. Calum had done it. Gordin had been a good man, with a wife and children. He had slain many monsters, but in the end, he had become one of them. Calum had saved the skull as a reminder that the land of Kartakass could corrupt anyone.

Now he lay in the soft, smothering folds of his sickbed, propped up on one side like a spitted piece of meat, save that pillows and quilts kept him in place, not a sharp metal spike. But he was just as trapped. He stared at the skull of his long-dead friend and envied him his quick death.

Calum had survived all of the evils of the land for eighty years. It was a prodigious age to have lived to see. Foul sorceries, monsters, beasts, robbers, evil people of every description; all these he had survived. Old age was not so easily escaped.

For many months, he had been unable to sit at his desk and work. The pain of the disease that ate him alive made every movement agony. He had been a tall, strong man, but now he was a bundle of sticks clothed in loose skin. He had made his housekeeper take down the room's mirror. Calum no longer recognized the fragile creature that stared back at him. In his mind, he was still young and strong, but mirrors did not lie, so he banished the truth-telling glass. The pain, and what he could see of his own body, were reminder enough.

His friends had come to visit him. His good friends. It was why he was propped up on his side, so he could see them without having to move, without having to let them know how much even the smallest movement hurt him. His housekeeper was very good about such things. He planned to leave her what money he had and this house. After twenty years, she deserved more, but it was all he had. Fighting evil was not a particularly lucrative business.

His friend, his best friend, sat in a chair by the bed. Jonathan Ambrose was not really young, nearly fifty. There was gray in his beard. His hair had receded to a thin circle that he kept closely cropped. The fashion was to let what hair you had grow long, but Jonathan never cared much for fashion. He wore a simple brown robe, clean, well mended, but utterly plain. No one had worn ankle-length robes in a decade, but Jonathan found them comfortable. His clear blue eyes looked at Calum. His face was smooth, calm. There was no hint of horror or pity. For that Calum was grateful, but at the same time, irritated.

To look at him, Jonathan might have been here on any afternoon. No special reason. Calum wanted to shout, "Don't you know I'm dying, dying?" He was angry his friend could face him without showing the pain he saw on so many faces. So why had he gotten angry at his housekeeper for crying this morning?

Calum gave a careful sigh. Nothing would satisfy him. He wanted everyone to know and pity his pain, and yet not to show it. He wanted to have his cake and eat it, too.

"I am a cranky old man," Calum said in a scratchy voice that he barely recognized as his own.

Jonathan smiled that same gentle smile. "Never."

Calum had to smile. His anger dripped away. He was suddenly glad of the visit. Was it a sign of death's nearness, these swift-changing moods? He was not sure; he had never died before.

In a smaller chair, the one his housekeeper usually sat in to do her sewing while she kept him company, sat the only other woman he allowed to see him like this. Tereza was tall, lithe, dark. Her thick black hair spilled round the strong bones of her face like a raven cloud. Her short, more fashionable tunic was scarlet, breeches brilliant emerald green. One black-booted foot was drawn up on the chair, her strong hands holding the knee. The belt from which hung short sword and pouches was black but much embroidered, so that it gleamed rainbowlike. Jonathan had a matching belt that made his brown robe look even more ordinary. But Tereza had embroidered the belts herself, and Jonathan always wore his.

There were no more chairs, so Konrad Burn stood behind the others. He was the youngest, not even thirty yet. His face had been handsome once. His green eyes were fierce and glittering as jewels, brown hair caught back in a leather thong. He was dressed all in brown leathers of varying shades that matched the tanned skin of his face and arms. An axe rode at his hip, a small shield on his back.

Calum was not sure what had changed in the younger man. His face was still clean-shaven, still unlined, but the life had gone out of it. It was as though he were looking at a bad painting. The picture looked like a man, but there was no life to it. Only his eyes gleamed, alive with . . . rage: Konrad's wife and partner had been killed two years ago.

Calum's body was dying, but his mind and spirit cried out for life. Konrad's body was healthy, strong, but mind and spirit waited for death. Konrad lived, but it was only the motions of life. Calum would have changed places with Konrad in a moment. He wondered if the younger man would have agreed.

"The twins are just outside," Jonathan said. "They would love to see you."

"No," Calum said. "They are too young to see how all life ends."

Jonathan touched his hand, gently, gripping the fragile flesh. "It does not always end like this, Calum. You know that."

"Then why is my life ending like this?" Tears warmed his eyes. He tried not to blink, holding his eyes very still. Crying would have been the final embarrassment. His voice came out choked, and he hated it. "I was a good man, wasn't I, Jonathan?"

"You *are* a good man, Calum." Jonathan squeezed his hand as if holding tight could make it better.

Calum clung to his hand, the betraying tears spilling down his cheeks. "I have fought the evil of this land my entire life. I have nothing to show for it."

"You are Calum Songmaster, one of the greatest bards in all

of Kartakass. You could have been a meistersinger of any city or town if you had wanted it. You could have lived in luxury, but you chose to serve the entire land. To search out and destroy evil, to serve the brotherhood."

"But what have I accomplished, Jonathan? The evil still rules this land. The brotherhood is no closer to discovering who, or what, poisons Kartakass. The corruption will outlive me, Jonathan. It will grow and thrive, and I will be dead."

"How can you say that?" Jonathan asked.

Tereza knelt by the bed. "You are Calum Songmaster, who defeated the vampires of Yurt. Calum Songmaster, the slayer of the great beast of Pel. Savior of Kuhl."

Staring into the woman's dark eyes, Calum could almost feel his blood flow stronger. For a moment, he was not an old man at the end of life, but the young Calum, the Songmaster who had tamed the wilderness and slain his share of monsters.

The pain roared up from his belly. A red, burning tide of pain that filled his body, ate his mind. Nothing was left but to ride the pain. He was aware, dimly, of Jonathan's hand still gripped in his own, but the rest of the world vanished while he writhed and trembled with pain.

He lay, weak and gasping, on the bed. Sweat covered his body. His hand was limp, too weak to hold Jonathan's. Jonathan cradled the trembling limb in both his own. A single tear trailed into his beard.

Tereza stared at him; no tears, but he could see a deep roaring pain in her eyes. He had never seen her cry. He was glad this would not be the first time.

Konrad had moved away from the bed, arms folded, angry eyes uncertain.

"Let me bring in the others. They need to say good-bye." Jonathan's voice was a soft rumble.

"No," Calum gasped. He wanted to shake his head but was too weak. Talking was almost beyond him. "Young ones . . . should not . . . see me . . . like this."

"They love you, Calum."

"Frighten them . . . it will frighten them."

Jonathan didn't argue. He raised Calum's hand very gently to his face, pressing the weak flesh to his beard. "You have always been a good friend to me, Calum. I wish I could help you in this."

"Do you want me to get the housekeeper?" Konrad asked. "She said the doctor should be here soon." He seemed eager to leave, to have something to do besides stare at the end of all flesh.

"Go," Calum said.

Konrad did not wait to be told again. He went, his strong body striding across the rug, easily, unthinkingly. Calum hated him for it.

The housekeeper entered. She was a small, round woman, her hair in a neat bun on top of her head. She smiled at the room as if nothing were wrong. In front of company, she was always her same cheerful self. In private she had mastered his moods. When he needed sympathy, she gave it. When he needed matter-of-factness, she gave that. Calum had come to love that plain, smiling face.

The doctor followed at her heels. He was a small, bent man with a mane of snow-white hair. If Calum hadn't been twenty years older, the doctor would have seemed old. His face was professionally cheerful. Nothing showed on his face or body unless the doctor wished it to. Calum envied his control.

"I'm afraid this visit has to end," the doctor said. "I need to see how our friend here is doing."

Jonathan pressed his hand. "I'll see you soon, Calum."

Calum stared into his friend's face and said nothing. They both knew this might be the last time.

Tereza kissed him on the forehead, her lips soft. Her long hair fanned around his face, smelling of herbs: pinenut, rosemary, sweet lavender. She said something in her native tongue—musical, guttural. A blessing, or a curse. It mattered little now.

Konrad had never returned. He did not come to say good-bye. He had never been comfortable around the sick. Calum hadn't wanted any of them to see him like this. Now the fact that Konrad had not said good-bye filled him with rage.

The doctor's visit was mercifully short. He left another bottle of medicine, for what good it would do, and took his leave, still pleasant, still smiling. What do you say to a patient who is dying, and everyone knows it?

The housekeeper followed the doctor out. She would escort all his friends outside, see they had a cup of tea or a sandwich. Her glance paused on the far wall and the brilliant wall hanging that covered it. Her pleasant face flashed in disapproval, then she closed the door behind her.

In the silence of the room the tapestry pulled back with a soft, thick sound. A tall, slender man stepped from the hidden door. His hair was long, thick, and so black that the weak sunlight made blue highlights on it. His fashionably trimmed beard and mustache framed a handsome face, a face for women to sigh over in romantic moments. He had a graceful, swinging stride that brought him gliding into the room. He always entered a room as if it were his very own private chamber, as if everywhere he went he carried his own kingdom in a circle around his body, so that he was always at home, always at ease.

His shirt was white silk, covered by a scarlet vest with gold embroidery. His pants were also scarlet, stuffed into gleaming black boots. A basket-hilted sword rode his hip. A matching scarlet hat dangled from one hand, complete with a sweeping black feather. Rings glittered from his long fingers. "Well, Calum, what do you think of your young friend now?" His voice was a rich tenor that held something of the music he made his living from.

Calum lay on his back now, pillows cradling him so that he could only stare at the man. "Have you come to whisper more lies in my ears?"

"Not lies, my friend, promises."

"What do you want of me, Harkon?"

"Your help." Harkon Lukas laid his hat on the foot of the bed and leaned against the bedpost.

"I cannot betray my friends."

Harkon smiled, even white teeth flashing in his dark face. "I have given you my word that none of the others will be harmed. I want only Konrad Burn."

"Why him?"

Harkon shrugged, a somehow graceful gesture in the tall man. "He is handsome, young, strong. He can travel beyond the boundaries of Kartakass. You can't tell me as a bard you have not longed to escape this prison, to travel the lands your friend Jonathan and his gypsy woman have told you of. The songs I could sing. The tales to be told. Think of it, Calum."

"But to possess his body? What becomes of Konrad when you are inside him?"

"He will get my body." Harkon glided round the bed. Calum could only move his eyes to follow the bard.

"Don't you think my body a fair trade for his?"

Calum did. It was a strong, healthy body. "If you truly command some . . . sorcery that will switch your body with Konrad's, but not harm him, why not ask him? Why not gain his cooperation?"

"Do you really think he would agree? Our angry, honor-bound Konrad?"

"Would anyone agree?"

Harkon sat on the edge of the bed. The slight movement caused Calum to gasp. "Oh, my friend," Harkon said, "did my sitting down hurt you?" He leaned forward, face concerned.

Calum did not want the man to touch him. He knew the concerned looks would fade instantly, chased by whatever new emotion entered Harkon's mind. He was as changeable as a spring wind, and as reliable.

Harkon's hand fell back into his lap. He smiled down at Calum. "I have found a body for you. A man in his twenties. Tall, strong, in perfect health, handsome. He is a little shorter than you were in your prime, more slender, perhaps a shade more handsome, though."

To be young again, with his whole life ahead of him, but with the knowledge of a lifetime. To leave his pain-ridden body behind. To live. It was a tempting offer, and Harkon knew that. Why make it otherwise?

Calum licked his lips. "And what happens to this young man if I take his body?"

"Why, he gets yours."

"He would die, horribly."

"As you are dying?" Harkon stood and paced back to the foot of the bed.

"Yes!"

"But, Calum, don't you plan to give the boy back his body? As I plan to give Konrad back his?"

He stared into that handsome face. The dark eyes mocked him. He knew if he once tasted the freedom of a new, healthy body, he could never return to this dying shell. He wanted to live. But at what cost?

"No one would agree to such a trade."

"But I assure you, the young man will."

"How could I come back to this pain once I was free?" Calum closed his eyes. "I would not be strong enough to make such a choice."

"Then make another choice, Songmaster," Harkon said.

Calum opened his eyes to find the tall man looming over him. "What do you mean?"

Harkon smiled a knowing smile. "Keep the body, be young and healthy. Escape this dying husk."

"What of the young man?"

"He will die."

"You would kill him?"

The smile deepened. "I would do anything to see you whole and well again, my friend."

"You don't plan to give Konrad back his body, do you?"

Harkon gave a soft, purring laugh. "Oh, Calum, do you really want to know?"

No, Calum decided, he didn't, not really. What they were speaking of was evil. As evil as anything he had ever fought against. He did not know why Harkon pursued this sorcery, but he, Calum Songmaster, would not steal the youth, the life from another human being. It was monstrous.

Harkon leaned close, eyes drowning-deep, face solemn. "This might be our last visit together, Calum. Not that I wouldn't want to see you again, my friend, but you may simply not be here. If you die before our bargain can be struck. . . ." He leaned close, whispering against Calum's skin. For a moment, he thought the man would kiss him gently, as you would kiss a sick child. He was loathe for those lips to touch his skin. But only Harkon's words burned along his wrinkled cheek. "Once dead, I cannot help you."

A wave of bone-grinding, stomach-churning pain burned upward from his rotting gut. When the pain receded, he lay gasping, staring up into Harkon's dark eyes. "What do you need me to do?"

Harkon smiled. "Very little, my friend, very little."

Calum waited for the words to fall from Harkon's lips, waited to hear how he would betray his friends, how he would destroy one of them utterly. They both knew Konrad would not survive in Harkon's body. He, too, would be killed. Calum knew that, and yet he listened.

His eyes flicked to his desk and the waiting skull. He felt he should apologize to the bones of his friend for forcing them to watch his fall. He had fought the land his entire life, but finally it had offered him something too precious to refuse. He wanted to live. And he was willing to pay the price, even if that price was another person's blood. Even if someday he paid with his soul. For a second chance, even that seemed a small price to pay.

two

ELAINE CLAIRN KNELT IN FRONT OF THE HUGE KITCHEN fireplace. The children crowded close to the fire, not for the heat, but so they would not miss any movement of Elaine's hands.

Her small, slender hands passed in front of the flames. Fingertips fanned wide, so close to the flames that heat wavered round her skin. She stared into the leaping fire, the backs of her fingers touched together. Her wrists rolled outward like flower petals unfolding. From the tips of her fingers images leapt. A tiny, perfect man walked in the flames. It was as if the fire were a wavering mirror on which the man moved.

He wore a white fur cloak, hood thrown back to reveal shoulder-length yellow hair. The hair was the same pale gold as the winter sunshine. He strode through knee-deep snow, surrounded by black, winter-bare trees. Elaine whispered, "Blaine."

A second man walked with him, wearing a three-cornered hat tied round his head by a multicolored scarf. The grip of a great two-handed sword showed at his coat collar. "Thordin."

The two men passed under a tall tree. It was the great tree. It towered over the rest of the forest like a giant among dwarves. Lightning had killed it two years ago, but its dead, bare branches were still a landmark for miles around.

The branches twitched, swaying above the men. A branch began to move downward, a slow creaking effort that had nothing to do with wind. The skeletal bough reached for Blaine, icy twigs like daggers.

Elaine screamed, "Blaine!" She plunged her hands into the flames, as if she could grab him to safety. Flames licked at the sleeves of her robe. Her hands touched the back of the fireplace, flames flaring around her shoulders, her face.

Hands jerked her backward. "Elaine!" A blanket was wrapped around her smoking clothes, smothering the flames. Her skin was untouched, protected by her magic. The cloth was not so lucky. "Elaine, can you see me? Can you hear me?"

She blinked upward; a bearded face came into focus. The smell of stew hung thick and heavy in the air. Fresh-baked bread was cooling nearby. Elaine lay in the familiar clatters and smells of the kitchen and knew she was safe. But others weren't. "Jonathan, help them. . . ."

"Help whom?"

"Blaine, Thordin."

"I saw the vision." The cook's oldest son, all of eight, knelt beside them. The other children were huddled at a safe distance.

"What did you see, Alan?"

"The great tree attacked them."

Jonathan stared down at Elaine. "True?"

"Yes."

Jonathan did not argue that it was impossible. "Do you think your warning was in time?"

Elaine clutched at him. "I don't know."

"What do you want me to do?"

"Find Blaine and Thordin."

"Child, by the time we could reach them by the great tree, the fight will be won or lost."

Her hand dug into his tunic. Her eyes were wild. "Then bring back the bodies for burial."

He stared down into her face. He nodded slowly. "That we can do." Jonathan turned to the boy, Alan. "Find Tereza, tell her what you saw. She will know what to do."

The boy ran from the kitchen.

"Can you stand if I help you, child?"

Elaine nodded.

Jonathan stood, lifting her to her feet as he moved. The cook, Mala, pushed a straight-backed chair near the fire. Jonathan eased Elaine into the chair, tucking the slightly charred blanket tighter around her. Mala shoved a mug of hot tea in Elaine's hands.

Elaine cupped her hands around the mug, as if it had no handle, warming her cold hands. She was always cold after a vision. Blankets, hot drinks, bed for an hour or so, then she was as good as new. But today she had seen her brother's death. No, he wasn't dead, she'd know that, but he could be hurt, dying, while she sat and sipped tea. She didn't have time to recover, to be weak. She had to know what had happened to Blaine.

Tereza entered the kitchen bundled against the cold. A second coat was flung over one arm. She held the clothes out to Jonathan without saying a word.

He slipped into the coat and tucked a hat over his bald head.

"I'm going with you," Elaine said.

Jonathan froze in the middle of pulling on mittens. They both looked at her.

"You haven't recovered from your vision, Elaine. You aren't well enough to travel," Jonathan said. He finished tugging on his mittens.

"He's my brother, all the family I have. I have to go."

"You will slow us down," Tereza said.

"The fight will be over before anyone can help them. Jonathan said so. If that's true, then it doesn't matter if I slow you down, does it?"

It was very sensible. A great deal more sensible than Elaine felt. She could taste her pulse in her throat. If Blaine were badly hurt in the cold snow, they couldn't get to him in time. The cold would finish what the animated tree had started. So why was her stomach tight, her heart pounding? She had to go with them. She couldn't just wait here in the kitchen, safe.

Tereza looked at her husband. "Jonathan?"

He looked almost embarrassed. "It is the truth."

"We can't wait for hours. The wolves might find them, dead or alive."

"We can go now," Elaine said.

The look on Tereza's face said she doubted that, but she didn't argue. "I will fetch your coat. But you must be ready to go when I get back. We won't wait on you, Elaine." She left, back very straight. Tereza did not like waiting on anyone, especially if she thought it was silly.

It wasn't silly, but Elaine knew she couldn't explain that to Tereza. Or to Jonathan. Blaine would have understood, but he was out in the snow, bleeding, hurt, or worse. Elaine tried to convince herself she would know if her twin brother were dead, but somehow she didn't believe it. She wasn't sure. Once the vision was past, she didn't trust her feelings. Feelings lied; they could tell you what you wanted to believe, not what was true.

"She doesn't mean to be harsh with you." Jonathan took off his knit cap, a sheen of sweat already glistening on his forehead.

"I have to go, Jonathan." She gulped the last of the tea. It was too hot and burned the roof of her mouth, but she needed the warmth. She really didn't feel well enough to go. Tereza was right, but it didn't matter. Elaine would go. She had to go.

Tereza returned with a white fur cloak that was the twin of the one Blaine had worn in the vision. Elaine glanced up. She wasn't completely sure she could stand, but the look on Tereza's face was plain. Either Elaine got up now, or she didn't go.

Mala appeared, lifting the tea mug from her hand. Her face was neutral, but her eyes held concern. She was always on the side of the children, everybody's children.

Elaine gripped the chair arms and levered herself upward. The muscles in her arms quivered. The blanket slipped to the floor. Her hands stayed on the chair arms for a moment, then she pushed free. She was forced to grab the back of the chair to keep from falling. Her legs shook underneath the long skirts. It took all her resolve just to remain standing, one hand hooked onto the heavy back of the chair. She wasn't sure she could walk, let alone ride to the great tree.

Tereza held the white cloak out, at least three strides from the chair. She made no move to step closer.

Jonathan stood uncomfortably between them. "We have no time for games, Tereza."

"No time at all," she said.

Elaine took a deep breath and let it out slowly. She drew two more deep breaths, trying to calm the jerking muscles, willing the weakness away. She let go of the chair back, fingers lingering on the wood. Tereza sighed. Elaine dropped her hand to her side. Her legs were braced, and she hoped no one could see how they shook, but she was standing alone.

Tereza held the heavy coat at arm's length, arm steady as if the coat weighed nothing.

Elaine took a step forward on her shaking legs. She didn't fall down. She took one step, then another, then another. Her hand gripped the fur. Tereza laid the coat gently across Elaine's arms. She smiled at the girl, a smile that made her dark eyes shine.

"If you want to go that badly, we can throw you over a horse. No need to wait."

Elaine smiled. "Thank you."

"Bravery should always be rewarded."

Jonathan smiled broadly. "Virtue is its own reward."

Tereza slapped him on the shoulder. "Don't you believe that."

Konrad came into the kitchen, bundled to the eyes against the winter cold. "Are we ready to go?"

Tereza helped Elaine on with the heavy cloak. She tucked Elaine's pale yellow hair into the hood. "Let's go find Blaine and Thordin."

Elaine felt the smile fade from her face.

"You did your best, Elaine. You warned them."

"I went to the fire as soon as I felt the call."

"I know you did."

Konrad shrugged a small pack over his cloak. It held the healing herbs and bandages.

Tereza wound a multicolored scarf around her black hair. It was very similar to the one Thordin wore. Elaine and Blaine had learned how to knit last year. They had made gifts for everyone.

She had made Tereza's scarf of red and black stripes. Blaine had made Thordin's of every color yarn he could find, perhaps thinking the warrior wouldn't wear it, but he wore it proudly. The joke had ended up on Blaine. He had made matching mittens as a sort of apology, though the mittens were the same awful colors as the scarf.

"Let us be on our way," Jonathan said. His plain knit cap, in his preferred shade of brown, had been Elaine's handiwork. The scarlet cap Blaine had fashioned for Konrad had been eaten by a monster, or so Konrad claimed. He wore a fur hat with a thick, striped tail that curved over his collar.

Mala held out a small pack to Tereza. "Something warm for them. Good food's better than medicine sometimes."

She took the pack with a smile. "Your food, anyway."

Mala blushed at the compliment, and turned back to her stove. The smell of vegetable stew filled the kitchen as she raised the lid and stirred the pot. The back of her neck was still red with the compliment.

The kitchen door opened; snow swirled inward. A gust of icy wind sent the herbs in the rafters swinging. The fire flared, sparks dashing up the chimney. The stableman stumbled in and shook snow from his boots.

"Here, now, you're getting snow all over my clean floor." Mala stalked forward, shaking a spoon that dripped stew.

The stableman gave a loud, braying laugh. "Now, Mala, you know I can't come in through the front door. Where else am I suppose to shake the snow off me boots?"

She pointed the spoon at him, stopping the gravy-covered tip a finger's breadth from his nose. "Harry Fidel, you don't know your place."

"Me place is in this sweet-smelling kitchen as often as I can manage it."

Tereza interrupted, "Are the horses ready, Harry?"

He grinned at her, bringing his nose perilously close to the spoon. "Aye, that's what I come to tell ye."

"Then we can go," Konrad said. They all moved toward the door. The cold air pushed at them like an invisible wall. Elaine drew her cloak as tight about her as she could, shivering in the frigid air. She glanced back as Jonathan closed the door. Harry the stableman was sitting in the straight-backed chair, snowy boots stretched out before the fire.

Mala was dipping out a bowl of stew, her anger apparently gone. She had been widowed for nearly two years. Blaine said the two would be married before the end of the year. Elaine wasn't so sure, but then Blaine was better at guessing about people. He always joked that his hunches were better than her visions about matters of the heart. Her visions tended to be more violent than romantic.

The wind whistled just outside the door, picking up the crystalline snow, flinging it into the air. The icy crystals stung Elaine's face. She jerked away from the wind. The movement threw her hood back, and her hair streamed across her face, blinding her. The cold wind made her gasp. She struggled to pull her hood back in place. Strands of hair clung to her suddenly icy skin.

What warmth the tea and blanket had put back into her body the wind stole. Elaine stood in the snow-swept courtyard, swaying on her feet.

Tereza was suddenly beside her, taking her arm. She didn't ask if Elaine was all right. She just began to lead her toward the stables.

Elaine stumbled; only Tereza's hands kept her upright. "You need to go back inside, Elaine."

She tried to say, no, but no sound came out. She finally shook her head.

Tereza pulled her inside the warmth of the stable and leaned her against the wooden wall. "You can't go like this."

"You said . . . you could throw me . . . over a horse."

Tereza frowned. "I didn't mean it literally."

Elaine just looked at her, too shaky to do much else.

"What's wrong with her?" Konrad asked. He was already checking the horse's harness. Konrad always checked the horses, even though Harry was never careless. Konrad trusted nothing and no one.

Elaine remembered him before the death of his wife. He had smiled, even laughed. He had trusted others to do their jobs. Now he was a dour man who seemed to believe in nothing. His wife had been killed by an ambush, by betrayal. They never knew who had betrayed them. Blaine said that was what bothered Konrad the most, that someone they had trusted had betrayed them.

Elaine wasn't sure, but she knew something had died in Konrad. Some spark of warmth had gone to the grave with his wife.

Elaine's mare was a large, broad-hipped gray horse. Blaine said the mare looked like a plow horse, but Elaine was not the rider her brother was, so she was glad of the docile mare. A horse that would walk quietly all day, her broad hooves surefooted, her patience endless. It was on her broad back that all the children first rode.

Tereza helped Elaine mount the mare. She leaned over, hands grasping the stiff mane, cheek pressed against the smooth hair of the neck.

Tereza smoothed back the hood, touching her cheek. "Your skin is cold."

Elaine stayed slumped against the horse. She was so cold. The only warm parts were her eyes, where hot tears were forming. "Lead the horse."

Tereza shook her head but didn't argue. She slipped the reins over the horse's neck and mounted her own horse, reins trailing between.

"Is she well enough to go?" Jonathan asked.

"No," Tereza said, "but she's going."

Konrad made some negative sound, but not too loud. Arguing with Tereza was a time-wasting thing. The outer doors opened, and the horses moved forward. Elaine felt the horse move under her, but the cloak had fallen forward, forming a dim cave round her face. She saw nothing but a small sliver of ground. She closed her eyes, and even that vanished.

The wind slapped against the heavy cloak. Tiny tendrils of frigid air snaked under the fur, icy fingers searching her clothing, seeking her skin. Elaine knew it wasn't that cold. Winter, yes, but not a blizzard, not a killing cold. Even so the cold touched her everywhere and her skin seemed to freeze. Tears froze on her cheeks. It was as if the vision had leeched away all warmth, all protection from the chill. The cold seemed to know and to be hungry for the touch of her skin. Each breath was a painful pull of air.

The horse's hooves shushed through the powdery snow, and its swinging gait rolled underneath her. She clung to the warmth and movement as the cold sapped her with invisible mouths. There was nothing left in the world but the cold and the rhythm of the horse. In a small distant part of her mind Elaine wondered if she were freezing to death. No, she was so cold. Didn't you grow warm before you froze to death? The bones of her face and hands were more open to the air; they ached with cold.

She must have fallen asleep because the next she knew, they were struggling up a hillside. If they were in the hills, they had to be close. Elaine raised her head. She felt the wind smack her face, but it wasn't colder. She was already as cold as she could get. She couldn't open her eyes. She tried to raise a hand to touch them, but her hands seemed frozen to the mane. She settled for rubbing her eyelids against the back of her hands. Ice crystals had formed from the tears, gluing her eyelids together.

She blinked painfully into the winter dusk. They were in the forest. Bare, black-limbed trees surrounded them. The horses struggled through the blowing snow on what used to be a wagon track.

Elaine worked to sit up and found she could. The cloak blew backward, exposing one side of her body. It didn't seem to matter. She could see the great tree looming over the lesser trees. They were almost there.

A full, shimmering moon rode above the naked trees. The wind blew the snow in swirls and eddies across the road, and dry snow hissed against the boughs. The snow had stopped falling; only the wind kept it moving, hurrying it along on dry hissing bellies, to crawl through the trees.

Konrad's horse pushed forward, raising plumes of snow. He rode out of sight. If anyone had asked him to scout ahead, Elaine had not heard it. The only sounds were wind, snow, the creak of frozen limbs, the creak of the saddle under her.

Blaine was just ahead, close, so close. Elaine tried to form a prayer, but the cold had frozen her lips, slowed her mind. She couldn't think of a prayer. She couldn't think of anything. There was nothing but the cold. All the fear, the panic, had squeezed down inside her into a small, cold center. Elaine knew she was terrified of what they would find, but she couldn't feel it. There was nothing but the cold buried down inside her, shutting everything away.

A shout came over the snow, ringing, echoing. The horses began to jog as fast as they could in the dry, spilling whiteness. Elaine clung to the saddle horn with both hands. The mare was sluggish, not used to anything faster than a canter.

The great tree stood alone in a clearing it had made for itself. Its roots had choked the smaller trees, cleaning away the brush. Five grown men could link hands around the trunk. The branches that reached outward and moonward were as big around as small trees.

Clouds closed over the moon, leaving the clearing in gloom. Only reflected light from the snow filled the clearing, making it murky. Something hung from one of the naked limbs. Elaine couldn't make sense of it at first. Her eyes refused to see.

The clouds slipped away, bathing the clearing in silver light. The thing on the tree was black and heavy against the moon, arms flung awkwardly outward, one leg dangling toward the snow. The other leg was missing. A large dark stain splattered the snow under the tree.

Elaine screamed.

Tereza had dropped the reins. Her voice came soft on the heels of the scream. "Summer save us."

Konrad stepped out from the undergrowth on the far side of the clearing. "It's not Blaine, or Thordin."

Elaine stared at him. "Who . . . ?"

"They're back here. Hurt, but they'll be fine."

She didn't believe it. He was lying. If Blaine was alive, he'd come to her, hurt or not.

"Elaine, I'm all right." Blaine limped out of the bushes, leaning on Thordin's broad shoulders. He flashed his brilliant smile, the one that said everything was all right. The smile more than the words convinced Elaine.

She slid off the mare, falling to her knees in the snow. She tried to stand, to go to her brother, but the moonlit clearing whirled around her. Dark spots ate the moonlight. She fell forward into the snow. It clutched her face, filled her mouth and nose. Darkness swallowed her. And the darkness was cold.

tHRee

Blaine, wrapped in a quilt, slumped in his seat. A pillow was shoved against the back of the chair. Strips of cloth showed at the split sleeve of his left arm, and his leg was propped up on a small embroidered footstool. It had been the worst injury. Konrad had sewn the wounds shut, using herbal salve and bandages to protect them. Even a small cut could turn septic and cost a person his arm. Blaine trusted Konrad's battlefield dressings more than those of most doctors. Tereza had tried to get Blaine to go to his own bed, but he'd refused. He wanted to be there when Elaine awakened.

Elaine was always weak after a vision, but Blaine had never realized how weak. Her skin had been colder than the snow, cold as death. Only the rise and fall of her breathing had let Blaine know she was alive. Though blood had dripped down his arm and seeped from his leg, though the tree branches had torn his leg and he couldn't walk without help, it was Elaine who had nearly died.

He gazed down at his sister. Her pale yellow hair spilled out over the pillow. Elaine's face was like a mirror of his own. The bones were slightly more delicate, the eyes greener than his own blue, but the twins were still like two sides of the same coin. Their parents had been killed when they were eight; from then on, it had been just the two of them. They had survived for two years before Jonathan took them in. Two years with only each other to trust, to depend on. No matter how grateful they were to Jonathan and Tereza, they were each other's family.

He slumped lower in the chair, blue eyes fluttering closed, then open. He struggled to sit a little straighter in the chair. A sharp, stabbing pain ran up his leg.

Elaine's warning had come in time. He and Thordin had dived for cover, but the stranger with them hadn't understood Blaine's yell. He had been a villager from Cortton seeking Jonathan's help. They had been his escort, his safety.

When the tree grabbed the man, they had tried to help. But the tree hadn't felt pain, and where was a vital spot on a tree? No heart, no head . . . They had done their best, but the man was dead. He had screamed for a very long time before he died.

A small sound came from the bed—not a word, more a soft moan. Blaine straightened up. "Elaine?"

She moved under the heap of blankets, head shifting on the pillows.

He reached out, fingers touching her cheek. "Elaine, open your eyes, please."

She opened her eyes. A gentle smile touched her lips. It was the most beautiful smile he had ever seen.

"Blaine, you're all right." Her voice was soft, almost rough, as if her throat hurt.

"How do you feel?" he asked.

Her blue-green eyes blinked up at him. "I'm fine."

He smiled. "I don't believe you."

She glanced at his arm. "You're hurt."

"Konrad fixed me up. I'm more worried about you."

"Why?" She looked puzzled.

He smoothed her hair back from her forehead. Her skin felt blessedly warm. "We sent for a mage."

A frown line appeared between her eyes.

"You nearly died, Elaine. Your skin was cold as ice. We got you home and bundled you up with hot bricks, bed warmers, anything we could think of. But you stayed cold." He answered the question in her eyes. "We don't know what happened to you. Tereza sent for a mage. Even Jonathan agreed to it."

"He agreed to let a mage in the house?" Her voice held soft astonishment.

"We were all scared for you."

"But Jonathan doesn't allow mages inside the house. He almost put us out when he found out about my visions."

"Visions are not the same thing as real magic."

Elaine smiled. "I remember the arguments."

The household had been divided. No one really wanted a mage in the house, but neither did anyone want to turn two young children out. It hadn't been until Tereza sided with those who wished to keep the children that Jonathan had relented.

Jonathan Ambrose was a mage-finder. It was what he did, who he was. He had been a virulent antimagician. After he accepted Elaine and her visions into the household, he had become more understanding, not so quick to condemn everything supernatural as witchcraft. He accepted that Elaine could have unusual powers and not be evil.

Jonathan said Elaine had broadened his mind, and he would always be grateful for that. Without anyone saying it aloud, the twins knew they were loved.

"Is the mage here?" Elaine asked.

"I don't know. I've been here since they put you to bed."

"You're hurt. You need to rest, not sit in a chair."

He grinned. "Like you needed to rest in a warm bed after your vision, not go outside in the winter cold."

Elaine blushed. "I had to go."

"And I had to be here when you awoke."

Elaine reached her hand out to him. They held hands quietly, no more talking. They didn't need words.

There was a knock at the door. Konrad opened the door without waiting for an answer. "The mage is here. Does Elaine feel well enough to come downstairs, if we help her?"

"Why? Can't the mage come upstairs?" Blaine asked.

"Jonathan won't allow the mage out of the kitchen. He says just inside the back door is far enough."

"Do you feel well enough to go downstairs, Elaine?" Blaine said.

"I think so." She sat up carefully, arms bracing against the bed.

Blaine gripped her arm. "You're shaking."

"I'm not cold, but I feel weak. I'm not sure I can walk downstairs."

"Then I'll carry you."

"You'll be lucky to get yourself down the stairs," Konrad said. He stepped fully into the room. "I'll carry Elaine myself."

Blaine opened his mouth to argue, but he realized that Konrad was right. He might be able to limp down the stairs, but he'd never be able to carry anyone.

Konrad was already leaning over the bed.

"I'll need a robe," Elaine said.

Konrad straightened. "Of course. I forget sometimes that you're not a child anymore." He turned around in the room as if a robe would magically appear. Then he turned back to Elaine. "I don't see it."

"It's in the wardrobe."

Konrad moved to the tall, oaken wardrobe that stood against the far wall. He opened the carved doors. Clothes were neatly folded on the many shelves; dresses and a blue robe hung on pegs to one side of the shelves. He pulled the robe out and handed it to Elaine.

"Turn around, please."

"Blaine has only one good arm. Do you really think he will be able to lift you so you can dress?"

"I will dress myself," she said.

Konrad gave a soft snort. "You are too weak."

She clutched the robe in her arms. "Turn around." It was an order.

Konrad sighed, but turned his back, arms crossed over his chest. His straight back said plainly that he considered it all very silly.

Elaine raised herself on her arms, elbows locked. Her arms shook slightly with the effort. Her lips were a narrow line, breath held. The white gown she wore covered her more than some dresses Blaine had seen her in, but that wasn't the point. He didn't understand why a thick gown was more shameful than a low-necked dress, but it was to most women. Or at least to Elaine. He knew better than to argue.

He held the robe out so that one arm was partially open for her. Elaine leaned her back against the headboard, using it to prop herself up. She shoved one arm into the sleeve. He shifted as far as he could to tuck the sleeve on her shoulder. Pain stabbed up his leg. He fell back in the chair, gasping.

"If you would let me help, we could be headed downstairs by now," Konrad said.

"No," Elaine said. Her voice was loud, but breathy.

"Modesty is a virtue, Elaine, but this is ridiculous. Let me turn around."

"No!"

It began to dawn on Blaine, for the very first time, that Elaine wasn't this careful around any other man in the house, including the servants. Blaine was sometimes slow on such things, but once an idea hit him, it didn't leave. Elaine liked Konrad.

Blaine glanced from the man's stiff back to Elaine struggling into her robe. Konrad was a widower, able to marry again. He supposed that Konrad was handsome; Blaine had just never considered him in that way. Certainly not as a prospective husband for his sister. He'd never considered any man as that.

Elaine lay back, gasping, on the pillows, the blue robe pulled tight over her chest. Her blue-green eyes stood out fever-bright against her pale skin. Her light wavy hair fell around her face like a golden curtain. She looked almost ethereal. With a shock that went all the way down to his toes, Blaine realized his sister was beautiful. It was a shock, and almost frightening. How had he never noticed?

The question was, had Konrad noticed? He had never seen any sign that the tall warrior thought of Elaine in that way. Of course, until today he'd never thought of her that way, either.

"Can I turn around now?" Konrad's voice was thick with scorn.

Elaine seemed too tired to notice. "Yes," she said.

Konrad turned around. His darkly handsome face was set in a frown. Because he was looking for it, Blaine saw the wince in Elaine's eyes. It distressed her that Konrad frowned at her. Darn. That Konrad's opinion mattered to her that much bothered Blaine. It was silly, but he was jealous. The moment he realized it, Blaine pushed it away from him. He let it go. If the dour Konrad could bring his sister happiness, then who was he to complain? Of course, if Konrad hurt her, that was a different matter. Keeping one's sister safe was a brother's job, wasn't it?

Konrad pulled back the covers. Elaine drew the robe closed over her gown. Without being asked, he picked up her slippers from the floor and slipped them on her stockinged feet. It was a curiously intimate gesture.

He tied the robe's sash with abrupt hands, as though she were yet a child.

Two bright spots of color burned on Elaine's cheeks. She was careful not to look directly at Konrad's face; she couldn't bear to meet his eyes.

He lifted her in his arms, as if she weighed nothing. Elaine put her arms around his neck, face pressed against his shoulder. She looked pale and ill and lovely in Konrad's arms. And entirely too much at home for Blaine's liking.

"Can you make the stairs by yourself, Blaine? If not, I can come back up and help you down."

Blaine shook his head. "I can make it." He would make it down the stairs by himself, or with someone else's help. Blaine would have taken anyone's help in the house before Konrad Burn's, right now.

Konrad nudged the door open and walked out with Elaine in his arms. He never glanced back or asked again whether Blaine needed help. Blaine had said no. It would never occur to Konrad it might not be true.

Blaine levered himself up from the chair, hopping, leaning on the heavy frame. A sharp pain slapped him every time he jarred his injured leg. His arm hurt with a persistent, bone-numbing ache. A crutch with cloth wrapped around the top leaned against the wall. He grabbed it and placed it under his arm. It was his crutch, carved for his height. Monster fighting tended to be hard on a body. As Tereza said, they were all temporarily able-bodied.

Blaine hobbled out the door. Konrad and Elaine were out of sight down the stairs. He balanced a moment in the empty hallway, letting the pain in his leg subside. It hurt to stand with the leg dangling, but it hurt much more to move.

He stood, getting his breath back, preparing himself to hop down the stairs. It had been childish to refuse Konrad's help. He would pay for it in pain. But it was his pain, his privilege not to accept help from the man who made his sister's eyes flinch. He doubted Konrad even realized how Elaine felt. Blaine wasn't sure if that made things worse or better. Probably neither.

He balanced at the head of the stairs, one hand tight on the bannister. A deep breath, and he took the first step. The pain flared up his leg like fire. By the time he reached the bottom of the stairs, he would be nauseated, weak, and feeling almost as badly as Elaine. What price, pride?

Blaine hopped another step down, gritting his teeth to keep from crying out. He'd make the same choice again. A slow, unreasonable anger had settled in his heart against one Konrad Burn.

four

a strange man sat before the kitchen fire. His hair was white as snow, his face dominated by a yellowish beard and a beaklike nose. He smiled at Elaine, gray eyes gentle.

Elaine sat in a chair on the other side of the fire. Mala had put another cup of tea in her hands. The cook was a great believer in the restorative powers of tea.

The man was also sipping tea. A plate of cookies balanced on his knees. It was the treatment any guest would receive, except that most guests would have been seen in the parlor.

Jonathan stood in the middle of the floor, arms crossed, frowning, staring at the stranger. He stood like a guard. Apparently, the kitchen was good enough for this particular guest.

Tereza sat at the table with Konrad and Blaine. They were the audience. Whether they were here to see a real live mage or to witness what Jonathan would do in the presence of one was unclear. It was certainly going to be entertaining either way.

"I am Gersalius, a wizard. I am told you have some magic of your own, Elaine."

She glanced at Jonathan's scowling face. "I don't think of it as magic."

The mage settled back in the chair, one hand steadying the plate of cookies. "Then what do you call it?"

She shrugged. "Just visions."

"Tell me about these . . . visions," Gersalius said.

Elaine sipped the hot tea, not sure what to say. "Do you want me to describe them?"

"If you like."

She narrowed her eyes, trying not to frown. Jonathan was doing enough of that for everyone. But the mage was being . . . frustrating.

"What do you want of me?"

"To help you."

"How?"

"For someone who has magical abilities, you are very suspicious."

Elaine looked down. "I don't know what you want me to say."

"Enough of these word games," Jonathan said. "Can you help her or not?" He stood over them like a tall, disapproving cloud.

"Mr. Ambrose, if Elaine had fallen ill and you had called in a doctor, would you be telling him how to do his job?"

"So far, you have done nothing."

Gersalius sighed. "The girl has magic powers. She sparkles to the eye that can see it."

"She has visions; that is all."

Gersalius stood, tea and cookies in hand. "If you insist on arguing with me at every point, I cannot help her."

"Good, then go," Jonathan said.

Tereza said, "Jonathan." That one word held something hard, almost threatening.

Jonathan turned to her. "He has done nothing but speak in riddles since he entered our house."

"You have not allowed him to do much of anything, Jonathan."

"Elaine is not a mage."

"Jonathan," Tereza's voice was gentle but firm, "she nearly died today. It was her vision that nearly killed her. The visions are magic of some kind. We need to know what happened."

"She is not a mage," he said.

"And if she is?" Tereza asked.

Jonathan closed his mouth with an audible snap. He turned away from them all.

Elaine huddled in the chair, the tea forgotten in her hands. Would he send her away if she were a mage? Would she be cast out of the only home she'd known?

Mala came up behind her, placing her hands on Elaine's shoulders. "You'll not be sending her away."

"If we're not wanted," Blaine said, "we can go." His voice was warm with anger. He was struggling to his feet.

"Sit down, Blaine," Konrad said. "No one is sending Elaine away." His voice was very firm when he said it.

Elaine turned in the chair to see. Konrad's green eyes were sparkling, the lines in his face tight with anger.

Would he have been this outraged over anyone's leaving, or was this especially for her? Elaine's face lit with a heat that had nothing to do with the potential loss of her home.

Tereza stood up. "Jonathan, you had better make yourself very clear on this issue."

He spread his hands wide. "Well, of course, Elaine will stay, no matter what. This is her home." But there was something in his voice that made Elaine shrink against the chair back. A hesitation, as if he had more to say but left it unspoken. If she were indeed a mage, Jonathan would never make peace with it. Not really.

She didn't want to be a mage. The visions were bad enough.

"Sit down, Gersalius," Tereza said. "Jonathan and I were just leaving so you could get on with your work."

Jonathan opened his mouth to protest. She stopped him with a small gesture. "We need to talk, Husband. And the wizard needs to see to Elaine."

She rarely called him husband. When she did, it was usually the beginning of a quarrel, or at least a disagreement.

Jonathan stood very straight. "If you say so, Wife." Anger was plain in his voice.

"I say so." She left the room first, and he followed.

There was silence for a time, then Gersalius sat down and said, "Describe one of your visions for me, Elaine. Please."

Elaine sipped her tea. She didn't want to talk to the wizard. It wasn't just wanting to avoid strife. Jonathan had taught them well. Magic could be useful, but it was easily turned to evil.

"I don't want to do magic," she said softly.

Gersalius's smile widened. "Child, magic is not a choice. I have known men who wanted more than life itself to do magic but had not the talent. You cannot force magic into your body, nor can you rid yourself of it if it is a natural ability."

"I have seen people who bargained with evil things to gain magic," she said.

"That is not natural magic, Elaine. That is abomination."

"Magic is magic."

"Those are not your own words, child."

She stared down into her cup. "I don't know what you mean."

"Elaine, magic—true magic—is not intrinsically evil. It is like a sword. The steel itself has no leaning to good or evil. It is the hand that wields the sword that dictates whether it will be used for good or evil. The weapon itself is neutral."

"But . . ." She searched his face, trying to find something that was not there. She could sense no trace of evil about him. Elaine wasn't sure she had ever been around a wizard that didn't bear some taint.

"You can feel I mean you no harm."

"Yes."

"It is magic that allows you to detect whether I am telling the truth or not."

She shook her head. "I can't always tell who's lying and who isn't."

"With practice you could."

"Can you?"

He grinned. "Most of the time. There are those with greater powers than my own. They can fool me from time to time."

"Magic is unreliable."

"Everything is unreliable, from time to time."

A small smile flashed across Elaine's face before she could stop it.

"See, not so bad," he said.

Elaine swallowed the smile, but couldn't quite chase away the warmth that had accompanied it.

Mala refilled Elaine's mug without asking. She motioned to the mage. "Would you like some more, sir?"

"Yes, please." He held out his mug. He offered her the empty cookie plate, as well.

"Would you like some more sweets?"

"Some more of those excellent cookies would be quite nice."

Mala blushed and dropped a rough curtsey. It wasn't as though Mala weren't complimented on her cooking often by the entire household.

Elaine watched the plump cook hurry away. Did Harry the stableman have a rival? No, that was silly. Mala would know that Jonathan would never let a wizard court her.

Elaine's stomach clenched in a cold, icy knot. Would Jonathan be able to abide a wizard under his own roof? Even if it were her?

Mala returned with a plate of cookies for both of them. She set it on a little stool before the fire.

"Thank you, Mala," Gersalius said.

Mala giggled.

A mere thank you, and she giggled. Elaine had never seen the cook like this, not even around Harry.

Mala left to stir something at the stove. The back of her neck was red with a blush of pleasure.

Was the mage that charming, or was it a spell? Elaine wanted to ask but didn't want to embarrass Mala.

Gersalius sipped his tea and looked at Elaine. There was a twinkle in his eye that seemed to say he knew what she was thinking.

"Do you know what I'm thinking right now?"

"Yes, but it is not magic."

"How, then?"

He leaned forward, lowering his voice. "Your body posture was very disapproving when your cook catered to me just now. Your face is like a mirror, child. Every thought chases across it."

She frowned at him. "I don't believe that."

"You don't want to believe it," he said. "The thought that your thoughts, your feelings, are so easily read by a stranger frightens you."

She opened her mouth to deny it, but didn't. It wasn't so much the mind-reading mage that bothered Elaine, but the others. Did Konrad know how she felt? Did everyone? Was she that transparent?

"I am a very noticing kind of person, Elaine. Most people aren't, even people that see you every day. In fact, I have found, people that have watched you grow up are often oblivious to you. You know what they say, 'familiarity breeds invisibility.' "

"I thought it was, 'familiarity breeds contempt.' "

"Well, yes, maybe it was, but I don't think he has contempt for you, do you?"

"You are reading my mind," she said. She sat very straight, hands gripping her mug tight.

"Perhaps I am, a little. The fact that you are an untrained mage makes it easier for me. Strong emotions are also easier to decipher."

Elaine's hands trembled. Hot tea sloshed onto her skin. Mala darted forward, scooping the mug from her hands and dabbing at the spill with a clean towel. "Have you burned your hands?"

Konrad knelt beside Elaine's chair. He pressed a cloth to her hands. She started at the coldness. He had scooped snow into the cloth. "Cold is the best for a minor burn."

His hands enfolded hers, pressing the snow to her skin. Her chest was tight. The weight of his hands round her own chased the last of the cold from her body. Even with snow touching her skin, Elaine felt warm. She felt the warmth creep up her neck, and she knew she was blushing.

Konrad stared only at her hands, at his task as a healer. He never looked at her face.

Elaine's eyes met the mage's gaze. Gersalius was right, Konrad didn't know. He didn't see what a stranger had noticed easily.

"How do your hands feel?" Konrad asked.

She stared down at him. The blush had faded with knowledge that Konrad felt nothing when he touched her. When he'd carried her downstairs, the feel of his body against hers had thrilled her. To him it was just another task. Another sick person to be tended.

"They don't hurt," she said.

He nodded and stood, taking the cloth to clean it and set it to dry. He never glanced back.

"Do you want the tea, Elaine?" Mala asked.

Elaine shook her head.

Mala took the offending mug away. She didn't even flirt with the mage.

"Tell me of your visions," Gersalius said. His voice was gentle, as if he knew what she had just realized. Since he was reading her thoughts, he probably did know.

Her first reaction was anger. How dare he spy on her feelings? She opened her mouth to tell him to get out, to leave her alone, but the look in his blue eyes was too kind, his face too understanding.

"I would not hear your thoughts quite so clearly if I could help it. You give off your thoughts like the sparks from a fire. You shine, Elaine. You shine with so much talent. When I learned how old you were and that you had never been trained, I thought your abilities would be small. How else could the magic have stayed so controlled for so long?"

His face was suddenly serious. He leaned toward her, and

Elaine found herself moving closer to the mage. "The strength of your will is fierce, Elaine. You did not want to be a mage, so you squashed the magic down inside of you. You locked it away with pure, shining determination. If you could turn that strength toward learning magic, you would be formidable. And you would learn quickly."

From inches away, she stared into his eyes. He was whispering to her before the fire, a conspirator. His power glided over her skin like wind. The hairs on the back of her neck and along her arms rose. Her skin crept with it. She felt something inside herself flare upward, something neither fire nor cold nor anything she had a name for. Whatever it was, Elaine felt it pouring up through her body, responding to the mage's magic. Like calling to like.

Elaine took a soft, shallow breath. She'd been holding her breath without realizing it. Her fingertips tingled as if magic would pour from her hands. She had the urge to touch the mage, to see if the pull of magic was stronger with a touch. She suspected it would be. She wanted to touch his hand. Her skin ached with the need to see what would happen. With the need came the fear.

She crossed her arms over her stomach, hiding her hands against her body. They balled into fists, digging into her sides, as if they would burrow out of sight. It took all the determination Gersalius had spoken of not to reach out to the mage.

She sat back in her chair as far from him as she could get without standing up.

Gersalius leaned back from her, giving her room. "It can be stronger when mage touches mage. It depends on what sort of magic a person possesses. Yours, even more than mine, is a laying on of the hands, I think."

"How can you tell that?"

He shrugged, smiled. "It is one of my gifts to judge talent in others. Most mages can spot power and judge potential strength, but few can decipher the actual method the magic will choose to come out."

"The magic chooses the way it will come out?" She made it a question, so he answered it.

"Often. If you had been trained earlier, perhaps you could have chosen the path of your own power, perhaps not. But now the magic has made some of the choices on its own. Your visions, for one."

Elaine shook her head. "You make magic sound like a second being inside of me, with a will of its own."

"I do not mean to. It is not separate from you. It has no thoughts or feelings of its own." The wizard frowned, thinking. He smiled as if something pleasant or clever had just occurred to him. "Say you had a talent for sewing—not a learned talent, but something you were born with. You were born to be a seamstress, or a tailor. But you were never allowed to study sewing. Then one day you made a beautiful ball gown. A week later you made another even more lovely than the first.

"Now, if you'd been allowed to study sewing from a young age, you might have decided to sew ceremonial robes, or winter woolies, but because you left your talent unused, the talent chose to make ball gowns. You might be happier knitting shawls or designing simpler dresses for more modest occasions, but it is too late. Your sewing has decided to make party dresses for the rich."

He studied her face for a moment, as if trying to gauge whether his analogy was working.

"Why don't you know what I'm thinking now?" she asked.

His voice broke into a lovely grin. "Very good, Elaine, very good. When you drew away from me that last time, you closed off more than just your body. You closed your thoughts as well. It was neatly done. But I think the fact you so quickly figured out I could no longer read your thoughts is even more promising."

"But I don't know how I did it."

"Think to how your body felt when you drew back. Think of the sensations. What did it feel like?"

Elaine thought about that for a moment. Had it felt like anything? She couldn't remember. She had moved away from him physically, but had she done anything else? Elaine closed her eyes, trying to recall what it had felt like. The sensation along her skin had retreated when she moved backward. The magic itself had moved back with her, inside her. She had broken contact with Gersalius. She had closed off her mind and her magic to him. That was a comforting thought.

She opened her eyes.

"Tell me," the mage said.

Elaine told him what she had felt.

"You have a wondrous grasp for the basics. What a pupil you would be." His face was eager, as if he had just this minute invented her.

"What would it mean to be your pupil?" She was amazed at her own question. Was she really contemplating studying magic? Yes, she was.

"The more time you could spend with me, the faster you would learn. The faster you would be able to control your powers."

"Would I need to move to your home?"

"You would be most welcome, or I could move here. I would be willing to do that. Under normal circumstances with someone as quick to learn, I would teach from her home. I would not willingly separate a young mage from her family and friends."

The thought sat unspoken between them: these were not normal circumstances.

"Jonathan will never allow a mage to live under his roof."

"Even if it is you?"

Elaine shook her head violently, and her hair whipped across her face. She didn't want to think about it. "I don't know."

"If we could not convince him to let a strange mage live under his roof, perhaps it would be easier to accept after you are trained."

It was logical, but Jonathan's hatred of wizards was not logical.

Blaine called from the table, "It might work."

"And I thought we were having a private conversation," Gersalius said, but there was no anger to his voice.

Blaine came to stand beside them, grinning. "If you move in here, there are no private conversations."

"There is that small hut on the grounds," Konrad said. "We would help you make any repairs and move your things in."

"Do you really think Jonathan would allow a mage to live inside the fort walls?" Elaine stared up at the tall warrior. She tried to find some hint that he wouldn't have made this effort for just anyone, that it was special just for her. His face was unreadable. Could she read his thoughts, as Gersalius had read hers?

The mage lightly touched her hand. No magic, just enough contact to gain her attention. "I would not try it, were I you. We often find out things we do want to know. Besides, how do you think Jonathan would feel knowing you were already trying to use magic on members of the household?"

"You can read my thoughts again."

"I told you, strong emotions make it easier."

Konrad and Blaine were frowning from one to the other. "What are you two talking about?" Blaine asked.

Gersalius smiled. "If Master Ambrose will allow me to stay here, even in the little hut, I will do so. For such a student, I would leave my own snug home even in this snow."

"I'll speak with Tereza," Konrad said. "If anyone can convince Jonathan to say yes, it will be her."

"Do you think he will say yes?" Elaine asked. She leaned toward him, wanting to touch his folded hands, to touch his bare skin, and have it thrill him as it thrilled her.

Gersalius tapped her hand again. He shook his head ever so slightly. Elaine frowned at him. "I wasn't . . ."

"Untrained magic has a tendency to reach out for things desired," he said, so soft that perhaps no one else heard. Heat crept up her neck to her face. She found herself blushing furiously, angry that her emotions were so obvious. She glanced up at Konrad, but he seemed merely puzzled.

"Why is the magic coming now? Why not before?"

"It has been leaking round the edges for some time. I am here now and can tell you when it's happening, and what the power is trying to do. But it has been manifesting for some time."

Elaine thought about that—Wild magic floating around her body, reaching for what she desired. "Am I dangerous?"

"Mostly to yourself, right now. But that will change, Elaine. With or without training, that will change."

Fear chased over her skin like an icy wave. "I can't risk the people I care about. If Jonathan will not let you remain here, I will have to leave."

"And I'll go with you," Blaine said.

"No, Blaine, we can't both leave."

He had that stubborn set to his chin. "I won't let you go alone. You know that."

"No one is going anywhere," Konrad said. "I'll find Tereza. If you can wait until we get this settled, Master Gersalius?"

The mage bowed his head. "Gladly, if I can have some more of those excellent cookies."

Mala came forward with a newly filled plate. "We'll not lose our Elaine for Jonathan's stubbornness."

"No," Konrad said, "we won't." He turned and left the room in search of Tereza.

"I'd best go with him. You know Tereza has a hard time saying no to me." Blaine left with a grin and a wave, all confidence, at least on the outside.

Mala was stirring the big pot on the stove.

"Konrad would do it for any of us, wouldn't he?" Elaine asked softly.

"I fear so," Gersalius said.

"I'll be able to read his true feelings someday?"

The wizard's eyes held sadness, as if of some old, remembered pain. "In very short order, I'm afraid."

"Did you read his thoughts?"

"No, child, that is unethical unless it is another mage. If the person cannot read your own thoughts, then it is unfair, like reading a person's private letters."

"You don't think I'll like what I find, do you?"

"Truth between us from the very first, Elaine Clairn. No, I don't think you'll like it."

Elaine looked away from his kind eyes. The fire glistened in unshed tears until the room danced in orange shadow. She closed her eyes, and a single tear trailed down each cheek. There were more pitfalls to learning magic than she had thought. She would learn how to read thoughts and feelings, and no matter how Gersalius cautioned her, Elaine knew someday she would read Konrad. She would not be able to resist. There would be no more guessing, no more hope, or fear, just the truth. And her heart would break, just like that.

five

JONATHAN AMBROSE SAT ALONE IN HIS STUDY. HIS window looked down into the inner courtyard of the fort. He could see the shed that the mage had been given. Strange lights danced over the snow, spilling from the shed's windows and open door. Dust flew in gray plumes out the door to dirty the snow. A neat pile of debris magically marched itself outside to be stacked by invisible hands on one side of the door.

There was a golden radiance that shone from the small, dirty windows. Not lamplight, but magelight. How had he let them talk him into this? How? He knew better than to let a magic-user inside his walls. They were weak creatures, easily turned to evil. All of them craved power, and darkness offered easier paths to power than did light. Not more power, but less effort. Jonathan had never met a mage yet that could resist the temptation.

Which brought him to Elaine. Little Elaine. All this time, he had been harboring a mage under his roof. Jonathan sighed and leaned back in his chair. A broken table levitated through the shed door, turning itself effortlessly to fit through the narrow opening. Would Elaine be able to do that, someday?

He had known deep inside that she possessed power, but he

had pretended. He had not wanted to know the truth. She had nearly died. When he touched her, she had been icy, like the long dead. It had not been Tereza's words that had decided it for Jonathan. It had been Elaine's ghost-pale face. Her immobile hand like death in his warm one. The memory of her lying in the snow had decided it for him. If her magic could kill her, she had to be trained. He would not risk her dying because of his prejudices.

A circle of sparks like multicolored fireflies danced against the shed's windows. The question was, could Jonathan stand a mage under his roof? A trained, powerful mage in his household? He had never had children, and never regretted it. What he had not admitted, even to himself, was that Elaine, Blaine, even Konrad—they were his children. Or, at least, his family.

Tereza had lost two babies in childbirth. The doctors said another might kill her, and the baby would most likely die. Thordin told of healers in his own land, those who could heal with a touch—could bring life, true life, back to the dead. Jonathan would have given much to have such a healer bring life to his dead children. To heal the pain he saw in Tereza's eyes, and in his own.

A whirlwind danced out through the shed door. In and among the swirling dirt and debris, magic lights whirled, so fast that the individual lights became stripes of glowing color. Snow blew upward in white plumes, reflecting the colors. Dirt mixed with the blowing snow, obscuring the bright lights. All that whiteness and the rainbow lights turned dark. The whirlwind rose above the snow, leaving its load of trash behind, then floated back in the open door.

Magic was like that. Pretty, even beautiful, but it dirtied what it touched. Then it floated away, untouched.

With a sigh, Jonathan turned away from the window. He scooted his chair up to his desk. The top was surprisingly clean. Tereza had recently made him go through all his papers. There had been something comforting about the familiar stacks of papers, and now the bare desktop looked somehow intimidating.

A letter lay in the center of that smooth, dark surface. The heavy vellum bore only a few scrawled words. Calum Songmaster's bold, theatrical hand was reduced to a wavering line. It was the handwriting of a sick man, an old man, a dying man. Jonathan slammed his hand on the chair arm, three hard blows. It wasn't fair. It simply wasn't fair.

He shook his head, a soft smile peeking through his beard. Jonathan Ambrose, mage-finder, bemoaned the fact that the world was not fair. As if he hadn't known that for years. It was funny, and bitter. No matter how wise in the ways of the world, some things are too awful to understand or forgive. Calum's declining days in a sickbed was one of them.

Thordin claimed there were healers in his homeland who could save Calum, could make him whole again. Jonathan shook his head sharply, as if to clear such thoughts away. Brooding would not help. Answering the letter might.

The note said simply:

Dear Jonathan,

The village of Cortton has fallen under an evil spell. They have asked for the brotherhood's help. Please aid them.

Yours in Devotion,

Calum Songmaster

Jonathan reread the letter. It said the same thing. No new information appeared. It was not like Calum to be so brief, but if it was painful to write . . . Still, it bothered Jonathan.

Calum was their contact, their only link to the rest of the brotherhood. It was he who passed to them assignments from the rest of the brotherhood. Jonathan had served with them for most of his adult life, but he knew none save Calum and a handful of others. That handful took its orders from Calum. The original intent had been to protect the brotherhood's leadership. If an operative were caught, tortured, he could reveal only a few names, and no one who was irreplaceable. The movement itself would not be hurt. Now Jonathan chafed under the restriction. Calum was dying, and if he died without passing his own contacts to someone else, they would all be cut off.

Jonathan could still battle evil, but as a vigilante going from one disaster to another. There would be no long-term goal to work toward. Fighting individual evil was a good thing to do with one's life, but ultimately useless. The evil sprang up faster than any one person or small group could destroy it. But if they destroyed the evil that infected the land, cut off the maleficence at its source, there would be no new monsters. If the evil stopped breeding, the monsters could be hunted down one at a time and killed. Even the evil magic might fade, the evil that corrupted all magic-users. Jonathan was not sure he believed that wholeheartedly. Mages were a weak lot, easily tempted. He sighed.

His thoughts turned back to Elaine. He shifted his chair toward the window. A soft amber glow filled the hut. It took a moment for Jonathan to realize it was fire—healthy, normal fire gleaming against the windows and open door. Flickering shadows caressed the snow outside the door.

The piles of debris were gone. The snow looked as if some great broom had brushed it clean. Where had all the broken pottery, the warped furniture, the dirt, the rotten cloth, gone? He shook his head. He was not sure he wanted to know. He hoped Lilian, their maid, had not been watching. If she saw how quickly magic could clean, she might be tempted.

Of course, as far as Jonathan knew, a person had to be cursed with the magic from birth. She could not simply choose it.

Gersalius came to the shed's open door. Firelight bathed him in warm colors. He had a broom in his hands.

Jonathan sat up straighter in his chair. If the old wizard was going to take to the air on the broom, Jonathan wanted to see it. He had heard of such things, but never been witness.

The wizard bent over the broom, hands a foot apart on the stick. Orange fire shadows turned the ordinary broom to gold, or perhaps that was its true color. The wizard breathed a great fog into the air—a word of command?

Jonathan stood, leaning close to the cold glass.

Gersalius propped the broom against his body, rubbing his hands against the cold. When the broom was once more firmly grasped, he began to sweep the stone stoop.

Jonathan stepped back with a snort of laughter. Perhaps the wizard heard him, for he looked up. He must have, for he waved, then went back to sweeping the snow. It had not been some giant hand that had cleaned the snow, but one old man with a broom.

Gersalius stooped and picked up a small bit of cloth. He shook it out, frowned, then made a sharp flicking motion with his hand. The cloth vanished. No light display, no wind, no tricks; it simply was no more.

Jonathan stepped back from the window so he could no longer

see the disturbing old man. Perhaps Gersalius could not fly on a broom, but what he could do was bothersome enough.

There was a solid knock on the door. "Enter," Jonathan called.

The door swung inward. Thordin entered. His square shoulders filled the doorway. His round face looked too small atop his powerful shoulders. Both the roundness and the size was heightened because he was totally bald. His head gleamed softly in the lamplight. The bones of his skull seemed thick under his skin. Thordin held the door while Blaine limped in behind him.

"Blaine, you should be in bed, resting," Jonathan said.

"I haven't made my report on what happened in the forest."

"Thordin can report for both of you."

"I tried to tell him that." Thordin's voice was painfully deep. A jagged edge of scar curled under his jaw to show why his voice sounded like rough sandpaper. "The boy would not listen to me."

The younger man shook his head. "The man was under our protection, and now he's dead. I owe him at least this much: to report in person."

"The dead do not care about grand gestures," Thordin said. "They are just as dead."

"His name was Pegin Tallyrand, and he'd never traveled more than a few miles from his home. He traveled for days in the dead of winter to find us; then we let him get killed."

"We did no such thing, boy. You nearly died trying to save him."

"And you, Thordin—did you take no wounds? You are not one to let a fight pass you by."

Thordin grinned. "Ah, that is a fact." His face sobered as if a hand had wiped it clean. "I fought, but it was a great, bloody tree. You can hack at it, but you can't rightly wound it. And I thought the lightning had killed it already."

"It was dead," Blaine said, "nothing of life inhabited what we fought."

Jonathan stared up at the younger man. He had never really questioned that Blaine had a feel for the land. He knew things about what grew or crawled or flew, knowledge observation could not account for. Like Elaine's visions, Blaine's intuition was something they had relied on without questioning its source. Was it magic, too? Was Blaine a budding mage?

Jonathan searched the familiar face. The gleaming lamplight showed the same earnest eyes, the handsome, if somewhat delicate, face. Nothing had changed, but suddenly Jonathan was looking with fresh eyes.

"How did you know the tree was not inhabited by some life-force?"

Blaine shifted on his crutch, frowning. "I don't know." He tried to shrug but couldn't quite manage it with only one good arm.

"For pity's sake, Blaine, pull up a chair and sit down."

Thordin drew two straight-backed chairs from the corner of the room. He steadied one chair for Blaine to ease into. When the boy was settled, he sat on his own chair. Thordin looked too large for the thin chair.

Blaine let out a shaky breath. Lines showed at his eyes and mouth. The candlelight gleamed on the sweat on his forehead and upper lip. He was hurt, only staying upright through sheer determination. Tonight was not the time to question his abilities, magical or not.

"Make your report, Blaine, before you collapse and we have to carry you off to bed."

"I'm not . . ."

Jonathan waved the protestations aside. "Tell me what happened."

Blaine drew a deep breath, nodded. "We were in Chebney."

"Was the report of a monster just fancy, or true?"

"All too true," Thordin said.

Jonathan did not prompt him. He knew Thordin would continue in his own good time.

"A ghost walked the corridors of the meistersinger's house. A phantom beast with poisonous breath that had stolen the meistersinger's voice. He was said to have a lovely voice, but we heard it not, at least not from the man. The ghost stalked the halls, singing in beautiful, mournful tones, like a great ringing bell that tolled the hours of darkness. With daylight, it vanished, and the meistersinger could speak with us. But he could not sing."

"A meistersinger that cannot sing cannot defend his seat."

Thordin nodded. "That was why he was so frantic for us to come, I think. It was only a matter of time before some young upstart challenged him. Without his voice, he was lost."

"The beast had a spark of life to it," Blaine said.

"Thordin said it was a ghost. Ghosts are shades of the dead."

"The ghost had once been part of a living being," Blaine continued, finishing Thordin's story for him. "I could feel its life-force, faint, but there. It wasn't just some evil conjuration."

"Had an evil conjurer died recently?"

Thordin grinned again. "Not exactly. You might say it was the evil person who lived."

Jonathan shook his head. "It grows too late for riddles, Thordin. Just tell me." He did not like Blaine's talk of living ghosts and conjurations.

"It seems the meistersinger had poisoned his last rival, not to kill him, but to steal his voice, to close off his throat on the day of the challenge. It worked. He became leader of the city soon after the old meistersinger died of apparently natural causes. The poison had worked too well. Soon after his death, the beast appeared."

"Justice beyond the grave," Jonathan said.

"Yes."

"How did you banish the creature?"

"We got the meistersinger to confess what he had done in the public square. Once the truth was known, the beast never appeared again."

"Is he still meistersinger of Chebney?"

Thordin nodded. "Yes. There are no rules about how you win your challenge in Chebney. Even though he cheated, he is still their leader."

"It isn't fair," Blaine said.

Jonathan looked at the boy. "Life in Kartakass is not fair."

"Life anywhere," Thordin said.

Jonathan acknowledged that with a nod. "How did you meet the man that died?"

"He came to the inn where we were staying," Blaine said.

"You were not housed by the meistersinger?"

Thordin gave an abrupt snort of laughter. "After we humiliated him—hardly."

"He turned you out into the streets?" Jonathan asked.

"No, but it was made clear we were not welcome."

"The next time the meistersinger of Chebney needs our help, perhaps we shall not give it?"

"We destroyed his beast," Blaine said. "He won't need our help again."

"Evil, ambitious men make the same mistakes over and over, Blaine. If he attracted evil to him once, he'll do so again."

Thordin nodded. "He has a beautiful voice, but he is not very bright. I doubt he's learned his lesson."

"What drove this man Tallyrand out into the winter night to find you?"

"His village has been struck with a terrible plague," Thordin said.

"The dead walk the streets at night," Blaine added.

"Truly, or just tales to frighten children?"

Thordin shrugged. "You know how it is, Jonathan. A plague hits, and people are too hastily buried. They come awake in the ground, shout for help, and are thought to be fiends in the ground. It could be something as simple, and as awful, as that."

"He said the zombies didn't smell bad. He seemed surprised at that. The walking dead don't stink in the cold because they don't rot. If Pegin had made it up, the dead would have stunk, perhaps breathed fire." Blaine leaned forward, wincing as his leg took more weight. "The story would have been embellished more. You know how stories grow.

"The man was very blunt and matter-of-fact. He didn't seem to be an imaginative sort. He talked of burying his own daughter, and a week later she was at his window trying to get inside."

"Was he sure she was truly dead?"

"Yes, of that he was sure."

"How many people have died of this plague?"

"Over half the village," Thordin said.

Jonathan shook his head. "Why did he not send for help before?"

"He heard a bard singing of your defeat of the beast of Mandriel. When the bard told him you were living and not some legend, the town decided to send for you."

"If half of them are taken, it is a serious problem, indeed, but I have had a missive from Calum. He has given us a new assignment. I can't put that off."

"I will go back to Pegin's village," Blaine said.

"Alone?" Thordin asked.

A stubborn frown made Blaine's face seem very young, like a child told he could not do something. "He died to save his village. We can't let him have died for nothing."

Jonathan sighed. There were times when duty to the brotherhood and larger goals chafed in the face of more immediate needs. This was one of them.

"What does Calum say in the letter?"

Jonathan handed it over.

Blaine stared at the floor, anger beginning to show through the pain and tiredness.

Thordin looked up, an odd expression on his blunt face.

"What is it?" Jonathan asked.

"Cortton is the village Pegin Tallyrand came from."

Blaine looked up. "You mean the brotherhood is sending us to help Pegin's village?"

Thordin handed the letter to him. "It would seem so."

"Well, now we know what is wrong in Cortton," Jonathan said.

"A plague of the dead," Thordin said in his deep, ruined voice.

"When do we leave?" Blaine asked. Eagerness showed on his face. He sat straighter in the chair; even his wounds seemed to hurt less. They were going to save Pegin's village, repay the debt that Blaine felt, assuage his guilt at the other man's death.

Jonathan understood all that. He could watch most of it dance across the younger man's face. Blaine's face was always like a mirror. Strangely, it was Elaine who was harder to read, more private.

"A few days to gather supplies and pack, to let you heal. To try and determine what caused the great tree to come to life. If there is some evil magic coming so close to our home, we must know of it. I don't want to leave the others behind in danger."

"If we cannot determine what happened, what then?" Blaine asked.

Jonathan had to smile at his enthusiasm. "Then we leave for Cortton in three days' time, with or without that particular mystery solved. If we huddled at home before we had deciphered every evil that befell us, we would never leave these walls."

Blaine grinned. "Good."

Jonathan looked at the younger man's eager face. Had he ever been that young? No, he decided, he had not. There was an answering gleam in Thordin's eyes. Looking forward to the next battle. Perhaps Thordin had been that young; perhaps he still was.

Jonathan stared at the two warriors. Perhaps those who lived by steel, like those who lived by magic, suffered the same delusion, that their abilities could solve every problem. Come to think of it, once upon a time, there had been a certain mage-finder that thought his abilities were proof against all evil. That had not been so long ago. Before Calum's illness—a few months.

He wanted to touch Thordin and Blaine, to shake them until the eager light died from their eyes. Didn't they realize that steel was not always enough? Magic was not enough. Intelligence was not always enough. There were some horrors for which nothing was enough.

They had fought the walking dead before and conquered. But a plague of the dead? Half a village brought to unholy life? Would they finally meet something they could not overcome? For the first time, a tiny worm of doubt began to gnaw at Jonathan Ambrose, mage-finder. Doubt . . . and fear.

SIX

THE MAN'S BODY LAY ON ITS BACK, HANDS AT ITS SIDE. He had been average: medium height, brown hair, an unremarkable face, neither handsome nor ugly. Perhaps, alive, there had been some humor that had animated that face, a divine spark that had brought beauty to ordinariness. Elaine had seen enough dead to know that was often the case. It was hard to recognize a friend, a loved one, in the face of the dead, even the newly dead.

The shed was a mere lean-to, one wall missing, open to the winter night. Snow skittered across the body, sounding dry as sand as it gathered in the wrinkles of the dead man's clothes. The back of the shed was filled to the ceiling with wood. The snow dusted the cut wood.

Tereza stood over the body. The lantern at her feet cast a golden swath on the dead face. The icy wind gusted inside the lantern with a whoosh that sent flickering shadows trembling in the shed. The amber light seemed almost as uncertain as the shadows themselves, like colored darkness.

Elaine huddled inside her hooded cloak. There had been much yelling about her braving the cold so soon after nearly dying, but in the end, they had listened to Gersalius. He said she would be fine. It was magic, and on that, like it or not, Gersalius was the expert.

The wizard moved up beside them, kneeling by the body. His thick cloak spread like a dark pool on the hard ground. One pale hand appeared from his cloak to trace the man's cold face. His fingers were very long and graceful: musician's hands, poet's hands. They traced the bones of the cheek, the chin, the forehead, the bridge of the nose, the fleshy lips. Without looking up, he said, "What do you see, Elaine?"

"I see a dead man," she said.

"Look with more than your eyes."

Elaine shivered, drawing her cloak tighter. "I don't know what you mean."

He looked up. His eyes were thrown into shadow, like blind holes. His face was strange, somber, no longer friendly or even approachable. Kneeling there in the fire-kissed dark, fingers touching the corpse's up-turned face, he was suddenly a sorcerer, with all that one word implied.

"Come, Elaine, we have had this discussion before. You are a budding wizard, a witch, if you prefer. Tell me what you see."

His voice filled the shed, beating against the darkness. It was not a shout, and yet it was, as if his voice shouted on other ears besides her normal ones.

"We haven't got all night, wizard," Tereza said. She stamped her feet against the cold. "Question her later, in the warmth."

Gersalius did not even look at her; his black-hole eyes never wavered from Elaine's face. "She must learn."

"I asked if you could discover why the great tree had come to life. You asked to see the corpse. I brought you. Now you go all mysterious on me. Why is it that wizards can never do anything like normal people?"

He turned to her at last, a slow move of his head. As his eyes moved out of shadow, they gleamed with a greenish light, the color of nothing in the shed.

His eyes weren't really glowing, were they? Elaine did not want to know if they were.

"You wanted me to discover something about the spell that killed this man. I am trying to do just that," the mage explained patiently.

"I asked you about the spell that animated the tree. We know what killed the man," insisted Tereza.

"Do you? Do you really?"

"The tree tore him in half, old man."

"That is how he died, yes, but not what killed him."

"It is too cold for riddles."

"And too cold for interruptions, gypsy."

Elaine's eyes flicked to Tereza. No one used that tone with her, not and lived a long and happy life.

Tereza drew a long breath that steamed in the air. Her eyes looked away from the kneeling wizard. "You are right. My apologies."

Elaine couldn't have been more astonished if Tereza had sprouted a second head. The woman never apologized, not for anything.

"Is that a spell?" She blurted it out before she had time to think. If it were a spell, saying so was not a good idea. Or perhaps it was. Gersalius shouldn't be bewitching them with his eyes. Surely Jonathan would disapprove of that.

Tereza smiled. "It is not a spell. The mage is trying to teach you sorcery, and I am questioning his methods. If I were teaching you swordplay, I would not want to be second-guessed." She made a small bowing motion with her arms. "Pray, continue, wizard. I will merely stand here freezing while you play schoolmarm."

"Graciousness becomes you, Mistress Ambrose." His voice held a familiar lilt of humor. It was the voice that had been so comforting in the kitchen. Then he turned back to her, and as his eyes crossed into shadow, they gleamed. They seemed to merely reflect the glow of the lantern, but Elaine knew better. His eyes shone with sparks of blue and emerald, the color of no honest flame.

When his eyes were safely shadowed, and that disturbing light quenched from her sight, he spoke. "Now, Elaine, tell me what you see."

She released a long breath that wavered and fogged near her face. It was so cold. Her body trembled in the warm shell of her cloak. Why was she suddenly so cold?

"Elaine, your magic seeks to control you. You must control it."

"I don't know how."

"You must learn, or perish. There is no other choice."

"Why am I so cold?"

"Because it's the bloody middle of winter," Tereza said.

Gersalius held up a hand. "No interruptions." Neither he nor Elaine looked to see what the woman thought of such an abrupt order.

"Your magic takes shape from two things, outside forces, like the fire or light of your visions, and your own body. It is trying to feed on the warmth of your flesh. Don't let it."

"I don't understand." The cold was growing worse. It was not the winter air. The cold was coming from inside her. She could feel it like an icy wind through her belly.

"Can you find the source of the cold?"

She nodded. "Yes."

"Explore it, Elaine. Tell me what it feels like."

She tried. She reached for the cold with something like a hand, with something that traced the cold wind back, back, deep inside her, farther and deeper than her frail body was wide. There, at what felt like the cold, dark center of her being, was something like a cave. She had no words for what it was, but she was human and needed words. So it became a cave, and with the word, the thought: It was a cave. A cavern of ice that had been built one crystalline layer atop another until it was like a great mirrored room. Each facet of ice glinted with reflected light. But there was no light. All was darkness.

No, there was light, but it was not reflected. It was in the ice, a flickering light that ran through the crystals like a fish through swift water. She turned and, with something other than eyes, saw blue and violet, purple, the liquid pink of sunset, and somehow it was Elaine. It was her power, as much hers as her own face.

"It is you, Elaine, your power, but you have let it run wild. It has built its own home, found its own way to freedom like water eating through the ground. It has chosen cold as its home, its brick. Heat is its mortar. There is nothing wrong with using fire, light as a catalyst for magic, but you must understand what you do, and why. You must reach for the flame to fuel your magic, not have the magic use your hand to feed it. Do you understand?"

She could still feel her body standing in the wind-bitten cold, but it was not as immediate, as important as that darting light inside the ice.

"Elaine, answer me."

There the light had stopped. She could almost reach it.

"Elaine!" The voice cut across her mind like a whip. She jerked and staggered. She was suddenly staring at the wizard's upturned face. The ice and flickering light inside was gone. She stood swaying in the winter night, frightened, but no longer unnaturally cold.

"Your power has been too long left to its own devices, Elaine. It is a destructive thing now, a hungry untamed child left too long in the dark. It has made its own world. It will take a long time to reclaim it completely. But it can be done, for tonight you must feed it, consciously."

"How?"

"Reach for the fire, Elaine, or reach for some reflected light. Reach for whatever would send you visions."

She extended a hand. The air was bitter against her bare skin.

The lantern flickered in a sudden gust of wind. Snow swirled, sparkling like silver dust, in the light. She felt the tug of a vision, a need to hold the light. But it wasn't just a vision; it was her magic, and it needed to be fed.

Her hand slowly turned, palm upward. The light and shadows trembled around her like struck gold. It was as if the light drew a shaking breath and bent toward her palm. It folded downward into the skin of her hand like water going down a drain. The light leaked away into her skin. It sucked downward into that cold, iciness, and the cavern filled with life, warmth, and the ice sucked it down greedily.

The lantern went out in a sputtering rush of sparks. They were left in darkness. The only light was the cold gleam of stars. But, strangely, that was enough. Everything seemed to flicker and glow with a faint edge of silver light.

"Look at the body, Elaine."

She did.

The man lay on the frozen ground. His face was no longer ordinary. There was some spark left, not of life, but of what he had been. He had been a man who laughed often and was often afraid. What need had driven him out in the darkest part of the year? The question gave the answer—love. He loved his remaining family, his people, his village. She saw the recent loss of his daughter like a shadow across his still face.

How did she know all this? How could she be so certain?

"Do not question yourself, Elaine. You will spoil it if you do."

She tried not to, but it was hard. Hard to stand there and stare at the flickering light that traced the corpse and gave up all the man's secrets. She knew him in that instant as no one else had, not even his family, perhaps not even himself. She saw him stripped and pure before her, faults bare to her magic, but strengths there, too. His bravery, his kindness, his fear. Over all was fear. He had traveled far to die in such terror.

It was not fair. Fairness is for children and fools. That soft, sure voice was in her head, Gersalius's voice inside her head.

The flickering light on the body was the reflected gleam of Pegin Tallyrand's life. A good life, well loved, generous with what little he had. He would be missed by many. The light shuddered, stumbling as if it had feet to be tripped. The light circled round a small lump in the man's cloak. It was not a pocket, but something affixed to the lining, sewn in.

Elaine half-fell to her knees, hand reaching for that stumbling light. Her fingertips hesitated, hovering just over the cloth. There was a flash so bright it dazzled the eyes. A smell of burned cloth, and Elaine held a small piece of carved bone in her hand.

It was the finger joint of a human hand, carved and painted with runes she did not know. The light was gone. Everything was gone. She knelt on the frozen ground with the bone on the palm of her hand. The bone gleamed like a ghost in the dark. The silver glow was gone, and the starlight too faint to see by.

Gersalius leaned forward, peering at her hand. His eyes glowed in the dark. Tiny pinpricks of flame burned in his face, green to her violet, but it was the same kind of magic. Had her own eyes glowed just moments before? Elaine glanced up at Tereza. She stood silent and unreadable in the dark. Elaine did not ask if her eyes had glowed with violet flames; she was not ready to hear if the answer were yes.

"Very interesting," Gersalius said.

"What is it?"

"What did your magic tell you?"

"It wasn't part of the man. He didn't know he carried it."

"Very good, what else?"

She thought it would be hard to recall what the light had shown, now that the light was gone, but it wasn't. It was easy, as if each moment were carved behind her eyelids where she could never forget it.

"It was a spell. A piece of death sewn into his cloak. It was dormant, waiting, until he touched the great tree."

"Why did the tree set the spell off?"

She thought about that for a moment, rolling it round in the remembered light. "Its power was death. It had to wait for something dead to come along."

"And the great tree was dead, killed by lightning."

"Yes," she said softly.

"Would a dead body have triggered the spell?" he asked.

"Yes."

"The spell animated the dead with a terrible purpose. What was that purpose, Elaine?"

"It wanted Pegin dead."

"It?"

"The maker of the spell wanted him dead."

"Why?"

Her hand closed over the piece of bone. "The spell's creator didn't want Pegin to bring help. He, or she, fears Jonathan, fears the mage-finder."

"How do you know that?"

"The bone reeks of fear."

"Could that not be the fear of the hand from which the bone came?"

Elaine nodded. "It could be that, but the maker of the spell is afraid also."

"Is it only the mage-finder that the spell's caster fears?"

"No."

"What else?"

"Death, he fears death." She squeezed the shard of bone until the edges bit into her skin. The bones in her hand trembled in sympathy with the thing she held. The pain was sharp and final, the injury so great that the body deadened the nerves. It was not her own pain she was remembering. The finger had been severed while the woman still lived. There had been many spells, many bones, much blood.

Fingers curled around her hand. "Let go, Elaine." Gersalius tried to open her hand. "Let go."

"I cannot."

"Tereza, help me."

Tereza did not ask questions. She just knelt, flinging her gloves to the snow, helping to pry Elaine's fingers apart. One finger at a time, they opened her hand.

Gersalius turned her hand palm down, spilling the bone to the snow. Blood welled in a small cut where the bone had bitten into her skin.

Tears trailed down Elaine's face. She wasn't sure why she was crying. "What happened?"

"Your magic feeds on light, heat. Other magic feeds on other things," Gersalius said.

"What other things?"

The wizard held her hand up to the dim starlight. He smeared his thumb through the darkness on her palm. "Blood, Elaine. It feeds on blood."

seven

JONATHAN SAT AT HIS DESK, ARMS CROSSED OVER HIS chest. He could feel his face set in a scowl, but didn't care. If anything was worth scowling about, it was this.

Tereza stood against the far wall. Her arms were also crossed, tucked tight against her stomach, angry. Her long, dark hair gleamed like fur in the lamplight. The rich colors of her clothing glowed with reflected radiance. The strong planes of her face were set in high relief by the light and shadows. The sight of her made his body ache, but what she asked was impossible.

"No, Tereza, I cannot condone it." His voice sounded firm and reasonable. He was right, and she would see that.

"You did not see Elaine in the shed tonight, Jonathan. Now that she knows she is a mage, her magic is coming out stronger, faster. If Gersalius had not been there, she might have been sucked to death's door again."

"From what you tell me, if the wizard had not urged it, she would not have tried this . . . magic."

"No, but the next vision would have endangered her. At least now she knows how to control the magic, a little." She pushed away from the wall and began to pace the small room. Her energy seemed to fill the room, making it shrink and pale compared to her. She was so very alive, all nerve endings and emotion, all physical. Jonathan was aware that she balanced him, his careful calculation to her impetuousness, his thinking to her heart, his age to her youth. Even as he argued, part of him wanted to say yes just because it was her. But no, not this time. He would, by the gods, stand his ground.

"Before tonight, I would have agreed with you." She stopped in front of him, hands on hips. "Gersalius must accompany us to Cortton."

He shook his head. "No." One simple word; why couldn't she understand it?

Tereza paced away from him, stalking the room as though it were a cage. "Then Elaine must remain behind, with the wizard."

"No."

She whirled. "Why not?"

"I do not trust the wizard here at our home with us away. He could bewitch the entire household, including Elaine, before we return."

"Do you really believe that?" She was standing in front of him again, dark eyes gentle and searching. The anger was seeping out of her. Tereza could never stay angry long, at least not at him. Frankly, this new reasonableness was more dangerous. As long as she ranted and raved, he could simply fight. But how to argue with reason?

He looked away from those searching eyes. It was a bad sign that he could not meet her gaze. He was losing, and not sure why. "Surely you see that we cannot take a wizard along on our work. I am the mage-finder. I cannot cart a mage along to aid me."

"He won't be there to aid you, Jonathan. He will be there to see that Elaine does not inadvertently kill herself."

"It can't be that serious. She has gone on all these years."

Tereza shook her head, dark hair sliding along her shoulders. "I told you what happened tonight. She was like a stranger, Jonathan." Her face when she turned to him showed something he had not expected . . . fear.

He reached out for her without thinking, touching her arm. "Are you truly afraid of our little Elaine?"

She cupped her hand over his, pressing gently. "She would never harm us on purpose—I know that. Before tonight I was only worried for her safety, but now. . . ." She knelt at his feet, hands encircling his hand. She gazed up at him. "She is going to be a powerful mage, Jonathan. We cannot change that."

He opened his mouth to argue, but her fingertips touched his lips and the protest died, unspoken.

"We cannot change it, Jonathan. After what I saw tonight, I know that for a certainty. All we can do is train her to be a power for good and see she does no harm to herself or anyone else by accident."

He pulled her hand away from his mouth. "There is no such thing as good magic. It is all evil."

"Then Elaine is evil," she said softly. "But you don't believe that. We've raised the girl for eight years. You know her heart is kind and gentle. You know that."

Jonathan stood, pulling away from her hands, the smell of her skin. He would not be persuaded by beauty to override his common sense. He walked to the window, staring down into the cold courtyard.

There was a gleam of firelight in the wizard's cottage. He

smashed his fist into the wall beside the glass. "Magic corrupts all it touches. I have seen proof of that, again and again."

He felt her approach behind him. He did not need eyes to sense her movements. He could sense her like some great irresistible force. Love and passion can be as strong as any star.

Her strong hands touched his shoulders, her body pressing against his back. "We cannot change what has happened to Elaine. All we can do is protect her as best we can, as any parents would."

He leaned his forehead against the icy glass. A wizard was sleeping just below, behind stout walls that Jonathan had built. A mage inside his defenses. It was outrageous.

"Leave Elaine here in Gersalius's care, or bring them both with us. Those are our choices, my love." Her voice was soft and warm against his neck.

He straightened. Her arms encircled his waist, and he pressed his hands over hers. "They will come with us." Her arms tightened against him, snuggling closer. Why was that small movement worth losing a dozen fights?

"Perhaps we might have the wizard look at Blaine."

Tereza was very still against him. "What do you mean?"

"His ability to feel animals, plants; he said the tree was dead, even when it attacked them, he knew it was dead. You tell me Elaine's magic said the same."

"You think Blaine might be a mage, as well?" Her voice was very soft, very careful.

"I don't know."

"But you fear it?"

"I fear we have harbored serpents in our midst without knowing it."

"You can't believe the twins are evil, Jonathan." Her arms tightened around him. "You can't."

"I don't know what I believe anymore, Tereza. If you had told me two days ago that I would allow a wizard within my home . . ." He let the thought trail off.

She softly kissed the back of his neck. "You were very brave to allow Gersalius inside."

"I cannot let Elaine die because of my prejudices. That would be evil all its own."

Tereza turned him away from the window to face her and the warm, familiar room. "You are a good man, Jonathan Ambrose."

"Am I? If Elaine is not evil, then what of the other mages I have destroyed over the years? Were some of them good? Has my own conceit murdered the innocent?"

She gripped his arms tightly. "No, it is not just magic that earns them death. It is evil magic. In all the years I have been with you, I have never seen you persecute someone that had not committed some terrible evil."

"I wish I could be certain of that."

"In Cortton, someone has conjured up a plague that has killed half the village. The dead walk the street, preying on the living. That is evil, Jonathan, and only one man can stop it. The mage-finder. You will hunt down this rogue magic-user and see that he is stopped." She stood just an inch or two taller than he, her face earnest, eyes searching his.

"Will Gersalius come with us to persecute one of his own?"

"If Gersalius will not aid us against a necromancer, he is the wrong wizard to be tutoring Elaine." She seemed to think of something that made her smile. "If the wizard agrees to come, surely that is proof that even a mage does not approve of murder and raising the dead."

He knew she meant it to be comforting. If Gersalius agreed that it was evil, he was probably not evil, and if a mage approved of the mage-finder, Jonathan was not wrong to hunt them. But what if Gersalius only went along to spy for the other wizard? What if he used his power over Elaine to corrupt them all? And what was he, Jonathan, thinking to give the mage power over Blaine, too? But if Blaine had magic, wasn't he in danger of its emerging at odd moments? Wasn't Blaine in as much danger as Elaine?

Jonathan shook his head. Tereza hugged him, pressing her strong arms tightly across his back, trying to comfort. He clung to her, taking the warmth offered, but he was not comforted. Too many doubts had been raised. Too many things he had been certain of were now as fragile as thin ice.

He was the mage-finder, but now, for the first time, he wondered if he was also a murderer. Tonight, and for many nights to come, he would be reliving past events. He would be searching for evil in the people he had helped destroy. He would go over every job, to see if the magician had been truly evil, or just misguided, to see if there had been a way short of killing them, or causing others to slay them.

Just a few short weeks ago, if Tereza had told him of someone else doing what Elaine had done in the shed, someone showing that much uncontrollable magic, he would have had her imprisoned, tried to see if she were a danger to others. And he would never have allowed another mage near her, to aid her, to teach her.

Jonathan clung to his wife, breathing in the scent of her skin, the warmth of her body. He clung to her like a drowning man. Guilt began to eat at his mind, feeding the doubts. Guilt and doubt; they were two things the mage-finder had never dreamt of, until now.

Eight

The snow grew deeper the closer to Cortton they rode. The horses slogged through drifts that dragged against their bellies. The gentle mare Elaine usually rode was safe at home in its stall, too old, too fat, too slow. In its place, a slender brown horse capered through the deep snow, or as close to capered as it could. Elaine was glad of the snow. It would make a fall a little softer.

She hadn't fallen yet, but she clung to the saddle horn with both hands, reins laced through her gloved hands. There was a look in the young horse's eye that was almost laughter, and Elaine was sure she was the butt of the equine joke.

Blaine drew up beside her, one hand on his reins, the other free to gesture. "Isn't it beautiful?"

His gesture pointed at everything. Ice clung to every tree limb. Every bush was an ice sculpture with bones of black wood. Bright sunlight dazzled the eye, sparkling and dancing from every twig. Elaine squinted against the brightness. There was nothing but light and brightness and a harsh beauty as far as she could see.

She stared into her brother's smiling face. "It is pretty."

The smile faded. "What's wrong?"

Her horse nipped at Blaine's knee. He avoided the snapping teeth without seeming to think about it. She sighed, breath fogging, joining the ice crystals already clinging to the fur of her hood. "Nothing."

He cocked his head to one side, hood sliding backward. His yellow hair was almost as bright as the sun-kissed ice. "Elaine, something's wrong. What is it?"

"This horse."

He prodded its hip with his foot. The horse gave a little jump. Elaine made a very unladylike squeak. "Blaine Clairn! What the blazes do you think you're doing?"

He looked instantly contrite, worried, sorry. "You're really afraid of the horse, aren't you?"

"Yes."

Blaine, who had never been afraid of an animal in his entire life, touched her shoulder with his mittened hand. "The horse doesn't mean any harm. It's just young and full of vinegar."

"If it were full of vinegar, it'd be a pickle," she snapped.

He let his hand drop back under his cloak. "I'm sorry I scared your horse, Elaine. I wouldn't have done it if I'd known it'd bother you like this."

She shook her head, the fur of her hood sliding against her face. An ice crystal scratched her cheek, a sharp bite. She touched the spot with her fingertips. A spot of blood showed on her gloves. She was suddenly unaccountably angry, as if it were Blaine's fault, though she knew it wasn't. It was a small cut, so why was she furious? Something was wrong.

"Get Gersalius."

"Why?"

"Just do it!" She turned away from the hurt in his eyes. His every emotion was always there in his eyes. She had no time for it.

Blaine rode forward in a cloud of snow. His cantering horse sent ice crystals sparkling in the air. The sunlight lit the gushing snow like diamond dust. A dim rainbow danced in the spilling snow. The sparkling light hurt her eyes.

She turned away from it, to find a small bush that glowed with silver fire. The light ate into her head. All she could see was silver light. It burrowed into her brain like a stabbing sword. She wanted to turn away, to close her eyes, but couldn't seem to do it.

"Elaine, can you hear me?" It was Gersalius's voice, warm and pleasant, the voice from the kitchen.

"Yes."

"What are you seeing?"

"Light."

"Describe the light to me."

"Silver, white."

"Is it just reflected light from the ice?"

"I don't know."

"Can you see anything else besides the light?"

She shook her head, and the light swung and trembled like a metal mirror that been struck. Nausea burned at the back of her throat. She took deep breaths of the cold air, swallowing convulsively.

"Could this be one of your visions trying to come through?"

"It doesn't feel the same," she said.

"You are beginning to control your magic, Elaine. Where before visions came of their own accord, without your control, perhaps now they will only come if you ask them to."

"How do I do that?" Visions had always been easy in a way, effortless. It was like falling once she'd decided to jump. Once she let herself go, she couldn't do anything but experience it. She certainly couldn't stop it or change her mind. Pressure was building behind her eyes. The light was expanding to fill the inside of her skull with cold, hot, white light.

"The magic is asking permission, Elaine. Let it come."

"I don't know how."

"Concentrate on the light. Feed the light to your magic; let them intermingle. It is what you have always been doing, but now you are doing it on purpose. You are simply aware of the process. Nothing else has changed."

She knew he was lying, but couldn't think how. She concentrated on the light, the brightness. As soon as she did, she could see again. She was still looking at the ice-covered bush. Sunlight beat sparks from it until it ran with silver flame. Elaine concentrated on one twig. She memorized the way the ice molded to the dark wood, the faint blue highlights that chased the white light. She could almost feel it against her fingers, slick, cold, smooth. No, there was a little bump in the ice where a twig stuck out, a tiny imperfection. Elaine could not possibly have known that. She could not see it, and she was still sitting on her horse, not touching the twig.

She could feel the wood at the center of the ice, feel its cold, and very faintly the waiting life, the warmth waiting for spring to come and give it life again. She grabbed that warmth to herself. It spread through her body like a rush of heat. The vision rode that warmth. . . .

A man lay in the snow. He was like no man Elaine had ever seen. High, thin bones shaped his face. It could have been just a high-cheekboned face, handsome, but nothing more, but there was a delicacy to the face that was more than bone. The skin was silver, nearly the color of the sun-warmed snow. His skin was truly silver, metallic in color, spread over the snow like silk. It wasn't a man at all. She didn't know what it was, but it was no man. Was it a monster? A beautiful monster?

A woman knelt by him. Long brown hair fell around a thin face. There was something of the other's alienness in the woman's face, but her skin didn't have that awful paleness. But her eyes gleamed like fire-shot brass, making mock of the ordinary hair and skin.

She tipped a small glass vial to his lips, rubbing his throat to make him swallow. Why was Elaine watching this? The woman was caring for the wounded creature? Was that it? Were they meant to destroy it? Was it dangerous?

The woman looked up at something Elaine could not see. Her strange eyes widened. She scrambled backward, floundering in the snow. She drew a knife from her belt, on her knees in the snow beside the fallen creature.

Elaine wanted to see what was frightening her. For the first time, Elaine moved her sight through the vision, moved away from the girl to what she was looking at. Elaine thought it was a wolf at first. Then it rose upward, towering on two bent legs, clawed hands flexing. Breath snorted out of its gaping, jagged jaws in a cloud of white smoke.

Blood decorated the snow like crimson lace. A man lay torn and twitching at the beast's feet. Wolves the size of small ponies stood at the beast's back, waiting their turn, waiting for their master to let them feed.

"No," Elaine said. The beast turned to look up into the sky

as if it had heard her. Had it? "Leave them alone."

The beast searched for the source of the voice, seeing nothing, but it did not attack the woman.

"Blaine, find them. Go to her. Help her."

"Where is she?" came his distant voice.

Elaine felt her arm move, slowly pointing.

She heard horses surging out through the snow. The jingle of harnesses, the snick of blades drawn. "Hurry," she said.

The beast stalked toward the woman, and the dire wolves surged forward. The creature whirled with a roar. The wolves cringed, tails tucked tight, belly-crawling on the snow. The great canines groveled; they should have been terrifying, but the man-beast made them seem small and ordinary. An ordinary horror, compared to it.

Elaine turned back to the woman. She felt her head move, but it was not her eyes that saw. The woman still knelt by the fallen man. She stood now, knife ready, but her hand trembled. One knife was no match against such evil.

The beast bounded forward, impossibly fast on its twisted legs. It slashed at her, and she screamed, backing up a step.

Where was Blaine? Why didn't he help her?

The alien man moved on the snow, a soft movement as if he were waking. The great beast knelt, claws reaching for the closer victim. The woman rushed it, slashing with her small knife. Blood flew, and the creature reared back, bellowing. Red flowed from a deep wound in its arm. The girl seemed surprised that she had hurt it.

Lips drew back from its teeth. A low, terrible snarl rumbled up from its chest. It had been playing with her before now, thinking her no danger. That had changed.

It circled her, trying to force her away from the wounded man, to force her out into the open. Once her back was to the dire wolves, she would be dead; she could not stand against them all.

The woman wouldn't leave her wounded companion. She stayed, standing over him as he struggled to wake from something deeper than sleep.

The beast waved its arm, and the wolves advanced. Where was Blaine? They were going to be too late.

The wolves plunged forward in a snarling rush. The beast urged them on, muzzle pointed skyward, howling.

Elaine screamed wordlessly, hand outstretched, as if she could touch them, protect them somehow.

The wolves, a near-solid mass of fur and fangs, surged in on muscled legs, running like a dark wind that rushed toward the woman, but fell back in a shower of violet sparks. The wolves lay in a stunned heap, inches from the wounded man. There was a faint violet-blue glow in the air in front of the woman and the man.

The beast stalked nearer, kicking at the fallen dire wolves to clear its path. It waved a cautious claw at the air. Violet sparks followed the tips of its claws, falling in bluish rainbows to the snow. Sparks sizzled there.

The beast turned slowly, searching the trees. It pivoted all the way around, giving the girl its back. She had cast a powerful spell to save herself, but the beast considered her no longer. It sniffed the air, breath foaming in the cold. Suddenly, it stared straight at Elaine. She wasn't sure what had changed, or how she knew, but it saw her, knew she was there.

She was jerked roughly. Her face stung. She blinked, and someone slapped her, hard and stinging. Gersalius was half holding her. Jonathan drew his hand back to slap her again.

Elaine put her hand up to protect herself.

"I think she's all right, now," Gersalius said. He lightly touched Jonathan's shoulder. "I don't think you need strike her again."

"You told me to hit her," Jonathan said. His voice sounded defensive.

"I know," the wizard said. "Elaine, are you all right?"

"I was having a vision. Why did you break my concentration?" She was suddenly angry with them. "Now I don't know if the woman is safe. Why did you wake me?"

"Some great darkness had found you, Elaine. I could feel it searching for you. I yelled, tried to break your hold before it found you."

"What are you talking about?"

"The man-wolf, it is not just a monster. It is a great evil, more than it seems."

Elaine blinked at him. "How did you know about the man-beast?"

Jonathan answered. "Your . . . vision was visible on every reflecting surface. We watched it all in the twisted mirrors of the ice."

There was something in his voice that made Elaine stare. Disapproval. He disapproved of her. There was a wariness in his eyes, something close to . . . fear. That one look pierced Elaine's heart like a dagger. She turned away, burying her face in Gersalius's shoulder. She hid the tears against the wizard's cloak, wanting Jonathan not to see.

"If she can ride," Tereza said, "we must go and help the others."

Elaine felt Jonathan rise and walk away. She raised her head slowly.

Gersalius touched cold, bare fingers to her face, gathering the tears. "He does not mean to hurt you."

"I know." She sniffed, wiping at her face with her gloved hands. Gersalius helped her to her feet. She couldn't remember getting off her horse, let alone falling to the snow.

"I've never had a vision that lasted so long," she said.

"It was not just a vision."

"We must help the others," Tereza said. "Mount up."

"Do you feel well enough to ride?" the wizard asked.

"Yes, I feel fine. I don't feel tired or cold, or bad at all. Why?"

"You are learning to control your magic."

Tereza led Elaine's horse over to them. "I'll hold its head while you mount."

The horse's eyes rolled to white. It did not look happy.

"There is no time to be squeamish, Elaine. The others have ridden ahead. They may be hurt, needing our help."

Elaine nodded. She grabbed the saddle horn. The horse danced away, only its head stationary by Tereza. Gersalius lifted her from behind, and the momentum carried her onto the horse. She settled into the saddle with the horse fidgeting under her.

Tereza released its head and kicked her way forward, leaving Elaine struggling with the reins. She knew Blaine was safe. One thing her visions always told her was if something truly awful were happening to those she loved. Like her parents' death. Nothing final would happen without warning, though the warning was often useless. But it gave Elaine a certain confidence that disaster would not strike unawares.

Jonathan followed Tereza. Only Gersalius waited. She let the horse have its head. It gave a bound that made her shriek, then rushed forward. It ran full out, stretching its muscled body to entire length. It leapt over a fallen tree. She swallowed the scream that rose in her throat. She passed Tereza's mount and realized the horse was running away with her. The harder she pulled on the reins, the faster the blasted thing ran.

Her hood fell backward. Her hair streamed in the icy wind. The trees rushed by at blurring speed. Hands clutched at the saddle, clawing for a hold, for anything to hold to.

Over the whistling wind, she heard sounds of fighting—a snarling, snapping, yelling chaos. The horse was running straight for it.

The horse ran full-out toward a stream, a wide, swift-running stream with crumbling, snowy banks. Elaine watched in horror as the horse bunched up beneath her and leapt. It sailed over the stream, and Elaine was airborne as it dropped away and scrambled for the farther bank.

She slammed into a tree and fell, crumbling at its base. She couldn't breathe, couldn't make her body work. She was helpless and dying. The stupid horse had killed her at last.

NINE

SOMETHING CRASHED THROUGH THE BRUSH. ELAINE tried to face the sound but couldn't move. She struggled just to breathe. If it was some great beast come to eat her, she could do nothing to save herself. The thought made her angry. She took another painful breath and fought to sit, leaning against the tree that had nearly broken her back.

Blaine stood knee-deep in snow, sword out, shield gripped close to his side. Two wolves circled him. He struggled in the deep snow to keep them both in sight, but they seemed to know that and turned opposite each other. Neither Blaine nor the beasts had seen Elaine.

She sat on the cold ground and watched her brother. What could she do to help him? She was no fighter. She did not even have the fighting knife that the woman with gold eyes had had in her vision. She had a small dagger for cutting food, stripping wood for a fire, but not fighting.

One wolf leapt at Blaine. He slashed it, and it yelped, falling back; fresh blood seeped onto the snow. The other wolf lunged onto Blaine's back before he could turn, bringing him down under its weight. Fanged jaws opened wide to crush his skull.

Elaine screamed, "Nooo!"

The wolf whirled, still pinning Blaine with its weight but not biting. It turned amber eyes to her.

She struggled to her feet. The wounded wolf stalked toward her, stiff-legged. The other wolf turned back to Blaine, lips drawing back from fangs. Blaine managed to get one shoulder up. The wolf bit down. Blaine screamed.

Elaine looked around for something, anything, to use as a weapon. She pulled a tree limb from the snow. The wounded wolf crouched, haunches tense, ready to spring. There was another scream from Blaine, but Elaine had no time to spare for him. The wounded wolf hurtled toward her. She held the tree limb out before her like a sword.

The wolf hit the branch, and though Elaine managed to hold on to it, the weight shoved her back into the snow, the snarling wolf atop her. The wolf was caught on the stick like a tent on a pole. It struggled, claws flaying, scratching at her face and arms. Elaine screamed.

A sword slashed out and down. The wolf's head tumbled away, and blood sprayed out into the snow, over Elaine's face. She threw an arm up to protect her face. The tree limb collapsed; the wolf dropped atop her. Blood pumped out on her, down her neck, soaking into her clothing.

She screamed. Blood poured into her mouth and eyes. The wolf slid to one side. Hands lifted her to a sitting position. She struggled, screaming, throwing her head from side to side, scraping at her face.

"Elaine, Elaine." Blaine's voice.

She blinked up at him. Her eyelashes were sticky with blood. He cradled her against his cloak. Blood smeared along the white fur.

"I thought the horse might have killed you," Tereza said. She stood over them, cleaning her blade on a bit of cloth. "I didn't know you'd be fighting wolves."

Elaine swallowed, tried to think of something to say and coming up with nothing. Blaine was alive. She was alive. The wolf was dead. There was nothing to say, except, "Where're Konrad and Thordin?"

"Here I am." Thordin stepped out of the trees. He held a rawhide string in one hand, a necklace of fresh wolf ears threaded on it. They made a trail of crimson drops on the snow like bread crumbs.

"Where's Konrad?" Jonathan asked.

"The beast that led the lesser wolves took off through the trees almost as soon as we arrived." He frowned. "I've never seen a huge creature like that turn tail without a fight. Konrad chased it with me, yelling for it to come back. But our first task was to protect the travelers, not go glory chasing."

Elaine's stomach clenched tight and cold. "Konrad is out there alone with that beast. We must help him."

"Now, child, either Konrad is fine and will come dragging his tail home, or . . ." Thordin shrugged.

"Or what?" she asked, but she knew. Thordin's matter-of-factness was too callous for words. "You have to help him."

"Oh, aye, child, but first I heard you screaming. Konrad's better at taking care of himself than you are. And this brother of yours." He nudged Blaine with his foot, smiling.

How could they all be smiling when Konrad might be dying or dead? Elaine knew her visions would show her Blaine's safety, or lack thereof, but she wasn't sure of Konrad's. He could die without her knowing. The thought made her throat ache with unshed tears.

"He's all right, Elaine." Blaine helped her to her feet. He winced as he took her weight. She pushed back his heavy cloak. His left shoulder bore tooth marks. Blood trickled down his arm.

"Does it hurt?"

He gave a crooked smile. "It would have to be the same arm the tree tore."

"Can you move it, boy?" Thordin asked. He proceeded to manipulate Blaine's arm, making sure it had a full range of motion. The arm did, but Blaine was tight-lipped and sweating when it was done.

"He's hurt; can't you see that?" Elaine said.

"Yes, but he's not too hurt to fight."

A horse pushed through the underbrush. Konrad was on it. He seemed uninjured. His eyes widened. He leapt off the horse and ran to Elaine. "Sit down, for gods' sake. You're wounded." He pushed her back into the bloody snow, medicine pack already open. His strong, sure fingers searched her face, neck. Fingertips kneading her scalp searching for the cut. She'd never felt his hands on her body so strongly. She didn't know whether to say something, or not.

It was Blaine who said, "It's not her blood."

Konrad didn't even look up. His healer's hands still searched for the wound he was sure was there.

Blaine touched his shoulder. "She's not hurt." Then it was Blaine's turn to frown at her. "You aren't hurt?"

Elaine looked at Konrad's serious face, so close, but finally said, "I don't think so."

Konrad blinked as if just now paying attention. "You aren't hurt?" He sounded like he didn't believe it.

Elaine wished she were hurt. Some small wound that would

bleed a great deal and look more serious than it was. She started to say no, then realized she was. There were lines of dull, burning ache on her cheek, arms, ribs. She raised a hand to her cheek, rubbing at the wolf's blood. She gave a soft hiss.

Konrad turned her head to one side. "Scratches." He glanced down at the headless wolf. "This?"

"Yes."

His fingers held her chin firmly, but not hard enough to hurt. He poured water on a rag and rubbed the wound, trying to clean it. The rag's cold water was still warmer than the surrounding air. It stung.

"What happened to the beastie you were chasing?" Thordin asked.

"I lost it in the trees." He never took his eyes from Elaine, from his work. His concentration was pure; fighting, healing, whatever, he was totally absorbed in it, as he had been in his love for his wife, as he was consumed in grieving for her.

Elaine realized with an almost physical jolt that the very trait she loved most about Konrad was the one that made him oblivious to her. His grief would live forever, as his love would have.

She stared into his green eyes, and he did not truly see her. He might never truly see her. That one thought hurt more than any wound.

Konrad lifted her arm. The claws had scratched through the cloth here and there. It was hard to tell if the wounds bled, for she was covered in wolf blood.

"Were you lying under the thing when it was beheaded?" he asked.

"Yes."

He made an exasperated sound low in his throat. "Who killed the wolf?" He looked up for the first time. "Blaine?"

"It wasn't me. I was too busy killing my wolf. In fact, after you see to Elaine, I've got a bite in my shoulder."

"Is anyone else hurt?" He bent back to Elaine. He'd unlaced her sleeve and was pushing the cloth back to reveal the white undersleeve. He traced the scratches. The cloth had protected her arms for the most part—no deep wounds.

"I'm living a charmed life of late," Thordin said. "Two encounters with evil and not a scratch."

"I slew the wolf," Tereza said.

Konrad rubbed salve into all the scratches he could find. "Why did you have to behead the blasted thing on top of her?"

"It was about to kill her," Tereza said. Her voice was warm with the first stirrings of anger. "If you hadn't gone off chasing boggles, you might have been here to help."

Konrad's shoulders hunched as if she'd struck him. Elaine stared at him. What was happening? What was he thinking to make that one remark hurt so much? His hands were smoothing salve on her cheek, touching her, the thought was enough. His mind opened to her like a door swinging wide.

He'd chased the great beast as though it had slain his wife, though Elaine didn't understand why. Beatrice hadn't been killed by wolves of any kind. He felt guilty for leaving them all, for failing them, as he'd failed his wife. Why failed?

His green eyes looked at her at last. They searched her face, seeing her, truly seeing her, as she had always wanted him to. But it was pity, not love. His thoughts filled his eyes like water and spilled into Elaine. She'd swallowed the wolf's blood. It was no natural wolf, and one way to become a werewolf was to drink the blood of one.

Elaine stared at him, mouth slowly opening in horror. Her eyes widened. "No, it wasn't."

The sudden tenderness on Konrad's face was too much. His pity was overwhelming. Why couldn't it have been love? The salty tears stung the cuts on her face.

"What's wrong?" Blaine asked.

"Did you swallow the blood, Elaine?" Jonathan asked.

She stared up at him with panicked eyes. "Yes." Her voice sounded strangled.

"No," Tereza said. "It was just a wolf."

"That size, in the company of a man-wolf," Jonathan said. He shook his head.

"No," she said again, voice strong and sure. "It was just a dire wolf, unnatural perhaps, but not a werewolf."

"How do you know that, Wife? How?"

Tereza shook her head stubbornly. "It doesn't have to be a werewolf."

"But what if it is?" Konrad said.

They all looked at Elaine. Blaine fell to his knees beside her, tears running down his cheeks, freezing in tiny silver beads on his face.

"But Blaine was bitten. Is he in danger, too?"

"I have a salve for scratches and bites if I can get to them before the poison has time to spread, but . . . if you swallow the blood, the salve cannot help."

"Surely a potion," Tereza said.

Konrad shook his head. "Most who drink the blood want to be a werewolf. There is no potion to save those who don't want to be saved."

"There is a way to tell if wolves are natural or not." Gersalius sat on his horse at the edge of the clearing. He had been so quiet Elaine had forgotten about him.

"What of the travelers?" Jonathan said, "Will they be safe while we linger here?"

"Safe enough," the wizard said.

"Jonathan, if there is a chance to know whether Elaine is contaminated, we must take it."

Jonathan turned to his wife. "Magic to save us from magic."

Tereza made a small pushing motion with her hands. "Enough of this argument, Jonathan. Do what you must, wizard."

Jonathan opened his mouth as if he would argue, but didn't. "I will go see to the travelers." With that, he took his horse's reins and walked back the way Thordin and Konrad had come.

With a sinking heart Elaine watched him go. Did he hate magic more than he loved her? She watched him disappear through the trees and feared it was so.

Gersalius pulled a small mirror from his pocket. He sprinkled a pale powder over the glass and spoke a few soft words. The sound raised the hairs on her body, like an army of marching ants. The air was too heavy to breathe, as if a thunderstorm hung in the air. Elaine looked at Konrad, but he was looking at the wizard. No one else seemed to feel anything out of the ordinary. There was an almost audible pop. Then Gersalius put his mirror away and said, "They are just wolves."

"Even I need more proof than that," Tereza said. "You spill some salt over a mirror, mutter some nonsense, and expect us to believe it's magic?"

"Look at your friend's trophies," the wizard said.

Thordin looked down at his necklace of ears. He raised it

slowly so all could see. Two of the ears were human.

Gersalius smiled. "It's a good spell. Not very flashy, but it gets the job done."

Tereza could only nod. Elaine could only stare at the two very human ears.

ten

ONE DEAD MAN WAS WEARING FULL-PLATE ARMOR. Elaine had seen such shining metal only twice before, on the wealthy, or the foolish. Much of what stalked the land was not kept at bay by armor. The wolves had been, though; four of the great beasts lay scattered around the dead man like a child's broken toys, four dire wolves killed by sword, not by arrows. He had been a great fighter. Now he was so much meat for worms.

She shook her head, huddling her cloak tight around her. With a little water, she had cleaned off what blood she could, but the blood had frozen in her hair in crimson ice. She needed a hot bath.

The second dead man was young, about the same age as Blaine and herself. His curly brown hair was cut unfashionably short. His face was handsome even in death, soft as if he had smiled often. Two wolves lay dead at his feet. One had been pierced through by two arrows. The fletching matched the pattern in the arrows in his quiver. Two arrows loosed, with the beast barreling down on top of him. It had died, and the second had come in. Barely time to draw a sword. He and the wolf seemed to have killed each other.

Only the woman and the wounded . . . man-creature still lived. They were still in front of the tree where they had been in her vision. The spell that had saved them was still in place. As it had kept the wolves out, it now kept them in.

Gersalius knelt in the snow in front of the spell. It glowed very faintly, the purplish-pink of wild roses. If he looked directly at it, there was nothing to see, but from the corner of his eye, half-glimpsed, it shimmered. Gersalius ran long fingers along its winking surface. Tiny sparks of violet-pink sizzled in the cold air. The sparks had a more solid color than the shield itself. That's what the wizard called it, a shield spell. Elaine had never heard of such a thing.

"I cannot dispel it," Gersalius said, at last. He stood slowly, as if his knees ached from touching the cold snow. He looked suddenly old. "You must help me, Averil."

"How?" the woman asked. Her unnerving eyes, the liquid gold of a gaudy sunset, stared at the wizard.

Elaine couldn't meet the woman's gaze. She had never seen a human with such eyes.

The rest of her was ordinary enough, if lovely. Her hair was a rich, chestnut brown with a deep copper gleam where the winter sunlight touched it. She was not overly tall, in fact thin, dainty as bird to look at. Her face was delicate, but human enough. Only the eyes gave lie to the rest. Her cloak was black, thick, but not expensive. The dress she wore was a reddish brown with white linen showing at its square neckline and wrists. Her only decoration was a golden chain with a charm on the end of it. It was the tiny carved figure of a stylized human.

The man still lay on the snow inside the shield. His left arm was gone, torn away in the fight. The arm lay by the shield, encased in its stout brown sleeve. Blood stained the snow from its broken end like a bloomed flower.

His skin was like the shield in a way. If you looked directly at him, he seemed pale, but here and there from the corners of your eyes, his skin was dusted with gold, like highlights in hair. But his hair seemed beaten gold, so metallic it didn't look real. His eyes were the same color as his daughter's.

Averil, the woman, was his daughter.

Averil had tied a tourniquet on the stub of his arm. Without it, he would have been as dead as the others. "How can she aid you, magic-user?" the elf asked. Elaine had heard of elves but never seen one. She found it easier to look at him, alien from the top of his head to his toes, than to meet Averil's eyes. The elven eyes in that human face were more disturbing somehow, as if the eyes had only borrowed the face and did not really belong there.

"If she would place her hands on the shield and try to dispel from your side, while I do the same out here, perhaps we can break it."

"If you saved us, Gersalius, why can't you dispel it?" Averil asked.

"I never took credit for this piece of work."

"This is not your spell?" Jonathan asked.

"No."

"It is not mine, either," Averil said.

"Whose then?" Jonathan asked, his voice thick with suspicion.

"Elaine's," the wizard said. As he said it, he turned and smiled at her.

She shook her head. "I didn't do it." Everyone was looking at her; most didn't look happy. "I've never heard of such a spell. How could I have done it and not known?"

"What did you do in the vision, just before the wolves leapt?" the wizard asked.

Elaine looked down at the snow as if it held some clue. "I didn't want to see them killed. I couldn't just watch." She looked up, staring at Gersalius. "I thought, 'I won't let it happen.' I remember reaching out to them as if I could touch her, save her."

"And so you did," he said.

Elaine shook her head. "I couldn't. I wouldn't know how."

"Whether you knew how or not, Elaine, you have done it. Now we must dispel it."

"Can I do that?"

"Yes."

"Then why were you asking Averil to help you, and not me?"

"Because I thought it would upset you that you had cast yet another spell without realizing it. If Averil and I had failed . . ." He shrugged.

"I know now, so how do I dispel it?" She walked toward him, the furred cloak whispering over the snow. The shield seemed brighter, the color of spring violets. With every step she took toward it, color flowed into it, until it bathed the snow in a soft purple glow.

"Your magic recognizes you," Gersalius said.

Elaine stared at the glowing shield. It recognized her? She tried to be afraid but wasn't. In fact, she wanted to touch it, to run her fingers along its gleaming surface. It was akin to the desire she'd had to touch the wizard's hands in the kitchen. Magic called to magic. Her own magic called most strongly.

"Touch it," he said softly.

Elaine reached out to it. Her hands tingled with its nearness. Her skin was stained violet, as unnatural-looking as the elf's, but she didn't care. Her hands sunk into the glow with a gush of sparks that flared and blinded her. She took a sharp breath, and as the air went into her lungs the spell went into her skin. She felt its being absorbed, like a tingling lotion. Then it was gone.

Elaine stood in front of Averil and her father, face-to-face, no shield. She felt clean and fresh, as if she had been bathed in the purest of water. She raised a hesitant hand to her hair and was surprised to find the blood still there. Her body felt clean, but her skin still bore the stains. It seemed wrong somehow, as if the magic alone should have been enough.

Averil's golden eyes stared at her. Elaine forced herself not to look away, not to show that it bothered her. That would have been the height of rudeness. The woman could not help what she looked like.

"How long have you been studying magic?"

Elaine thought about that. "Three days."

Averil's eyes widened. "Only three days? You are very accomplished for that short space of time. I still can't cast a shield spell after four years of study."

Elaine glanced at Gersalius. "He's a good teacher, I guess."

The wizard waved the compliment away. "It is not my tutoring but her natural abilities. Elaine had delayed her formal study of magic until recently, but she has been keeping her hand in, here and there."

Averil's stare was too intense, too thoughtful. It wasn't the alienness of her eyes that made Elaine look away.

"A person can study for years, but natural talent like that"—she shook her head—"it cannot be bought, or even learned." She looked envious.

"You are a good mage, Daughter."

She looked down at the elf still sitting on the snow. "But I will never have ease such as she has, such as Mother had."

The elf sighed. "Your mother was a great crafter, but what one can accomplish with talent, another can accomplish with sheer hard work. Is that not so, mage?"

Gersalius nodded. "Very true. You will find very few in Kartakass that have Elaine's natural flare."

"Kartakass?" the elf said. "Is that the name of a nearby town?"

"I am afraid not," the wizard said.

Thordin strode forward. "I thought you all might be new to the land." He didn't sound happy about it.

"What land?" Averil asked. "We crossed no borders."

"I'm afraid you did," Gersalius said.

With his daughter's help, the elf stood. "Something has happened, hasn't it?"

"Yes, my friend," Thordin said. His face was very sober, even sad. "You are in a new land unlike whatever land you came from."

"Since you do not know our land, how can you be sure of that?"

"I am as sure of that as I am of my own nightmares," Thordin said.

"Nightmares?"

"Welcome to Kartakass," Thordin said softly.

Eleven

The elf, Silvanus Brilliantine, took a deep, shaking breath. He held up his remaining hand. "Will this be a long explanation?"

Thordin exchanged glances with Gersalius. "Yes," the warrior said, "it will be long."

"Then let me see to my friends before night finds us in this accursed place."

"You are right on that," Thordin said.

"On what?" Silvanus asked.

"The land is cursed."

Silvanus waved that away as if he had no time for it. "My oldest friend lies dead; that is curse enough for now." He walked toward the armored man.

Elaine expected the elf to kneel in prayer over the body, to add some last word of comfort to his friend's dead form. He did kneel, but then he laid his one remaining hand on his friend's chest. He closed his eyes and let his head fall back. His golden hair streamed down his back in a glimmering exclamation point.

"What is he doing?" Elaine asked.

Thordin had a strange expression on his face, a look of both bitterness and wonderment. Gersalius's look was one of resignation, as if he knew a great disappointment was coming and could not stop it.

"What is happening?" she asked again.

Tereza shook her head. "I don't know." She was looking from warrior to mage. "You know what he is doing." It was not a question. "Tell us."

It was Averil who said, "Have you never seen a cleric before?"

"No," Thordin said, "she never has—not a real one."

"What do you mean a 'real' one?" she asked. Her voice was uneasy, almost fearful.

Gersalius gave a deep sigh. "He seeks to raise the dead to life. It will not work."

"I have seen my father raise the dead many times," she said. "Why should this be different?"

"It is the land, itself," the wizard said. "It will prevent it."

"We cannot permit him to raise a zombie," Jonathan said. "That is evil magic of the worst kind. He must desist or be imprisoned."

"Not a zombie, Jonathan," Thordin said. "He believes he can bring his dead friend back to life—true life."

"He is mad," Konrad said.

"No," Thordin said, "I have seen it done myself, in my home world."

"The wizard is trying to do what?" Tereza asked.

"Raise the dead," the wizard said, as if it were quite mundane.

"Can wizards raise the dead?" Elaine asked.

"Not wizards, holy men," Gersalius corrected.

"No one can raise the dead to life," Tereza said.

"I have told you that healers could mend wounds by laying on of hands," Thordin said.

"Yes, but that is different," Tereza said.

"Not so different," Gersalius said. "I understand the principle behind the spell, if not the actual mechanics."

Elaine stared at the kneeling elf. Something was happening. It wasn't the skin-tingling, overwhelming rush of the magic Gersalius had shown her. This was something softer, fainter. It didn't dance along her skin, it tugged at something deep inside her. It did not touch the cavern of power that Gersalius demonstrated. This quiet building of power called to something outside Elaine, almost as if the magic did not come from the elf at all, but from something beyond him.

"We should stop him," Thordin said. "The cleric that came over with me tried for months. She fell into despair and tried to harm herself."

"Some take it better than others," Gersalius said.

"But he is doing magic," Elaine said.

The wizard turned to her. "What do you mean, child?"

"Can't you feel it?"

He shook his head. "I feel nothing but the cold."

She stared at the wizard. Was he teasing her? The look on his face said he was not.

"Tell me what you are sensing, Elaine."

"It is a slow, growing . . . feeling. The magic doesn't come from inside but outside." She frowned. "How can that be? I thought all magic came from inside a person. You said you had to be born with it."

"You do, child. Even a healer has to have a natural inclination for his work. But they can summon divine aid. Something we poor magic-users cannot do."

"I've known mages that consorted with the powers of darkness,"

Jonathan said. "They sought power outside themselves."

"Wizards are like everyone else, Master Ambrose. There are bad people in every profession. Even among mage-finders." The last was said with a soft smile.

Jonathan started to protest when Tereza gasped. They all turned to her, but her staring eyes were all for the elf. The armored body was trembling. The hands flapped helplessly against the snow; unpleasant scrambling motions.

"This is impossible," Jonathan said. He spoke for all of them, save one.

"I told you my father could do it," Averil said.

Elaine would have normally turned to see the woman as she spoke, common courtesy, but the body was moving. It had been dead. She had seen the walking dead, but never watched them be raised. She still did not believe in resurrection. That was impossible.

The armored figure drew a deep shuddering breath that echoed against the bare trees. The "body" gave a sound, almost a shout, and was still. Then a gauntleted hand rose slowly toward the visor. The hand pushed at the helmet. The elf tried to help him take off the helmet, but with only one hand, it was hard to get leverage. The dead man wasn't much help.

Averil went forward and slid the helmet off. The face that was revealed was human enough. It had none of the monstrousness of the undead. The man had a sweeping mustache of purest white. Short-cropped hair that looked like it might have curled if it were not so severely cut, sat atop a square face.

"Silvanus," the man said, his voice sounded breathy, but otherwise normal. "You brought me back, old friend."

The elf's too-thin face broke into a smile that transformed it.

Suddenly, Elaine was not aware of the alienness but only of the love and humor in the face.

"I could not let this be our last adventure, Fredric."

Fredric turned his head slowly to look at Averil. "Where is our young friend?"

Averil's face crumbled. "He was killed."

"Beyond retrieval?" He struggled to sit, but would have fallen back to the snow if Averil had not caught him. She was stronger than she looked, holding a fully armored man upright.

"Oh, no, not the boy." He looked ready to weep.

"He is not beyond help, Fredric," the elf said. He got to his feet, carefully, as if it were a hard thing to do. He stumbled and nearly fell. He stood there swaying slightly, then took another step toward the second body.

Tears slid down Thordin's cheeks. He was crying without a sound. Gersalius patted the bigger man's shoulder.

The elf staggered. Elaine ran forward and steadied him. His good arm was solid and more muscled than it looked. His golden eyes stared at her from inches away. Lines that had not been there before etched his face.

"Thank you." He let her help him to the second body. Elaine eased him to the snow. He took a deep shuddering breath.

"You cannot do it." Gersalius stood over them in his dark robe. "I may not be a healer, but I know you are sorely wounded. You risk your own health."

The elf looked up, still half-leaning against Elaine's grip on his arm. "I am a healer of Bertog. I have no right to hoard my gifts if they can help others." He believed utterly in what he said. The strength of his belief was nearly touchable. His truth was a shining, warm thing.

Thordin touched the wizard's arm. "He is a cleric, a true healer. Let him be." The tears had frozen in tracks on his face. Thordin's smile had a peacefulness to it that Elaine had never seen.

"He should not have been able to raise even one dead man back to life," Gersalius said. "He risks more than just his life here, and you know it."

"It is his risk."

"Not if he doesn't understand that risk."

"What does the wizard mean, Thordin, that the healer risks more than his life?" Jonathan came to stand over them. His eyes were wider than normal, a touch of wildness to them. Even the mage-finder had been impressed with this particular spell.

Gersalius shook off Thordin's grip. "The land corrupts everything that touches it. You know this, mage-finder."

"It corrupts all magic, yes."

"It will corrupt even this pure gift. Until this moment, I would have said no cleric was powerful enough to call divine aid inside Kartakass."

"If he truly can raise the dead, then surely he is proof against even this land," Thordin said.

The wizard shook his head stubbornly. "If that is true, all is well and fine, but if not, the healer must understand what he risks. If he does not fully understand, he has no real choice."

The elf leaned over the fallen man. "If I risked my very soul, I could do no less."

"And if that is exactly what you are doing?" Gersalius said.

The elf blinked up at the mage. His smile softened, and Elaine felt him straighten under her hands. "Then it is what I am risking. And it is my choice, freely made, freely given."

"You don't understand. You can't understand."

"Leave him, wizard," Jonathan said. "He has made his choice."

"If you like, mage-finder, but a few moments in Kartakass cannot prepare you for a lifetime here."

The elf pulled his arm, gently, from Elaine's grasp. "Thank you for your aid."

She gave a slight nod.

He placed his good hand over the man's chest. There was no armor here to hide what was to happen. Nothing would have drawn Elaine from her place at the elf's side.

His head slumped forward, shining hair like a curtain over his face. She fought the urge to brush the hair aside. She wanted to see his face, to watch his features as he performed this miracle. For it was nothing less. She had grown up listening to Thordin's stories of healers, but she had not truly understood. Now she did, and she hungered after this . . . magic was too small a word.

It was a growing thing, like the earth itself waking to the sun's warmth. A slow filling up from some unknown source; outside power met and mingled with a spark of magic inside the elf. Elaine felt it as if it were her own body. There was simple magic to this, but it was much more.

The dead man drew a painful breath, spine bowing upward as if a string pulled him. He blinked wide brown eyes and sat up like a startled sleeper. He looked around wildly.

"Where am I?"

The elf gave a second beatific smile and slowly toppled forward onto the legs of the man he'd just resurrected.

Elaine wasn't sure, but she thought she heard Gersalius mutter, "I told you so."

twelve

THE TENT WALLS FLAPPED AND STRUGGLED IN THE wind. The two men that had so recently been dead lay on piles of furs and blankets. The elf, Silvanus, was curled in a corner, quite unconscious. He had not moved so much as a finger when they carried him to the campsite. The two deadmen had been much more lively.

The larger man, Fredric Vladislav, hugged the furs to his bare chest. "It is not right that a woman should see me like this. Especially an unmarried one." The skin of his shoulders was milk-white. Many a lady would have been proud of such skin. The jagged white scar that traced the collarbone spoiled the effect somewhat, as did his strong hand clutching desperately at the fur. His eyes were the color of storm clouds, a soft, wooly gray. The sweeping white mustache went well with his impossibly broad shoulders.

Elaine had always thought Thordin a large man, but the paladin, for that was what he called himself, made Thordin seem small. One sword-callused palm could have covered Elaine's entire face. His feet pressed perilously close to the tent walls.

"I would not have disrobed if the healer had told me a young woman was going to enter."

"She's a . . . nurse. Isn't that what you called her?" Randwulf asked.

Konrad spoke from the back of the tent. He was laying out his salves and bandages on a clean cloth near the unconscious elf. "Yes, she's helped me tend the wounded many times." He never looked up, all attention for his medicines.

Once Elaine had thought that commendable. Now it was vaguely irritating, just another sign that she was of no real importance to him. She was just another tool, like a medicinal herb.

"I have seen a bare chest before, Master Vladislav," Elaine said, tugging on the fur. His strong hands held on. Short of cutting his grip free, she couldn't budge him.

"You have not seen my chest. Besides, girl, that is not the only thing bare under these covers." A rush of color crept up his neck, tinting him pink from upper chest to forehead.

Elaine smiled; she couldn't help it.

"Are you so brazen as to think that is funny? Are you a healer's aid or a camp follower?"

"I don't know what a camp follower is," she said.

"I would be happy to show you," the other man said. His voice had a happy lilt that made Elaine blush.

"Oh, you mean a woman of loose morals," she said softly. Her face was scarlet, and she looked away from the large man. She had tended the wounded, but it had mostly been her own family group. Truthfully, she'd never seen a complete stranger undressed. Konrad didn't seem to remember that, or perhaps he didn't care.

"Now, girl, I did not mean to embarrass. I would not do that for anything."

"I thought you'd tended the wounded," Randwulf said.

"Mostly my own family." She glanced at him. He was naked to the waist, arms behind his head as if he were posing for effect. His well-muscled chest was crisscrossed with scars. He half sat up, causing the furs to slide alarmingly. Elaine turned away.

"Have a care, you young idiot. She's not a camp follower to be impressed with your scars," the paladin said.

"Maybe a healer would be impressed with my scars, too."

Fredric made a sound halfway between a snort and a sigh. "Perhaps, but she is no healer. She is a young woman, and you are embarrassing her."

"If you do not let Elaine look at your wounds, then I will have to do it myself," Konrad said flatly. "That will mean leaving your unconscious friend's wounds until after I see to you. After what he did for you out there, I would think you'd cooperate."

Fredric raised up on one elbow, the other hand still clutching the furs. "Is he truly hurt?"

"He lost an arm and performed such magic as I've never seen. He is at least profoundly exhausted, if not worse."

The paladin frowned. "Do not leave his side if he is truly hurt. I will allow your . . . nurse to tend me, but perhaps she would prefer someone else to tend our wounds. She seems uncomfortable confronted with two nearly naked strangers, wounded or not."

"Elaine's all right," Konrad said. He never turned around. His voice was vaguely irritated, but nothing more. He treated her like a faithful dog.

It must have shown on her face because Fredric said, "If you want to send in one of the men, we will understand. I do not think your friend is aware of how uncomfortable you are."

She shook her head. "If Konrad says I will be all right, I will be all right." Her voice held a warm touch of anger she could not control.

"Ah," Fredric said. He lay down again, hands loose on the furs. "Some people are more oblivious than others to those they see every day."

That a perfect stranger could so quickly see how she felt, and how Konrad ignored her, wounded Elaine. She would rather the paladin had stabbed her with a dagger than looked at her with kind, pitying eyes.

"Will you let me see your wounds?" She would not meet his eyes. It was too painful to see how clearly he saw everything. Let him think it modesty, though Elaine feared this paladin knew exactly why she would not meet his eyes.

"I will." Those two words held a quiet dignity. She glanced at his face. It was neutral, careful. He would not purposefully embarrass her; she knew that as if he had spoken it aloud.

Elaine touched the edge of white fur. Fredric raised his hands slightly to allow her to pull the covers down. She drew them off slowly, a knuckle's length of pale flesh coming to light at a time. His left arm bore a bite mark that still leaked blood. It would leave a nasty scar, but it was not serious unless it became infected. Infection took many a warrior when the wound itself wasn't a killing blow.

There was a patch of scar tissue near the center of his chest. Elaine touched it gently with her fingertips. The skin was rough and thickened like any scar. She ran fingers over his chest, as if to test that the rest of his skin was soft and unblemished, then back to the scar. It was white with age, an old scar, right over the heart. Something large had speared him there, long ago.

"This was a killing blow," she said.

"Aye, Silvanus brought me back from that one." His thick fingers caressed the scar, eyes distant with memory. "It was a good blow, straight through the heart."

"How many times has he brought you back?"

"Three, counting today."

"But that's . . . that's . . . " Elaine had no words for it. She had seen so many die with wounds not half as serious as that one heart blow. But, of course, Fredric had also died, just not permanently. It was outrageous . . . and wondrous.

Elaine lowered the covers another handspan or two. Even his stomach was flat and strong. Low on the stomach was the wound that had killed him this time. She folded the furs carefully at a line just below his waist. In truth, perhaps just a fraction lower. She tucked the covers firmly just below his hip bones. The smooth white skin of his stomach was in ruins.

Claws had sliced him open in ragged furrows. Teeth had torn great gaping hunks of flesh from his stomach. Even if it hadn't been a murderous wound, it would never have healed. There wasn't enough flesh left to fill in the hole. The wolves had eaten down through the muscle, shoving their muzzles into his stomach and intestines. This wasn't like closing the edges of some great wound, or mending a pierced heart. Hunks of flesh were gone, swallowed, before he was healed. The scar tissue was a great pinkish mound that covered most of the stomach.

Elaine touched the wound. She could almost feel the new flesh sinking away under her fingers. Scar tissue held his stomach and intestine together, scar tissue where it should never have been.

"Is this—and your arm—your only wounds?" she asked.

"My left leg, I think." His hands were back, clutching the

covers. "You can draw away the furs from my leg." It was clear that pulling the covers farther down was not an option.

That was fine with Elaine. She lifted the furs from his left leg, folding them back to midthigh. It left his long body bare, save for a swath of fur across his groin, and one covered leg. His bare leg was long and muscled. His white hair had made Elaine think Fredric old, older than Jonathan, but this was a young body.

The claws had hamstrung him. The wound was partially healed, the deeper flesh knitted together in a pink mass. The lip of the wound still gaped where the claws had sliced, but the profound damage was healed.

"How did he heal only part of your wounds? How did the magic know to heal your worst injury? Is it possible to heal many lesser wounds and run out of spell before a killing wound is mended?"

Fredric laughed. "Girl, I don't know. I'm no cleric. I've seen Silvanus do many wondrous things, but I've never thought to ask how he does it."

Elaine looked at his laughing face. She was puzzled. "Didn't you want to know how the healing worked?"

He shrugged broad shoulders. "As long as it works, that's all that matters."

"Spoken like a warrior with no hobbies," Randwulf said.

Elaine turned back to what she'd assumed was a younger man. After seeing Fredric's body, she was no longer sure. Randwulf seemed younger at least in actions, if not in years.

Randwulf lay naked on the furs save for a white underpant. Elaine turned away, staring very hard at the tent wall.

"Where is the injury that killed you?" Just asking the question sounded ludicrous.

"Don't you want to search for it, like you did with Fredric?"

"I don't think so," she said.

"Elaine, can you help me over here?" Konrad asked.

She let out a breath she hadn't known she was holding. If Konrad needed her help, he would probably tend to Randwulf himself. The brown-eyed man with his curly hair was too eager for her hands.

She crawled over to Konrad, who was still kneeling by the unconscious elf. He had cut away the sleeve from the torn arm. Only a handspan of arm remained. The end should have been jagged with naked bone and ripped flesh, but it was smooth. The skin had pulled together, hiding the end of the arm in a smooth golden-skinned stub.

"Is it healing?" she asked.

He nodded. "I believe so."

"What do you need my help for?" she asked.

"I need a second opinion."

She glanced at him. His handsome profile was serious, no smile, no teasing. He turned to her, full-faced. His green eyes studied hers. If it had been anyone but Konrad, Elaine would have said he looked uncertain.

"If this were a normal amputee, I would cauterize the wound to stop bleeding and keep infection from the flesh." He ran his hand over the stub. "Feel it."

She didn't want to, but Konrad had never asked her opinion before. He had taught her to clean and bandage simple wounds. Her most common task was to preview the wounded and give Konrad a report of who was the worst injured. But once Elaine gave her report, she followed his orders, did as he directed. She would not be squeamish now.

Elaine ran fingertips over the stub. The skin was soft as a newborn babe's, smooth; no jagged bone jutted beneath the skin. The stub was fleshy, as if the end were filled up with meat. It was smooth, solid, and perfect.

"It's healed," she said, softly.

He nodded. "Should I burn the end of the stub, or not?"

"Oh, no. It's healed. Burning it would just injure it further. Don't you think?" Elaine knew that cauterizing the wound was the wrong thing to do, but she couldn't resist asking for his approval. She hated herself just a little bit for that last question.

He stared down at the elf, running his hand over the smooth stump. "I think you're right. But this is so far beyond my poor skills, I almost don't know how to tend them."

"You tend the wounds that aren't completely healed and leave the others alone," she said.

"Do I? Have you looked at the other two?"

"I haven't seen to Randwulf's wounds yet."

"Tell me of the first man's wounds."

She did. When she had finished, he sighed and went to Fredric. "See to Randwulf."

Elaine sat there for a moment, angry. She was not in the mood to be teased or tormented. She had been embarrassed enough for one day.

Konrad knelt by Fredric, hands seeking the wounds she had told him of. He did not second-guess her by looking for other wounds, but went only to the areas Elaine had mentioned. It was a measure of trust. Once he had searched each body himself; now he simply took her word. He might not love her, but he respected her, and that was worth a great deal, worth enough to risk the teasing Randwulf and much more. Just because he didn't love her, did not mean she didn't love him. Love is like that. Once it exists, it is not so easily killed.

Randwulf had cuddled back under the covers. Apparently, it was too cold in the tent for such blatant flirtation. The sight of only his curly brown head sticking out made it easier for Elaine to go to him. Perhaps he had been merely teasing, that when it came down to it, he would behave himself.

And pigs would fly.

Randwulf's smile was lovely, but there was a hint of evil in it, a knowledge in his eyes that was too intimate to be directed at a strange young girl. It seemed as if he knew what she looked like without clothes on, or wanted to.

Heat rushed up her face, but with the embarrassment came anger. Enough of this, she thought. She knelt before his covered figure, face set in a businesslike scowl. "What are your injuries?" She made her voice cold and distant.

He didn't seem to notice. "Oh, I am badly hurt, all over. I think you had best see for yourself." With that, he whipped back the covers, and Elaine looked down. She studied the ground as if her life depended on it.

Randwulf's face appeared in her line of vision. He laid his head in her lap, gazing up at her. "Don't you want to see my wounds?"

She stood up abruptly. His head thunked onto the frozen ground. He closed his eyes. "Now my head hurts, as well."

"I hope it does," she said. She was angry with him, but more with herself for letting him bother her so. She had tended a few strangers. But none had made it so difficult. It was easier to pretend her touch wasn't intimate if the patient pretended also.

"There, I've fixed it," he said.

Elaine was almost afraid to look, but she did. He lay covered to his chin. His face looked very young, peeking from above the furs. He looked boyish and adorable, but the gleam in his eye was a little too grown-up for the act to be convincing. At least he was no longer naked. Elaine would take what improvement she could get.

Elaine knelt beside him one more time. Her fingers curled around the fur to pull it back. His cheek rubbed against her knuckles. She lifted the fur and her hand out of easy reach. If he had tried kissing it, she would have jerked away and left him to his own devices, but the movement was one a cat might make. An overly friendly cat.

She lowered the covers slowly, eyes searching his body for injuries. His skin was not as pale as the paladin's. He looked as if he would brown in the sun. His chest and arms were shapely but slender compared to Fredric's. He could not boast nearly as many scars. He was either luckier, a better fighter, or newer to adventure. Elaine thought the last.

Both his forearms bore bite marks. It looked as if a wolf had grabbed each arm and held on. They were fearsome wounds, but nothing to die over. Randwulf's flat stomach was unblemished, skin smooth.

He lay back on the furs, a slow smile on his face. He looked very pleased with himself. Elaine fought the urge to slap him. It would probably have made him laugh. She did not want to amuse him. She realized, strangely enough, that she wanted to hurt him. Or at least make him as uncomfortable as he had made her.

Elaine took a deep breath and let it slowly out. She pulled the covers below his waist. She gave only a quick glance before moving on to his legs. If the death wound had been in a very intimate place, Konrad could bloody well search for it himself.

His legs were short, almost stocky, muscled from walking, but uninjured. A white scar like a bolt of frozen lightning traced his right thigh, but there were no new wounds.

Elaine sighed. "Please, turn over." Randwulf's wounds would of course be in an out-of-the-way place. He couldn't possibly have done it on purpose. She glanced at the slow curl of his smile. He stretched, arms straight over his shoulders. Every muscle in his body strained. He was like a contented cat that had already drunk its fill of cream. His dark eyes stared at her as if she were the proverbial canary.

Konrad and Fredric were just an arm's length away. He couldn't possibly do anything to her. He was simply flirting or teasing, or both. But it meant nothing—nothing real. Randwulf had only as much power over her as she gave him, and she'd given him far too much already.

"Turn over, Randwulf, now." Her voice was a good imitation of Tereza's when she'd had all she could stand of silly children and indoor games.

Randwulf blinked at her, his smile slipped around the edges. He rubbed his hands down his chest and across his stomach. Her eyes followed them, as he'd wanted them to. The hands started to slip farther, but she grabbed one bloody wrist, wrenching the skin in two different directions. He gave a hiss of pain.

"Turn over so I can look for injuries, or I'll put salt in these wounds."

"You wouldn't dare," he said, but there was doubt in his eyes.

"Salt cleanses a wound and prevents infection."

His eyes narrowed as if he didn't believe her. But there must have been something in her face that convinced him. He began to turn over, slowly, giving her time to admire the way his body worked.

Elaine kept her best no-nonsense look in place. She consciously pictured Tereza at her most cross. The look that had always sent Blaine and herself running.

Randwulf never took his eyes from her face, looking for some reaction besides disapproval. He didn't find it. He gave a small sigh and settled onto his stomach, though he did keep his face turned so he could watch her.

Elaine was staring, open-mouthed at the back of his neck. His hair had been just long enough to hide it from the front, but now . . . jaws had crushed the back of his neck, broken his spine. Tooth marks imprinted the skin, but the neck itself had filled back up, like a waterskin inflating. He moved well enough that it was clear the spine was not severed. The tooth marks filled with blood like miniature rain puddles with rain.

But the blood did not flow. The wound looked raw, but the blood seemed to be held in suspension by some invisible force. If the wound were swabbed with a damp cloth, would it bleed afresh? Would they start it to bleeding? Would it stop once it started? With magic healing, who knew?

Randwulf watched her face. "Is it that ugly?" He was young and handsome, and the horror on her face bothered him.

He had handed her a way to hurt him; all she had to do was lie. The one thing she could not do.

"It is not the appearance of the wound, but the terrible injury it must have been. Your spine was broken, snapped. How can you be healed of that?"

"I don't know," he said.

"Is this the first time you . . . died?" she asked.

His small white teeth bit his lower lip, his eyes uncertain. "The first time."

"Were you frightened?"

"Of dying?"

She nodded.

"I was frightened when the wolves grabbed my arms. They held me with their mouths the way two men would have held me with their hands. Then I heard the man-wolf behind me. His breath was loud and hot against my neck. I think I screamed. There was a moment of sharp, horrible pain, then nothing. I didn't feel a thing." He rubbed his hand over the back of his neck, fingertips tracing the tooth marks, ever so lightly. "No pain, but I felt myself slide away. I felt myself die."

Elaine just stared at him. She couldn't think of anything to say.

"Elaine, may I speak with you," Konrad said. He stood, forced to stoop by the low ceiling. He went to the tent flap. "Outside."

Elaine fought to keep to her face blank, stood, and followed him outside. The wind hit her face like a cold slap. She lifted her hood in place, struggling against the wind to hold the furred cloak close to her body.

Konrad's long hair spilled over his face, tangled by the icy wind. With his back to the wind, his cloak streamed out around him; no need to hold it next to his body—the wind did that on its own. The tent cracked and bucked in the rising gusts.

Konrad led her a few steps from the tent, hand half-draped over her shoulders. He drew her into the circle of his arms so they could talk above the wind and rippling tent hide. That was all. The physical closeness that made her chest tight meant nothing to him. Elaine reminded herself of that as he leaned near her cheek to speak.

"If we cleanse the wounds, will they start to bleed again and not stop? Does the magic used to partially heal them change how we should treat them?"

She wanted to say something clever and certain, but that would have been an outrageous lie. Lives might be at stake. It was not a time for lies. "I don't know."

"You know more magic than I do," he said. He was really looking to her for an answer. Elaine had never claimed more knowledge than she had. If she didn't know, she always said so, but now was sorely tempted. Konrad's face was close enough to kiss. His eyes looking at her, seeing her.

Elaine drew a deep sigh. "I've only been studying magic for a few days, Konrad. I'm no expert, but Gersalius is." She was rather pleased with that last thought, pleased to have come up with a good idea, if not a good answer.

"I cannot leave them alone. Could you speak with the wizard, then report back to me?"

"I could stay with them while you spoke with Gersalius." It was a generous offer. The last thing Elaine wanted to do was go back in that tent. Randwulf's serious eyes and his strange voice as he had related his death story had frightened her. She preferred even his teasing and flirting to that.

"No, if anything should go wrong, I am the best healer in camp—at least awake. And the wizard will speak more freely to you. Don't you think?"

Again, he was asking her opinion. This time she could give an answer. "Yes."

"Then go talk with the wizard. I'll wait here. I won't tend their wounds unless something goes wrong."

"I'll hurry," she said.

He gave an abrupt nod, almost a bow, and ducked back inside the tent. Elaine stood there for a moment in the rattling wind. Konrad had asked her opinion twice in one day. It was not only a record, it was a nine days' wonder. What was wrong with him?

thirteen

Gersalius's tent was smaller than the rest, with strange curlicues of carved wood mounted above the entrance. Elaine hadn't really inspected the wizard's tent closely. Now she looked at the wooden carvings. They were attached to the tent itself, not tied on. It was almost as if the wood grew straight out of the hide. She could make nothing of the carvings themselves. They were of no animal or image she was familiar with, just designs of wood and paint.

Elaine called, "Gersalius, it's me, Elaine. I need to speak with you." The wind gusted, making the tent strain and pull at the tiny tent stakes. The wood carvings swayed in the wind as if they were antlers on some live beast.

"Gersalius?" Elaine called. She waited in the cold, huddled against the wind. "Gersalius, please, if you're in there, answer me." When there was still no answer, she turned and walked back to the fire. Blaine was cooking the camp dinner—sausages in a skillet over the flames. They actually smelled good. Of course, even Blaine couldn't do a lot of damage reheating sausages. It was almost foolproof.

There was a smaller saucepan sitting to one side. Blaine stirred it with a wooden spoon. An odor rose from the saucepan and caught the back of her throat with a bitter taste. Before she could say a word, Blaine poured the foul sauce over the lovely sausages. He put a lid over the skillet and set it to one side. He'd probably say he was letting it simmer. Blaine was the worst cook in the world, but he had pretensions of being a gourmet. His 'improvements,' experiments with herbs, were legendary.

He smiled up at her, pleased with himself. "I'm trying a new sauce tonight. Want a whiff?"

"I already smelled it," she said, a brave smile in place. Blaine was not only the worst cook in the world, he was oblivious to the deficiency. No matter how much Thordin and the others complained, Blaine never quite believed them. He went on his cheerful way, crumbling dried herbs, chopping roots, and trying to poison them all.

"Have you seen Gersalius?"

"I think he's in Thordin's tent." He turned back to an earthenware bowl on the ground by his knee. A cloth was tied over it. He cut the string, lifting the cloth to reveal a grayish mass. "I made stuffing before we left. All I have to do is heat it."

"Did Mala help you make it?" she asked hopefully.

He grinned. "Of course not. You know I like to do all my own cooking."

"Of course," she said. She left him to ruin their dinner and went in search of Thordin's tent. He shared it with Konrad, so it was big enough to accommodate a visitor.

The wind died down as suddenly as it had sprung up. In the fresh silence, Elaine heard the murmur of the men's voices, a soft, rumbling sound that was somehow comforting. Elaine had spent a great deal of her life listening to that strong, bluff, blunt sound.

She bent over, calling, "Gersalius, are you in there?"

The tent flap swung open. Thordin's face and arm popped out. "Elaine, come join us. I think if we all squeeze there may be room."

It occurred to her for the first time that Thordin had seen clerics work their healing magic. He might know something valuable, too. She crawled into the tent, tugging her heavy cloak through the small opening.

Gersalius was sitting on a pile of bedding, smiling. He had a mug in his hands. "Elaine, what brings you in search of me?"

Thordin offered her a mug.

"Surely that is yours," she said.

"Yes, but I can get another." With a smile, he handed her the mug.

"Thank you." The mug was wonderfully hot to her hands. Steam rose from the cup like sweet-smelling ghosts. The tea was a strong spearmint faintly touched with sugar. Breathing in the steam was almost as refreshing as drinking the tea itself.

"How goes it with the wounded?" Thordin asked.

"That is why I have come," Elaine said.

Thordin poured a third mug of tea from a small earthware pot, then set it back on its warmer. He took a pinch of sugar from a small pouch at his belt, added the sugar to the tea, then stirred it with a small silver spoon.

"With a few comforts, any place can be home," Gersalius said.

"My sentiments, exactly," Thordin said.

"Why were you seeking me, Elaine?" the wizard asked.

"Konrad and I have never seen magical healing before. We aren't sure what to do."

"A cleric heals by laying on of hands. The wound just closes up and is healed," Gersalius said.

"Completely healed?" She made it a question.

"Yes," he said.

She shook her head. "But these injuries aren't completely healed."

Gersalius sat forward sharply, spilling hot tea on his robes. He gave a small yip, pulling the cloth away from his body. He set the mug on the ground. "Tell me exactly what you mean, Elaine. This could be very important."

She looked from one man to the other. Thordin appeared as worried as the wizard. "Are the wounds suppose to heal completely?" she asked.

"Yes," Gersalius said.

"Not always," Thordin said.

The wizard stared at the warrior. "A spell either works or it does not."

"I was a fighter long before I came to Kartakass," Thordin said. "A cleric can heal a wound, but when I had many wounds, not all of them healed. They were better, but some still bled a little, others were only partially healed. Kilsendra, the cleric that came over with me, said each healing has only so much power to it. It heals what it can, then stops. It might take several attempts to heal completely."

Gersalius frowned. "It is true I did not adventure much. I owned a little magic shop where others bought supplies, but with my magic, a spell either works or does not. If the spell components are insufficient, the spell simply does not work at all."

Thordin shook his head. "Healing is not like that, or so Kilsendra told me."

The wizard frowned. "Most unobservant of me, if you are right."

Elaine sipped her tea and turned to Thordin. He seemed to know more of healing than the wizard. "If a wound did not heal completely, what did you do to tend it?"

"I'm not sure what you mean."

"Did you cleanse it? Bandage it?"

"I think so." He looked puzzled. "Why couldn't you treat them as any other wound?"

"Normal wounds don't just sit there full of blood. Konrad's afraid if we cleanse the wounds we'll start them bleeding, and the blood might not stop."

"Why wouldn't it stop bleeding?" Thordin asked.

Gersalius answered, "I understand his concern. What if what keeps the blood from flowing is some sort of magic field. Would touching it destroy it? If the spell that kept the blood from flowing was destroyed, would normal methods be able to stop the blood, at all?"

"Yes, that is what we fear."

Thordin frowned. "I don't remember anything like that ever happening."

"Are you sure?" Elaine asked.

"I am sure I never knew of anything like that happening, but whether it ever happened. . . ." He shrugged. "I am not a healer."

"How did your friend, the cleric, handle partially healed injuries?" Gersalius asked. He was once again reclining on the furs, tea in hand. The spilled tea was a small wet spot on his robe.

"Kilsendra laid hands on me a second or third time. Sometimes she had to wait a day to regain her strength, but she healed us herself."

"And the wounds?" Elaine asked.

His eyes grew distant, as if he were seeing things long ago and faraway. "We did nothing to them. We waited until Kilsendra could heal us."

"So you don't really know what would happen if more mundane methods were used on magically healed wounds," Gersalius said.

Thordin shook his head slowly. "I guess I don't." He looked at Elaine. "Is the elven cleric awake yet?"

"No, he still sleeps, but the end of his arm has healed over so we didn't have to cauterize it."

Gersalius choked on his tea. When he was done sputtering, he said, "I wouldn't apply fire to any of the wounds. I think that might stop the flesh from healing further."

Elaine suddenly felt cold, and it had nothing to do with the winter wind. What if they had performed normal care? Would they have condemned all three men to being wounded forever? Konrad said that burns were some of the most painful of all injuries. The elf's arm would have been a burned stump instead of the smoothness it was. The arm looked for all the world as if the elf had been born without that arm, a deformity rather than an injury.

"What should we do?" she asked.

"Nothing," Gersalius said. "Wait until the elf wakes. Let him tend the wounds."

"What if one of the wounds begins to bleed? What if the men go into shock? Can we treat them with herbs, or would that be harmful?"

"Do what you must to keep them alive," Gersalius said. "But the bare minimum, I think."

Thordin nodded. "I agree."

"All right, I'll tell Konrad what you advise." She handed the empty tea mug to Thordin. "Thank you for the advice, and the tea." She stood, half-stooping, and lifted the tent flap.

Outside, the air was still as glass and cold enough to hurt when she drew a breath. She stood there for a moment, studying the sky. Clouds had moved in, turning the sky to a perfect whiteness. It threatened snow, but that stillness in the air felt more like thunder. She had only once before seen thunder and lightning in the midst of a snowstorm. It was rare, but so much that was happening was unusual, what was one more event? A little thunderstorm in the dead of winter was a minor thing compared to what she had seen this day. Whatever the cause, the air was close and threatening.

Elaine glanced at Blaine, still puttering before the fire. She almost asked him if he felt it, too, but if he didn't, she would be making him worry for nothing. If the sense was a vision, it would grow. If it wasn't, it would fade, and only Elaine need worry about it.

She clutched her cloak tight around her and hurried back to Konrad. He was kneeling by the elf, his back to the tent flap. He glanced back, a sound or the cold alerting him to her entrance. He motioned her to him.

She pushed her hood back and knelt beside him. "What's wrong?" she whispered.

His hand was feeling for the pulse in the elf's neck. "His heart is not beating like it should."

"Perhaps it is normal for an elf?"

He shook his head. "Before, it was strong and sure; now it is thready, fluttering under my hand. See for yourself."

He rubbed her hands together to banish the cold. She never touched the wounded with icy hands if she could help it. She felt the smooth skin of the neck. The pulse hesitated, then gave a few rapid beats, then settled back into a steady rhythm. She held her hand there for a few moments, but the pulse re-mained steady.

"I felt the flutter, but he seems fine now," she said.

"I don't like it. His heart was fine until just moments ago." He tucked a fur tighter under the elf's chin. "I don't know what's wrong. I don't even know why he won't wake up. I thought at first he was unconscious from his injury, and from doing such powerful magic, but now I . . . I'm just not sure."

"Thordin and Gersalius didn't seem alarmed that the elf was still sleeping."

"What did they say to do about the others' wounds?" he asked.

"As little as possible. When the elf wakes, he can lay hands on their wounds again and again, as many times as needed to heal them."

"An amazing gift, but only if he wakes to do it." He had dropped his voice so low that she had to lean into him to hear. His breath was warm against her face.

"Is something wrong with Silvanus?" Fredric asked. The big man had turned on his side, propped on one elbow.

Randwulf was looking backward at them, still lying flat on the bedding. "What's happening?"

"His heart is beating erratically," Konrad said, without candy-coating it. He was a good healer, but you didn't dare ask his opinion unless you truly wanted it, and wanted the truth, no matter how harsh.

Randwulf sat up, spilling covers to the ground, but Elaine didn't think he was being flirtatious. He looked too frightened to be teasing.

"Is he dying?" Fredric asked. His voice was low and almost matter-of-fact; only his eyes betrayed him. Grief was already licking round the edges of his gray eyes.

"I don't know," Konrad said.

"You're the healer. How can you not know?" Randwulf asked.

"His body is fine. His arm is even healing itself. I have never seen magic healing, and I believe his problem stems from that."

"Do either of you know anything of healing?" Elaine asked.

Randwulf shook his head.

Fredric said, "No, but Averil does."

"I thought she was a magic-user," Konrad said.

"She is, but she makes healing potions and sells them," Fredric said.

"Healing potions," Konrad said. He started to blurt something, closed his lips, then said, "Elaine, go get the girl. Bring her and her potions. Hurry."

Elaine stood and hurried from the tent. She ran, heavy cloak skimming the snow. Averil was in the tent that Elaine and Blaine shared. She was supposed to be resting.

Elaine flung open the tent flap. Averil sat up, blinking, hand clutching her knife. "What's wrong?"

"Your father is ill. Bring your potions and come, quickly."

Averil grabbed her backpack, scrambling for the tent flap. She was wearing only her shift, her dress neatly folded by the bedding. She didn't seem to notice, but pushed past Elaine.

Elaine threw her own cloak over Averil's bare shoulders. The girl began to run; the cloak slipped to the floor, and Elaine left it. She hiked up her skirts and ran with the girl. Elaine noticed the cold, but it didn't seem important, with Averil's fear pulsing in the air.

fourteen

Averil knelt by her father. It wasn't until then that Elaine realized the girl wore no shoes. She had run over the snow in her stockinged feet. Her bare shoulders were blue with cold, but her hands were very steady as she searched for her father's pulse. She undid his shirt and pushed her hand over his heart.

She glanced at Konrad. "His heart beats strongly. His color is good. She said he was ill." Averil glanced up at Elaine. Her eyes were accusatory.

"Keep your hand over his heart, and you will feel it flutter," Konrad said.

"Flutter? What do you mean?"

"The pulse is steady most of the time, but every few minutes the heart hesitates. The problem is growing worse, happening more often."

Averil shook her head. "I feel nothing."

Randwulf and Fredric were sitting to either side, covers tucked round their bare bodies. "He has never had a problem with his heart before," Fredric said.

"No," Averil said, "he hasn't." She kept her hand over his heart, but her liquid gold eyes were growing angry. After only a few hours, Elaine was finding it easier to read her expressions rather than just staring at the strange color of her eyes.

They waited. Elaine found herself willing his heart to falter, which was obscene, but she didn't want Konrad to seem a fool. Besides, she had felt it herself. It was there.

Averil stiffened. A small gasp escaped her lips. She fell utterly still, even holding her breath. Finally she let it out in a long sigh. "Yes, you are right."

She slipped her hand off his heart. Her hand lingered to caress his cheek. The movement was so gentle, so intimate, it was painful to see. "I don't understand this. He was not injured in the heart at all. Why would this be happening?"

"Could it be a strain from raising the dead?" Konrad asked.

Averil shook her head. "No, healers have the ability to heal their own bodies as well as those of others. His heart would mend itself before it got to this point."

"Yet," Konrad said, "something is wrong with his heart."

"I know," she said, her voice harsh. She looked down at her father, then up at Konrad. "I'm sorry. I have no right to snap at you. This is just so inexplicable. It should not be happening."

She opened her backpack and began rummaging in it. There was a soft clink of glass, and heavier duller sounds, like pottery. She extracted a small glass bottle. It was familiar, somehow.

Her vision. She had watched Averil force some liquid down Silvanus's throat in her vision. The girl unstoppered the bottle and raised the elf's head just a little.

"He's unconscious and may choke," Konrad said.

"I'll stroke his throat and get him to swallow it."

"He could still choke."

"I've done this before when the need was great." She looked at Konrad, her liquid eyes full of such sorrow that Elaine had to look away. Konrad did not. Elaine fought the urge to make him look away. Some pain was too private for a stranger's eyes.

"Lift his head for me, Fredric."

The paladin moved forward, cradling the elf's head in his lap. The gold hair mingled with the fur, framing the too-thin face in soft textures. Fredric, who earlier would barely let Elaine look at his bare chest, now was mostly naked to the waist and didn't seem to care.

Averil forced her father's mouth open.

"I'll hold his jaw while you pour," Konrad said.

Averil looked at him a long moment, then nodded. Konrad's strong fingers held the elf's mouth open, and Averil trickled the smallest of doses into it. "Let go now, healer."

Konrad let the lips fall together gently. Averil firmly stroked the elf's throat. He convulsively swallowed.

Moments passed. Silvanus's eyes fluttered open. He blinked up into Fredric's face. The paladin smiled down at him, big hands cradling his head.

"Good afternoon, old friend," Fredric said.

Silvanus smiled. He looked around at the gathered faces. When he found Averil sitting beside him, the smile deepened. She took his remaining hand, holding it in both of hers.

Elaine stared open-mouthed. Konrad made herbal potions, but nothing like this. This was as wondrous as the laying on of hands. A sip, and a badly injured man awoke smiling. She knew Konrad couldn't lay hands, but could he make such potions if he knew the ingredients?

"How do you feel, Father?"

He seemed to think about the question, more than he should have. "I am not sure."

"What do you mean, Father?" She leaned over him, face and voice demonstrating her concern. She touched one hand to his forehead. "I feel no fever."

"It is not fever," he said. He coughed, a great racking sound that doubled him over.

"Raise him up," she said.

Fredric did, cradling the elf in his strong arms. He held him against his bare, scarred chest until the coughing eased. Silvanus's voice was a harsh whisper. "Water."

"Elaine," Konrad said.

She broke the thin skin of ice on the bucket and dipped the wooden cup into it. She handed the water to Konrad, but Averil took it from her. No one protested.

Silvanus took a sip of water. It set him coughing again, but not so badly. He kept sipping water until he could drink without coughing, then he lay back in his friend's arms, exhausted.

"Oh, Father, what is wrong?"

"I'm not sure. I have raised the dead before. I feel so strange."

Averil turned to Konrad. "You are a healer. What is wrong with him?"

Elaine knew the answer; Konrad didn't. He took a deep breath as if trying to decide what to say. "I believe it is a reaction to his healing of the others."

"But he has healed me many times," Fredric said. "He has not been like this before."

"Yes," Randwulf said, "he is a cleric. They heal; it is what they do. It would be like my shooting an arrow and having it harm me. It's ridiculous."

"Perhaps, Randwulf is closer to the truth than he knows," Elaine said softly.

Everyone turned and looked at her. Even Silvanus's strange eyes were upon her face.

"Go on, Elaine," Konrad said. His expression was neutral. It didn't seem to bother him that she was usurping his territory. Konrad always wanted to hear what others had to say, if it would save lives.

Elaine licked her lips and took a shaky breath. Suddenly she felt silly. What if she were wrong? She looked round at their expectant faces. Silvanus's face was very patient, gentle even. What if she were right and did not speak up?

"Gersalius and Thordin say magic healing does not work in Kartakass. Not even laying hands on a wound will work here. But Silvanus has raised the dead. What if he can still heal, but it harms him as it helps others?" Spoken aloud, the idea sounded farfetched, the barest conjecture. She felt heat crawl up her face as they all continued to stare at her.

"That is ridiculous," Averil said. Her voice held the scorn Elaine expected.

"No, Daughter," Silvanus said, voice harsh with coughing. "Hear her out."

Hear her out, Elaine thought, that was it. That was all the theory she had. Averil's face was set in disapproving lines, but she waited. They all waited for Elaine to go on, but there was no more.

Silvanus took his hand from Averil's grasp and held it out to Elaine. The hand trembled slightly. She took it. The skin was cold, or perhaps it was her own hands. She almost apologized for not warming her hands first, but something in his eyes stopped her. She was babbling in her own head, trying desperately to think of something useful to say.

"Do not try so hard," the elf said softly.

What did he mean? "I'm not trying at all."

"Ease your mind. Empty your thoughts. Feel."

It was something Gersalius would have said and just as inexplicable. "I don't know what you mean."

His gold eyes seemed larger than they should have been, great molten pools of glittering metal. The dying light that beat against the tent walls glimmered in those eyes. That glimmer pulled her down. His hand in hers held her up, or she might have fallen.

"You are hurt," she said. Her voice sounded very faraway, even to her own ears. But with the words, Elaine knew she was right. "I feel something around you, in you, mingling with my skin . . . I . . ."

"Life-force, Elaine, you sense my life-force."

She nodded. Of course. His hand tightened around hers, squeezing until she gasped. Then he slumped back, hand almost limp in her grasp. His life-force pulsed and fluttered along with his heart. The heart was steady, but the life-force, that invisible something, was weaker.

"There is nothing wrong with your heart," she said.

"Of course there is. We felt it." Averil's voice was startling. Elaine jerked and turned to look at the girl. It was almost a shock to see those eyes so like what Elaine had just seen, but so unlike, as well.

"Elaine," Silvanus said. That one word brought her back to him. She was not lost in his eyes anymore, but something was happening. Something was growing between them. It held that same slow building of power that she had sensed when Silvanus raised Randwulf.

"If my heart is not injured, what is wrong?" His words were careful, leading her like a string of words through an unfamiliar maze.

"Your life-force is hurt. Something feeds on it."

"What feeds on me, Elaine?" His voice gentle, his hand firm in her grasp.

She could see the others, knew she still knelt in the tent. Elaine was still aware. It was not like the magic that Gersalius had shown her, where she had lost herself in herself. Now she was aware of power, but only the spark of it was inside her. She stared at Silvanus. "Am I drawing power from you?"

"No, Elaine," he said softly.

"Then where . . ." Even as she asked it, she knew the answer. She felt the earth under her move, roll like a giant waking from long slumber. "The land." That last was the barest of whispers. She wasn't sure anyone heard, but Silvanus's eyes said he knew. Whether she spoke aloud or not, he knew.

In that one instant, she knew one other thing. The land hated the cleric. The sensation was so strong, it escaped her lips in a soft moan.

"Elaine, are you all right?" Konrad asked. He touched her shoulder.

"Don't touch me!" The fierceness in her voice surprised even her. Hatred spilled through her, scalding. He did not love her. How dare he? Elaine shook her head sharply, as if trying to wake from a dream.

"You are still yourself, Elaine. You gain power, but you never lose yourself in it," Silvanus said.

That voice drove out the hate, let her think clearly again. It was this power that the land, Kartakass, despised. The cleric was stronger, in some ways, than all the land combined.

"Konrad, you must not touch me, not now." Her voice sounded almost normal, but the edge of anger was still there, roughening it, making Konrad's eyes widen.

"What is happening?" Konrad asked. He looked at Silvanus when he spoke.

"She is laying hands on me, to heal me."

"But she cannot do it," Konrad said.

"Oh, but she can," the elf said. His face was utterly serene, confident Elaine could do it. His belief was her belief. Her source was hatred, envy, but she was not. She was still Elaine Clairn, who had lived all her life in Kartakass. The land had fed and clothed and held her in its dark arms, forever.

She let those dark arms touch her now, aware for the first time that the very ground was alive with something more than next year's crop. It should have frightened her, but it did not. That lack of fear should have frightened her all on its own.

She felt her own body, beating, pulsing, living. She was aware as never before of the workings of her flesh. Over all that ran a force like water, running over and through her. That water ran into Kartakass and out again, like the source of a spring, though water was just a word to use where no words were sufficient. It was a device to hold in her mind what shouldn't have existed. Water, but it was not water at all.

"Look at me, Elaine. What do you feel?"

She looked at Silvanus, felt his skin, the bones of his hands against her own. There, a flutter in the water that ran round his skin. A patch of darkness that had attached itself to him when he healed here in Kartakass.

Elaine reached out her hand to that darkness, drawing power from the same source that sought to destroy him. She touched not his heart but that force that wove round him. Her hand hovered over his chest because that was the weak point, the place of attack, but it wasn't the heart she sought to make whole. It was his life-force, that invisible water that held him safe. The darkness was like a hole through which the water could seep away until there was nothing but an empty skin left.

But if it had been a hole, Elaine would have tried to plug it; if it had been a stain, she would have cleansed it; but it was more a thing to be plucked off, a piece of darkness attached to suck away life in bits and pieces.

She drew that patch of blackness into her hand, into the invisible force around her own body, and let it flow down her into the ground itself. Kartakass swallowed its blemish back into itself with hardly a murmur.

Then Elaine did lay her hand on his chest. She felt his heart underneath the cloth, the skin. It seemed she could have closed her hands around the heart and squeezed. Instead she poured some of that invisible force through her hand and over his heart. The power itself seemed to know what to do. It mended the damage the blackness had caused, healed without Elaine really knowing how it worked. It was not her hand, her knowledge. She was just a tool.

Silvanus took a deep, shuddering breath. Elaine raised her hand from his chest. He smiled, and she could not help but smile back. She released his hand and knelt back from him, hands clasped in her lap.

She was herself again—alone, aware of that invisible force, but distantly—and she felt the distant beat of Kartakass, almost like music just out of hearing. The sensation drifted away until it was gone, and she was herself again. The last thing she sensed was a vague pleasure. The land was pleased.

fifteen

THE NIGHT WAS BITTER COLD. JONATHAN SAT BY THE fire in their camp. He stared into the orange flames until his eyes ached, then turned toward the darkness, night-blind from the light. Tereza sat watch at the edge of the campsite, huddled in her cloak. Konrad had been on watch when Jonathan sat down. How long had he been by the fire?

He wanted to call his wife over to talk, but didn't. She was sitting in the cold dark so her eyes could see without being ruined by the flames, far enough away from the tents that she might see whatever might be creeping on them.

Tereza was guarding; he would not distract her from that. His brooding before the fire would bother her enough. She would worry about his frame of mind. When he sat for so long unmoving, thinking, it was often a bad sign. He tended to black moods, but this was not a mood. He was trying to make sense of what he had seen this day.

Jonathan had always believed magic to be evil, or at least weak, lazy. Most things that magic could accomplish could be done by honest work. The task was harder, perhaps, and took longer, but it could be done.

But this . . . raising the dead to true life. Jonathan held his hands close to the flames until the blood was like to boil. The fire did not seem warm enough. Perhaps it was not his body that was cold, but something deeper.

The extra tent they had packed for emergencies was set up against the soft rise of the hill behind him. The elven cleric and his daughter were tucked safely away behind the hide walls. And the two men, the two deadmen, had gone to their bedrolls cheerfully, tired, but not worse for wear. How could that be?

A soft sound behind him made him whirl, his heart pounding in his throat. It was Elaine. She held her white cloak tight about her. There were still bloodstains here and there on the fur.

She was the last person Jonathan wished to see.

She stood there, face uncertain, as if she knew she was not welcome. The hurt in her green-blue eyes cut him like a knife. He did not want to hurt her. For her, he had betrayed everything he thought he believed. He had saved her life, but had he endangered something more precious? And whose fault was that? His? No one's?

He extended a hand to her. She smiled and came to him, taking it. He drew her into the circle of his arm and his cloak, as he had when she was small.

With a sigh, she settled against him. It was the same sound she'd made when she was ten, the first time Jonathan had ever held a child and told the lies that all parents tell, that the world is fair, and adult arms can protect them from all harm. Her hair was soft against his face and smelled of herbs and . . . her. The warm scent of a child. No mere perfume could ever disguise it from him.

"Was it real?" she asked, softly.

"Was what real?"

"The elf, he brought those two men back from the dead. I saw it, but I still don't believe it."

"I wouldn't have believed it either, had I not witnessed it myself."

"Thordin and Gersalius said no cleric should have been able to raise the dead in Kartakass. Why is that?"

"I don't know."

"Did you know Gersalius was an outlander, like Thordin?" she asked.

"No, I didn't." Jonathan wondered what else he didn't know about the wizard.

"Could the elf heal Calum?"

Jonathan sat very still. He had been so busy worrying about magic and the state of souls, the matter of Calum had slipped his mind. It was Elaine, the corrupted magic-wielder, who had thought of Calum and his pain. Jonathan was ashamed of both his forgetfulness and his suspicions.

"I don't know. Thordin has spoken of them healing wounds, injuries, but not disease, not old age."

"But perhaps Calum would not mind being old so much if he were not in such pain." She looked up at him, her head still on his shoulder, a mere rolling of eyes. It was an old gesture; for a moment, the little girl looked out at him. Then she straightened, not pulling away, but looking directly at him. Her eyes were honest and unrelenting.

"Do you hate me?" She did not turn away after she had asked it, but met his gaze. Whatever his response, Jonathan would have to speak it into those familiar blue-green eyes.

"I could never hate you, Elaine. You know that."

She searched his face as if looking for some clue. "I know you hate magic and all who practice it. Now I am a mage, or learning to become one. You hate that I have magic in me." The last was statement, pure fact.

Jonathan had to look away from her searching eyes. He stared into the flames.

Her fingertips touched his bearded chin and turned his face back to her. "Tell me true, no half-truths."

"You are as dear to me as flesh of my flesh."

"That is not the question I asked." She was relentless. Tereza was the bravest woman he had ever known, but even she might not have pushed the question. Tereza might never have asked at all; most people wouldn't. They would fear the answer too much.

"I wish you were not a mage, Elaine."

"I know that," she said. Small frown lines formed between her eyes. "Do you hate it? Do you wish me to leave?" It was her turn to face away. She huddled against him, but would not meet his eyes. "I wasn't going to ask that, but I couldn't stand to watch you hate me, Jonathan." She looked up suddenly, the pain in her eyes so raw it made him gasp.

"I would rather go away than watch you grow to fear me."

"Fear you? I don't . . ."

"I saw the look on Tereza's face in the shed that night. I saw your face after my vision." She shook her head. "You were both afraid of me."

"Of your new powers, perhaps, but not of you." He hugged her to him, chin resting in her yellow hair. "Never of you."

"I know you're lying." Her voice was choked with tears. "I can read your thoughts like words on a page."

He pushed away from her, half-tumbling before the fire. His heart choked in his throat. His lips formed the word, and said it soundlessly, a silent hiss: "Witch."

Tears shimmered in her eyes like water at the brim of a glass. She widened her eyes, fighting so no tear would fall. "I have my answer." She stood, hugging her cloak to her as if it could protect from more than cold. "When we come back from Cortton, I will pack my things and go with Gersalius. We can go back to his home. I don't think he will mind that I can read his thoughts."

She turned and walked slowly back to her tent. Her spine was rigid, movements confident, proud, stiff with pain.

He wanted to call her back, to say he was sorry, and he was. He was sorry, so terribly sorry, but he had fought magic all his life. He could not change now. If she had not confronted him, they could have pretended. He could have pretended, but if she could read his thoughts . . . it was hopeless.

He sat up, folding his cloak closer about him. Tereza came to stand beside him. "What did you and Elaine talk of?" She knelt to warm her hands before the fire.

Jonathan did not answer right away. He didn't want to tell his wife what a fool he was, though if anyone knew his frailties, it was Tereza. The wonder was that she stayed with him.

"Talk to me, Jonathan. She was crying when she left."

"She asked me if I hated her for being a mage."

"And you said yes?" Her voice was outraged.

He looked up at her, anger flaring through him. "Of course not!"

"Then what happened?" Her face was already angry, frowning and suspicious.

"She read my thoughts. I can lie in words. I can lie even with eyes and gestures—but thoughts, Tereza . . . who can lie with thoughts?"

She stood up so abruptly her cloak trailed into the fire, sending sparks whirling skyward. She stalked around the fire like a caged beast, every movement etched with anger.

"And what did she say after she read your thoughts?"

"She said . . ." He could not say it. To say it out loud to Tereza would make it real. If he told anyone else, Elaine would leave, and he wouldn't have a chance to apologize, to beg her not to go.

"Jonathan," she stood across the fire, hands on hips. The flames bathed her face in strong shadows, leaping light. "What did she say?"

"I'll make it all right. I'll talk to her."

"Jonathan . . ." Tereza let her hands fall to her sides, cloak swinging closed. She stood there like a pillar of flame. "She's going away, isn't she?"

Jonathan wanted to look away, to not see the accusation in her eyes, but he forced himself not to move, not to blink, not to flinch. He would always remember the disappointment on Tereza's face. The contempt.

"I told her she was as dear to me as a daughter."

"But you couldn't hide your hatred of her magic." She bit off each word, spitting it at him. He had never seen her so enraged, not at him. It frightened him.

"She knew I hated the magic. That wasn't what bothered her the most," he said.

"What then?"

"It is the fact that we fear her powers. That is what she cannot tolerate."

"We?"

"She said you were afraid of her after the night in the shed."

Tereza glanced away, then back. The righteous anger slipped away from her face. "She's right."

"I know," he said softly.

They stared at each other over the crackling fire. A branch broke with a sharp sound, settling farther into the fire. Sparks spilled upward into the dark. The sound of the flame was loud like voices whispering in the other room.

"What are we to do, Jonathan?"

He shook his head. "Perhaps, we can ask the wizard for help."

"You would do that, turn to a wizard on such a personal matter?" She looked surprised.

"To keep Elaine with us, I would do nearly anything."

Tereza smiled, and something inside of Jonathan relaxed. He felt as if he'd been given a reprieve from a sentence of death. Tereza had forgiven him.

She walked around the fire to put her arms around his shoulders, resting her chin atop his head. "If neither of us wants her to leave, surely she will stay."

He said nothing, and it was nearly a lie, that silence. He had seen Elaine's face, felt her pull away from his arms. If she could read their thoughts, thoughts they could not control. . . . But he said nothing. He didn't want to fight with Tereza tonight. He needed her arms around him too much to risk it.

"Elaine asked if the elven healer could heal Calum."

Tereza grew very still against him. He knew she was rolling the thought round in her mind. "Could he truly save Calum?"

"He called the dead back, Tereza. I would believe him capable of anything."

She slid to her knees, arms still around him. "If he could save Calum . . . we must send him to Calum at once."

"He lost an arm today, a grave wound. Do you think he is well enough to travel days back in the cold by himself, with just his own people?"

"We would go with him."

"Calum gave us this task to perform. If the elf, Silvanus, cannot heal him, Cortton will be the last evil we ever fight at Calum's bidding. I cannot fail him now."

"But if he can truly be cured?"

"We can tell Silvanus tomorrow about Calum's illness. He may not be able to cure a disease, especially a disease of old age."

"My mother was years older than Calum, and she died quietly in her sleep. Old age does not have to end in such misery."

He patted her hand. "Good to hear."

She smiled suddenly. "You are not old."

"I am no longer young."

She hugged him tight. "That is not the same as being old."

He didn't argue; he didn't want to. Watching Calum's strong body being eaten away by pain and age had made Jonathan aware of his own mortality in a way that no battle ever had.

"We'll talk to Elaine tomorrow," Tereza said.

He nodded. "Yes, tomorrow."

Tomorrow they would talk with Elaine. Tomorrow they would speak with the healer. Tomorrow, perhaps, Silvanus would tell them he could save Calum Songmaster. But even after what Jonathan had seen this day, he did not truly believe. It was as unreal as a dream. He mistrusted anything that promised to give him his heart's desire. Healing was still a form of magic. Magic often promised exactly what a person most wanted, then found a way to cheat him. He feared he might have his heart's desire as long as he didn't mind fiends feasting on his heart.

"Let's go to bed." Tereza helped him stand. His knees were stiff from sitting so long in the cold, even with the fire so near. A few years ago the cold had not made his bones ache.

She kissed him gently on the cheek, as if she, too, could read his gloomy thoughts. "It will all look better in the morning, Husband. I promise."

He smiled and let her know he believed her. It was a lie. A lie that he told with his eyes. Perhaps if he practiced enough, he could fool Elaine as well. This reading his thoughts was harder. Perhaps the wizard would have a cure for that.

Could he really let a wizard, any wizard, work a spell on him? He did not think so. But he hoped so. For Elaine's sake, he hoped so.

sixteen

HARKON LUKAS WATCHED THE CAMPSITE. HE STOOD wrapped in a wine-dark cloak. A matching hat swept round his head, a hat more suited for a ball than winter travel. White ostrich feathers fluttered on it, and the wind tugged at the feathers as if trying to steal them. His long hair blew in tangles across his face. He should have been noticeable standing among the winter-dark trees in his ridiculous hat.

Harkon had watched the camp since Konrad had stood watch. Neither Konrad nor Tereza had seen the tall figure moving in the darkness. Now Thordin stood watch, and somehow he didn't see Harkon either. It was good to rule the land. It gave a person certain . . . abilities.

Harkon might even have loved his land of Kartakass were he not trapped here. The country was too small to satisfy his ambitions and appetites. He could trap others inside the borders, but could not free himself. The irony was not lost on him.

He sniffed the cold, tugging wind. He smelled . . . goodness. Not one, but a handful of shining goody-two-shoes lay in one of the tents. New blood come to the land. He had not brought these people over. Sometimes the land itself plucked away someone from another place. There seemed no logic to the land's choices, or none that he could understand.

Harkon ran fingers under his cloak, over a small bump in his tunic. It was a magic amulet, an amulet that allowed the wearer to switch bodies, whether the other person wished it or not. He had seen it used once, had killed the owner of the amulet, and kept it, until he found the right use for it.

He had been forced to flee from Konrad Burn. The warrior was a superb fighter, and Harkon had feared he might be forced to harm the man in order to save himself. It wouldn't have done to damage the very body he planned to inhabit. So he had fled, leaving his dire wolves to be slaughtered.

A growl started low in his chest, climbing up his throat to spill in a snarl from his lips. The sound should have had fur around it, and fangs. If anyone had been near enough to hear and see, they would have known him for what he was: a wolfwere. Harkon had never been human, but once he held Konrad Burn's body, would he be human? Would he lose his ability to shapechange?

He did not know. So much was unknown, but the gamble was worth it. If he could be free to travel all the lands, his power would know no bounds.

He stood contemplating his future conquests. It brought a smile to his handsome face. Killing usually did.

Konrad Burn was part Vistani. He didn't look it, but he was, and he could travel to any land because of it. Jonathan Ambrose's mother had been a gypsy, too, so he was also free to travel. But Ambrose was too old. If Harkon really did become human, he wanted as many years left to him as possible.

He had thought about taking his choice of gypsies, but something had protected them, as if the land itself kept them safe.

Harkon did not understand why, but he knew that to harm them was to risk much. Kartakass was his, yet there were some things the land would not allow. Harming gypsies was one of them.

Why had the land brought in these new people? They stank of goodness. The smell of it attracted evil. Harkon himself had been drawn to them. They had come so conveniently near to him and his wolves. Harkon wanted to feast on pure flesh, to crack the bones of saintly men and suck the marrow from them. There was nothing like fresh marrow to warm a wolfwere on a cold winter's day. Then it had all gone wrong. Had the land planned it that way? He was never sure how conscious of its own actions the land was.

They had killed the two that shone the brightest, extinguished that goodness forever. He had been far away in the forest when he felt what the cleric had done. It had felt like a great stabbing whiteness in his head. Even behind closed eyelids he could see the light. It had called to every evil thing in the land. If Harkon had not forbidden it, the creatures of Kartakass would have descended on the party like a plague. They wouldn't have survived a mile. But his future body was traveling with these interlopers. Harkon would not risk any harm coming to Konrad Burn until he himself brought it.

The wolfwere watched through the night, for he did not trust every evil thing that crawled or flew in Kartakass, not with so much shining goodness blazing forth. It was a candle flame to a moth, irresistible though it burned away the wings that bore the creature to it.

Harkon had made it plain he would punish anyone who harmed them, but there were things in the land that would care more for the killing than the punishment afterward. Harkon sympathized, and once he had the body, the land could slaughter every man and woman among them.

But for now, Harkon Lukas stood knee-deep in snow—cold, irritable, and watching over them all. The bard of Kartakass guarded the sleep of Jonathan Ambrose, mage-finder.

Harkon, who enjoyed irony when it was at someone else's expense, chuckled in the winter's dark. Perhaps he would tell the mage-finder what had kept him safe in his travels, tell him, watch his face crumble in disbelief, then kill him. A low, growl trickled from his lips. Yes, that sounded like fun. A poor wolfwere was entitled to a little fun in the middle of a larger plot. A little frivolous cruelty always made him feel better.

seventeen

THE NEXT MORNING, THE SKY WAS AN UNRELIEVED white that promised snow. Beneath that sky came Elaine's horse, wandering back into camp without the slightest hint of apology for nearly breaking the girl's back. There was a gleam in its eyes that said it would be happy to give it another try. Elaine had hoped it had been eaten by wolves.

Thordin spooned stew into thick pockets of bread that he had made to hold the stew. It was an invention of his from his homeland. He called them "kangaroo sandwiches." A much younger Elaine had asked what a kangaroo was, and his description had been so funny, she hadn't believed him. Carrying its young around in a pouch, indeed. It was a tale to enthrall travelers who could never check one's story. But she, like all the others, dutifully called them kangaroo sandwiches.

Elaine sat on a log by the fire, Blaine beside her. He was on his second sandwich. Silvanus and Averil sat across the fire, eyeing the morning fare.

"How are you this morning?" Elaine asked.

"I feel quite myself again." Silvanus gave her a small nod.

Konrad had convinced the strangers not to mention anything

to Jonathan of Elaine's new talent, fearing that one more magical ability would make the mage-finder send her packing. Elaine had told no one of what she and Jonathan had discussed before the fire last night. She doubted Jonathan could think less of her than he already did, nor she of him.

Fredric and Randwulf reclined before the fire, wrapped thickly against the cold. Konrad had bandaged the wounds that still bled. Silvanus had been too weak to heal them yesterday, so Elaine had volunteered, but the elf thought she was too new. He had helped her heal himself. Neither of the warriors could do that.

Fredric took a small bite of the kangaroo sandwich. He rolled it around, tasting. Then a broad smile spread across his face. "This is wonderful." He finished the rest in three bites. Randwulf matched him, bite for bite. Being wounded clearly hadn't affected their appetites.

The elf and his daughter took smaller bites, but seemed to enjoy the food. Anyone who had eaten Blaine's dinner of gray stuffing, herb-sauced sausages, and rock-cake cookies was grateful for the simpler but more edible meal. Thordin had no gourmet pretensions, but he could cook anything and make it tasty. On really long trips, it was best not to ask what was in the stew. There were some meats that, despite their pleasant flavor, turned the knowing stomach.

Elaine glanced back at Silvanus. There was something different about him, some change overnight that her eyes noticed but her mind could not make sense of. What was it? Something had changed in his appearance. Not that she had become an expert on what elves, even this particular elf, should look like.

Silvanus had no trouble eating the sandwiches one-handed.

Had Thordin made them knowing the wounded could eat them easily? Probably. Thordin was thoughtful and courteous, when he could be so quietly.

"Which one are you staring at?" Blaine asked. He spoke low, face nearly touching her hair.

She felt the heat climb up her face and knew she was blushing. It was like an admission of guilt though she was entirely innocent.

"It is impolite to stare at people," she said. She was now staring fixedly at the ground. No matter what had happened between them, Silvanus was a near stranger, and she had been staring. It would be too awful if Silvanus thought as Blaine did, that she was staring at him.

Blaine grinned. "Then what were you staring at?" His grin was the crooked one he wore when he was determined to tease.

"There is something different about the elf this morning, but I can't figure out what it is."

Blaine glanced across the fire. Averil caught him looking and smiled. He grinned back, not upset in the least to have been caught looking at a pretty girl.

"You two look a fine pair, whispering before the fire." The voice made her whirl. The wizard was behind them. He had come quiet as a cat, unheard through the snow.

He smiled. "I didn't mean to frighten you."

Elaine wanted to say he hadn't, but her heart was beating in her throat, and she didn't trust herself to speak.

"I've never heard a man move like that. Silent as a spy," Blaine said.

The wizard shrugged. "Live long enough and you learn a few useful tricks."

"That was no trick," Elaine said softly.

"Nor was it magic," the wizard said.

She frowned at him. She didn't believe him.

"We all have inborn abilities, Elaine. I was called Gersalius Catpaw in my youth. I once thought of being a thief, but my mother said she'd cut off my ears if I disgraced the family." He laughed. "She was always threatening such dire things. I don't think she ever took a switch to any of us."

The wizard sat down next to them. Thordin handed him food. "I hope your old bones find this traveling easier than mine," the fighter said.

The wizard nodded. "It isn't only age, Thordin. I have hidden away in my own cottage for years. I haven't gone on a long journey for over a decade."

"You don't complain much," Thordin said.

"Complaining about hardship doesn't drive it away, though it does drive away one's companions."

"True."

Elaine leaned close to the wizard and whispered. "Is there something different about the elf? I think there is, but I can't quite see it."

Gersalius nodded, mouth too full to speak. He swallowed and said, "Observant girl. His arm's longer."

She sat very still, looking at him. "What do you mean, his arm's longer?"

"The wounded arm is growing back." He ate more sandwich, smiling and happy as if what he had just said were perfectly possible.

"But the arm was torn off, completely. It's gone."

The wizard finished his sandwich, wiping his hands on his

robe. "You saw him call the dead back from the beyond. Why shouldn't the arm grow back?"

"I . . . don't know, but . . . but . . ." She just stared at him. She wanted to sputter and say it was impossible. She had half convinced herself that the two men hadn't really been dead, just gravely injured, and he had healed them. That was miracle enough. But the elf's arm was longer. The arm had been missing above the elbow, now there was almost a whole joint there. It was a hand-span longer.

Was the skin still smooth and thick with flesh? Elaine had an almost overwhelming urge to unwrap the arm, to see it bare. Was bone poking through the skin? Did it bud like a flower?

Silvanus met her gaze. "Do you have a question for me, Elaine?" His liquid-gold eyes were calm and smiling. There was about him an aura of peace that Elaine found intriguing.

"I didn't mean to stare."

"It is all right to stare when your intentions are to learn. I see a question in your eyes. Ask it."

She took a deep breath and asked the question quickly, as if it would sound less strange if she rushed through the words. "Is your arm truly growing back?" No, even fast, the question seemed ridiculous. And yet . . . she could see for herself that the arm was longer.

He smiled. "Yes, it is growing back."

"Does it hurt?"

"No, but it does itch abominably." He gave a small laugh like the distant ringing of bells. Human throats did not sound like that.

"How does it grow back? I mean . . ." Elaine tried to think how to phrase the question.

"Elaine, just ask, the perfect words for such questions are never found," Gersalius said.

"Is the arm growing back in stages? Is the bone growing first, then the flesh covering it, or does it grow all at once like a tree limb?" It sounded a very personal question, but she wanted to know. Her hands itched to touch the growing stump.

Elaine looked down at the ground, afraid he would see the eagerness in her eyes and mistake it for something else.

"Would you like to see it?" Silvanus asked.

She looked up at him, studying his face. Was he teasing her? No. His face was pleasant, but serious.

"Yes, very much." Elaine was surprised by the eagerness in her own voice. She had to learn magic, for it would control her otherwise, but healing . . . she wanted to learn healing, too.

Blaine was looking at her strangely. She had not told him she might be a healer, like Silvanus. It wasn't that she had tried to keep it from him. It was more that she herself didn't believe it yet. It was both too wonderful and too frightening to share, even with Blaine.

She touched his arm, leaning close to whisper. "I'll explain all later. I don't want Jonathan to know."

Blaine tipped back from her to see her face, then leaned in, breathing words against her skin. "Is it another magic?"

She nodded.

He hugged her briefly. "You must tell me everything later." His face was very serious when he said it.

"Promise," she said softly. She caught movement from the corner of her eyes. Jonathan was walking toward them, his cloak held close to his body against the cold. It was hard to see his expression with the hood up, but Elaine thought he was scowling.

Of course, that could have been her own insecurity. She hadn't realized she did anything differently, but Blaine touched her arm. "What's wrong?"

What could she say—that Jonathan was afraid of her? That he hated what she was? Elaine shook her head. "Jonathan is unhappy with me."

"With the magic?"

She nodded.

Blaine squeezed her arm. "It'll be all right. He'll come around."

She looked into his face, trying to see if he were just saying something to comfort her, or if he believed what he was saying. His eyes, his face, his touch were utterly sincere. He believed. Elaine wished she did.

Silvanus's sleeve was tied up with string. He undid the string and began to push back the cloth.

"What are you doing?" Jonathan asked.

"Elaine wishes to see my arm. She is curious about how it grows," the elf said. He said it as if it were an everyday occurrence.

Jonathan stared down at him. "What do you mean, your arm is growing?"

"It is growing back," Silvanus said.

Jonathan shook his head. "I do not think I can face another miracle before breakfast."

Silvanus smiled and continued to roll up his empty sleeve.

Jonathan put a hand outward as if to push something away. "Please, I do not wish to look at your . . . injured arm while I eat."

Silence fell on the little group. An appalled silence. Thordin stood, spoon dripping stew on the ground. "Jonathan, the cleric is a guest at our fire."

"I have no problem with him as a guest, but surely it is rude even in your homeland to show wounds at a meal."

Put like that, Jonathan might have a point. Yet he should have let it go. They were guests. You did not make a guest uncomfortable, not deliberately.

Silvanus gave a small bow from the neck. "I have no desire to be offensive." Averil had to help him refold his sleeve and tie it in place.

Elaine felt her face burn with shame. Silvanus didn't seem offended, but she didn't know him well enough to know if it were just a polite act.

She stood. "I asked him to show me his arm." She faced Jonathan across the fire, not flinching from the disapproval in his eyes.

"Then you should have gone to a tent. I do not see why you would want to see it."

"It doesn't bother you that the arm has been cut off. It bothers you that it is growing back. That it is magic." There was scorn in her voice, scorn bordering on hate. She still loved Jonathan, but she was beginning to detest his narrow-mindedness.

Jonathan stared at her. His expression was unreadable.

"You're afraid of it," she said.

"What do you want of me, Elaine?" His voice was suddenly tired.

She suddenly realized what she wanted. She wanted him to be someone else. To be fair. Elaine was beginning to realize that he might not be able to be fair, might not be able to move beyond his vision of evil. Her eyes stung with unshed tears.

"I need to finish healing Fredric's and Randwulf's wounds," Silvanus said.

Jonathan and Elaine looked at him as if he had just appeared before them. They had been intent on each other. The elf's voice was an intrusion. Whether a welcome one or not, Elaine wasn't sure.

"I had planned to heal them out here in the open, but if it will make you ill, we can retire to a tent."

Jonathan shook his head abruptly. "No, heal them. It was unfair to protest just a moment ago. I am unaccustomed to such strange magic. It is . . . uncomfortable for me."

Silvanus looked at him, his face thoughtful. "Thank you, Jonathan. I will heal them here by the fire. It is warmer here than in most of the tents."

Jonathan gave a curt nod. He took his sandwich from Thordin and sat down on the opposite side of the fire, his back to them so he could not see. But Elaine could see his face. That one look was enough to know what it had cost him to let the elf heal by the fire. He was trying. Maybe he was sorry about last night, too?

He glanced up and caught her eye. They stared at each other. Elaine gave a small smile, and Jonathan answered it. The first stirrings of "magic" tickled over her skin. She turned from Jonathan's smile to the cleric, the healing. She wanted to see the wounds close, instant healing. It was the stuff of legends. Hopeful stories told round winter fires when the wolves howled at the door.

Elaine stood and took a few steps toward the cleric. She did not glance back at Jonathan. She was afraid he'd be frowning. She didn't want to lose what good will they had gained, but she didn't want to miss seeing this miracle, either.

Silvanus clasped Fredric's bandaged arm in his one good hand.

He did not throw his head back, as he had to raise the dead. It was a simpler task he set himself. He merely touched the wound and drew power.

Elaine felt the power breathing along her body, but something was wrong. She wasn't sure what, but it felt different. Incomplete.

Silvanus hunched his shoulders. She could see the tension in his body. The effort shuddered along his collarbones. His hand trembled. He lifted his palm from the bandaged area.

"Take off the bandage," he said.

"What's wrong, Silvanus?" Fredric asked.

"Please, just take off the bandage."

Fredric didn't argue again, but did as he was told. When the bloody bandages came away, the wound was still there. It had not healed.

Fredric's eyes widened. "Silvanus, what has happened?"

The elf shook his head. "Randwulf, bare one of your wrist wounds for me, please."

The younger man had no teasing words, he simply unwrapped his right wrist. The wound no longer bled, but it was still an open bite, nasty to look at and painful. Without a word, Randwulf offered his arm to the cleric.

Silvanus touched the wound, delicately, fingertips alone. He traced the laceration as if exploring it. Randwulf winced, but made no sound.

The elf closed his hand over the wound and bowed his head, concentrating. Again the soft, growing magic built, fluttering in the air like a trapped bird, a bird that had no where to fly. Something was very wrong. Elaine had no words for exactly what, but she knew it shouldn't happen like this. Even without the ability to sense the healing, the looks on the two fighters' faces were enough. They were shocked, frightened.

Averil knelt by her father. He was still shuddering, struggling to heal. She touched his shoulders, gently. "Father, Father, please."

He shook her hands off and half fell to the ground. His cloak trailed into the fire. Elaine knelt and rescued the cloth. It hadn't begun to burn yet.

He turned to Elaine. "I cannot do it. I cannot heal them." His face was raw with anguish.

"Of course you can," she said. It was a lie, even as she said it, she knew that, but she said it anyway.

"Wizard," Silvanus said, eyes searching for Gersalius.

Gersalius came to stand in front of the elf. "Yes, my friend." His voice was full of a deep pity.

"You said I should not be able to heal here in Kartakass. Why was that?"

"I do not know why, Silvanus, but I know that it is so." He turned to Thordin, who was kneeling by the fire, stirring his stew but watching the cleric. "You had a cleric friend who came over. Did she know why she could no longer heal?"

"Kilsendra said she could no longer reach her god, that she was somehow cut off from her deity." Thordin's voice was heavy; he didn't like saying it.

Silvanus shook his head. "That is not possible. Bertog cannot be separated from his clerics. No, that is not it."

Thordin shrugged. "I can tell you only what Kilsendra told me. I was never a healer."

Silvanus turned to Elaine. His glittering eyes searched her face. "Elaine . . ." He let the sentence trail off. He did not look to where

Jonathan still sat. He did not have to. Konrad had explained some of Elaine's plight, and the cleric had promised not to reveal that she, too, knew some magic.

Elaine glanced back. Jonathan was watching. His squeamishness forgotten in the novelty of it all. His face was watchful, curious. If he hadn't been so terribly afraid, he might have been nearly as curious as she was, as he was curious about everything else. But his fear stood like an unbreakable wall.

If Jonathan knew what she had done, she would be even less human to him. She turned back to Silvanus. He watched her with quiet eyes. He would not berate her if she refused. She knew that. If he had argued, or threatened, Elaine could have said no, but those quietly patient eyes . . . she could not say no to them. More than that, she didn't want to say no. She wanted to know if she could do it, if she could close a wound with a touch.

She nodded. "Show me how."

Silvanus flashed her a smile that warmed her like the glow of the sun itself. "Touch Fredric's wound."

"What are you saying?" Thordin asked. "Elaine is no healer."

"Oh, but she is," Silvanus said. "She helped heal me yesterday."

"Elaine," Gersalius said, "that is wonderful."

"Why didn't you tell us," Thordin said.

Elaine glanced at Jonathan.

Thordin said, "Oh."

They all turned back to the cleric, determined as far as possible to ignore the mage-finder—if one could ignore a storm that might break any minute.

"Touch the wound, Elaine, explore it. Memorize the feel of it in your fingertips," Silvanus said.

Elaine hesitated, hands just above Fredric's bare flesh. Her skin ached to touch the wound, to explore it, but . . . "Won't it hurt him?"

"A little, but you are new at healing. You must understand the nature of the injury before you can heal it. You must be free to touch the wound as much as necessary." He glanced up at the big warrior's face. "Fredric takes pain well. He won't hold it against you."

"If you can heal me, girl, I will have only praise for your name."

Still she hesitated. "And if I can't?"

"Then you will have tried, and I will sing your praises for that." A smile peeked from behind his mustache.

Elaine gave a nervous smile in return and let her fingers touch the wound. The skin folded back on itself where the teeth had torn it. She ran fingertips over the gash, over bumps in the skin with slick holes underneath.

She glanced at Fredric's face, but it was blank, unreadable. "If I hurt you, tell me, and I'll stop."

He shook his head. "I've had far worse done to me than to suffer a lady to touch a small wound."

The injury was not small, and they all knew it. The partial healing that Silvanus had managed yesterday had given him use of the arm, but until it was healed completely, he would not be at full fighting strength. He wore a great two-handed sword strapped to his back and needed two good arms to wield it.

She had trailed over the surface of the skin, but her fingers wanted to go deeper. Elaine glanced at Silvanus. "I don't want to hurt him."

"Do you remember in the tent how you explored my life-force until you could sense the darkness?"

She nodded.

"You must explore the wound the same way. You must know if the damage is shallow, or if muscles or bones are involved. What you did yesterday is really much harder, for you cannot hold an aura in your hands. You can't even truly visualize it. You can see the bite with your eyes, touch it with your own skin. When you know the surface of the wound, reach inward, but not with your fingers. Yesterday, you felt like you could hold my heart in your hand, didn't you?"

"Yes, I did."

"Search this wound until you can feel your fingers melting into his flesh, searching his muscles for injury."

Elaine bent back over the wound. She took a deep breath, then pressed her fingers deep into the teeth marks. Fredric let out a sharp, soft exhalation of air. Elaine didn't look up. If she saw pain in his eyes, she wasn't sure she could do this. And she wanted to do this. She could feel that same growing power. It flowed through her, from Kartakass. The land was with her. She could feel it, almost as if it were curious.

Her fingers dug into flesh. There was a soft grunt of pain. Elaine closed her eyes, pressing her hands around the arm. She pushed her hands over the wound, fingers half-curled, searching the torn flesh, sinking deeper through the injuries. It was as if her fingertips slid inside the wounds and kept going. They traveled through layers of muscle. Blood flowed around them, all safely below the surface, like a hidden river. She touched the bone itself, fingering it like a piece of jewelry, trying to memorize the feel of it.

"Is there any injury below the surface?" Even Silvanus's soft voice made her jump. She lost that feel of slick bone, and working muscle. She blinked and dropped her hands to her lap.

"There is some bruising, but nothing more. Nothing's broken."

Silvanus smiled. "Good, now it is time to close the wound."

"How do I do that?"

"You must heal it from inside out. Find the bruised flesh and heal it, then come outward and close the wounds behind you."

She stared at him, frowning. "I think I understand healing the inner bruising, but how do the wounds close up behind my fingers? Wouldn't it make more sense to smooth the wounds shut, like making pottery, and mending holes in the wet clay?"

"If that makes sense to your mind, do it, Elaine. I do not know about wizardry, but healing is a very individual thing. Each healer uses her own imagery. You use visuals similar to my own, but I know other clerics that go entirely by feel. As long as it works, it does not matter how it works."

Elaine reached for Fredric's arm again. She gave a quick glance to his face, then back to the wound. She had hurt him, she knew that, but it was more important to heal the wound than to ease the pain.

It was easier this time for her fingers to flow into the flesh. The tips of her fingers ran down the length of the bone in its muscle-and-blood sheath. She opened her eyes, just to see, but her hands sat on top his arm, looking ordinary. If she hadn't been feeling it herself, she wouldn't have known anything unusual was happening.

Now that she had opened her eyes and could still feel the bone, she kept them open. It was odd, almost dizzying; sight told her she was merely holding Fredric's arm, but touch told her her fingers were deeply imbedded in his flesh. She shouldn't have been able to see her fingers at all, but there they sat.

"Do not become distracted," Silvanus said softly. He was kneeling by her, shoulder almost touching hers. She hadn't felt him come up so close beside her.

"Keep your hold on the deep sensation, but remember why you are there. You are there to heal, not to simply sightsee."

Heat crept up her face. She had been playing inside the man's arm without healing him at all, simply enjoying the sensation. She glanced up at Fredric's face. His face was calm, but puzzled.

"I am sorry," she said.

"No, Elaine," Silvanus said. "Do not become distracted—not even by words or pity. Concentrate on the injury. Heal it."

"How?" Elaine started to turn to look at the elf. He touched her gently and turned her face back to the wound. "See only this. Feel only this."

She took a deep breath and did as she was told. She felt the bruising; it went all the way down to the bone. A breaking of blood vessels, a near crushing of flesh. She wanted to heal the broken blood vessels, to smooth the flesh inside as well as out. She drew her invisible fingers through the tissue, as if combing them through putty.

The broken flesh closed behind her touch, like a wall mending itself. Her fingers drew outward until Elaine could feel them resting on Fredric's arm. She stared down at the torn flesh.

Elaine drew her hand over the tears. She smoothed the outer skin, and it moved under her touch like clay. The flesh melting together, mending itself as she ran her fingers and thumb over the wound. She ended by holding his forearm between her hands and smoothing her palms down his arm, as if working in lotion.

She lay his arm in her lap and looked at it, turning it from side to side. But Elaine didn't need her eyes to tell her it was healed.

With that last smoothing motion, she had felt the flesh whole, of one piece, with no imperfections in it.

"It is done," she said. Her voice sounded a little surprised, even to her own ears.

Fredric lifted his arm before his face, turning it, staring. He ran his hand over where the bite mark had been. "There isn't even a scar. Silvanus, there's no scar."

The elf crawled forward and grabbed the arm. He ran his fingers over the healed flesh. "Bertog be praised. It is as if the skin were never broken."

"I knew a healer that could do that," Thordin said, "but he was a temple elder."

Silvanus looked up at the fighter. "I have known only two clerics that could do this." He traced fingers back and forth over the smooth flesh. "Are you experiencing any pain?"

Fredric raised his arm, flexing the hand. "It feels wonderful, almost better than new."

"My turn next," Randwulf said. He held out his wounded arms. He wasn't smiling when he said it, no teasing now. Elaine didn't know him well enough to read his expression, but it was solemn, perhaps impressed.

"How do you feel, Elaine?" Silvanus asked.

"Fine."

"Do you feel at all tired?"

She shook her head. "No."

"Not at all?" Silvanus asked. "Be sure you are not tired, Elaine. You have just done your first major healing. You must be careful to conserve your strength."

Elaine sat back and thought, how did she feel? She wasn't tired. In fact, she felt wonderful. Refreshed, alive.

"I'm not tired at all. I feel wonderful."

Silvanus stared at her, as if trying to gauge her reaction. "Don't feel you must be strong for others. If you are too tired to heal Randwulf, you could harm yourself."

"I feel fine."

"How could she be harmed?" Jonathan was standing just behind her, tall and forbidding, though he was asking after her safety. Even after last night, he was worried about her. Elaine reached out to touch his hand, to let him know his concern meant something to her. Jonathan jerked his hand away, as if her touch burned him.

Elaine let her hand fall back into her lap. She stared at his face. She would not look away, would not make this easy for him. Jonathan would not meet her gaze. He stared fixedly at the elf.

"If she is too tired and persists in trying to heal, she may tap into her own life-force. Elaine could use up her own life, spilling it away into Randwulf. She is new enough to healing that she does not know the signs. She could kill herself giving others life."

Jonathan finally did look at her. He stared into her face. He took a deep breath and touched her hair with his fingertips.

Elaine raised her hand slowly. He didn't move away. She touched his hand, and he returned the touch, squeezing the fingers gently. "I would not want anything to happen to you, Elaine."

"I feel fine, truly." She laid his hand against her cheek as she had as a child. He smiled, and she felt better than she had in hours.

"Then heal him, but be careful." He patted her cheek and pulled his hand gently from her own.

Elaine turned back to Randwulf. "Do I heal him just the same?"

"Yes," Silvanus said, "it is nearly the same type of wound. You can either heal one wrist at a time or both together."

"How do I heal them both?"

Silvanus smiled; it held almost bitterness. "You are eager, child, aren't you?"

"It feels . . . wonderful."

Silvanus touched her face, looking into her eyes as if they would give away secrets. "Are you saying it feels good to heal?"

"Yes." There was an expression on his face that made her say, "Don't you feel that way when you heal?"

"No, Elaine," he said, softly, "I do not."

"Is that bad?"

"Not at all. It is merely rare."

"How rare?" Jonathan asked.

"Rare enough that I've read of such things but never known of anyone who could do it," Silvanus said.

"I don't understand," Elaine said. "Why should the fact that I feel better after healing Fredric's wound be so unusual?"

"In a battle situation, you could heal many more people than I. I would grow tired and begin to draw on my own life-force. If you are doing what I believe you are doing, you will never grow tired. You will always be able to heal, over and over again. It is a great, great gift."

"Enough talk about magical theories," Randwulf said, "I'm tired of these wounds." He held his arms out to her once more.

"Randwulf, you are being impertinent," Silvanus said.

The young man smiled, then winked at Elaine. "If you all quit talking, this beautiful woman will lay her sweet hands on my bare flesh. Sorry if I'm impatient."

Elaine stared into his smirking face. She didn't like Randwulf, but she wanted to touch the wounds. The injuries were what was important. It didn't matter whom she was healing.

"Apologize immediately," Averil said. She sounded outraged.

"No," Elaine said, "it's all right." She should have been embarrassed but wasn't. She wanted to heal, not just Randwulf, but any ruined flesh, touching it and making it whole. Her hands itched with desire.

Elaine ran her fingers over Randwulf's wrists. The flesh was punctured, but not torn as badly as Fredric's arm. The wolves had simply bitten down, held him so the death blow could be dealt.

She clutched one of his wrists in either of her hands. Randwulf brought his arms up, putting the backs of her hands in a position to be kissed. Elaine plunged fingernails into the open bite wounds. Randwulf drew back with a hiss. Elaine's invisible fingers plunged into his flesh, tickling along his bones. It was almost disappointingly easy to heal. She drew out the bruising, and her hands sat on his skin. She squeezed down until Randwulf gasped, then pulled downward, smoothing the teeth marks in one hard movement.

Randwulf drew his arms to his chest, grimacing. "Silvanus never hurt me like this."

"You never tried to kiss my hand," Silvanus said.

"I promise not to tease her anymore. Just don't be as rough with the wound on my neck." He touched it lightly as he spoke. "It hurts already."

"If you behave yourself, I promise not to hurt you on purpose," Elaine said.

He placed a newly healed hand over his heart. "My word of honor," he said.

"Is the skin as perfect as mine was?" Fredric asked.

Randwulf offered his arms to the big fighter. Fredric rubbed his hands over Randwulf's arms. "No scars." The big man seemed amazed. He glanced at Elaine. "If I'd had you around, my body wouldn't look like a map of every fight I've ever had."

"Father did his best," Averil said.

Silvanus patted her hand. "He is teasing, Daughter."

"Ah," Fredric said. "I'd be dead a dozen times over if not for your father."

"I am in some pain here," Randwulf said. "Could she heal me now?"

Averil slapped his newly healed arm. "You are an ungrateful wretch."

He grinned. "Yes, I am."

"If you could just heal him before he makes a bigger fool of himself," Silvanus said, "we'd be most grateful."

Elaine looked at Randwulf, ignoring the smirk. She was thinking about the injury, visualizing it in her mind. "I think he'll need to lie down to be healed."

"Don't say it," Averil told him.

Randwulf ducked his head, pretending to be embarrassed but not succeeding. "I didn't say a thing."

"Keep it that way," Fredric said.

Elaine wasn't sure she had followed all the conversation, and didn't care. She wanted to see the wound again. She started to take off her cloak.

"What are you doing?" Jonathan asked.

"He'll need something to lie down on."

"I think we can fetch a blanket for that," Jonathan said. "We don't want your getting sick from the cold."

She retied her cloak.

"I've missed the chance to lie down on something warm and smelling of her body, darn."

Elaine looked at Randwulf. Last night his words would have bothered her, but not now. She was almost as eager to touch him as he was to touch her, but for very different reasons.

Blaine brought a blanket and laid it down before the fire. Randwulf knelt on the blanket.

"Could you loosen your collar so I can lay hands on the wound?" Elaine asked.

He opened his mouth to say some smart, teasing thing. She raised a hand, and said, "You are wasting my time. Do you want me to heal you or not?"

Randwulf looked as chastened as he was capable of and said, "Yes, please."

"Then loosen your collar and lie down before the fire."

He did as he was told. Elaine knelt over him, folding the fur back below his shoulders. She pulled the cloth away from the wound. Every tooth mark was like a small, frozen puddle of blood, except the blood trembled and shook, held in place by something more mysterious than ice.

"Your healing did this?" she asked.

Silvanus peered over her shoulder. "Yes. I did not have enough strength to heal it completely, but enough to heal the spine and the deeper injuries."

Her fingers hovered over the wound. "Will it be different healing a more serious wound?"

"Perhaps, perhaps not. You seem to have a quick grasp of such matters. Explore the wound and see."

Her hands fell against the skin, almost without her wanting them to. Her fingertips traced the edges of the sunken wounds.

Elaine almost expected to feel something holding in the blood, but her fingertips touched wetness. The blood was surprisingly warm, skin temperature.

The blood welled around her fingers, trickling in tiny rivulets down his skin. She dug fingers into the open wounds. Randwulf gasped, raising his head. Elaine forced his head down with one hand. Blood stained his curls.

Her invisible fingers slipped below the skin. The spine was not smooth. She could trace the joints between the vertebrae, but the neck vertebrae were thick with extra bone, scar tissue. Two of the vertebrae were fused together. No wonder his neck hurt. If the bones were left to heal bound together, he would lose some of the movement of his neck. Elaine wasn't sure how she knew that, but she could suddenly see not only his injury but what it meant for him, what would happen if it weren't fixed.

It was as if some window in her mind that had been closed had opened, and she could see things she hadn't before.

She touched the bone and rubbed it between her fingers. It wasn't like healing an injury. The bone was healed, but it wasn't right, and she sought the flaws. Blood flowed in a sheet across her hands, down his neck. She rubbed the bump down and down, until the vertebrae were even. Her invisible fingernails found the fused line and cut it open again. Her hands easily moved the neck back and forth.

"Does that hurt?"

"No, it doesn't." Randwulf said. He sounded surprised.

The blood flowing down her hands was so warm. It spread into the snow like red punch. She was fascinated with the crimson splashes. There was so much of it that the blood began eating through the snow like warm water.

"Close the wounds, Elaine." Silvanus's voice was still calm, but there was an undercurrent of urgency.

She turned to him, slowly. She didn't want to look away from the blood, wanted to stare at it, feel it pour down her hands forever.

Silvanus touched her shoulder. "Elaine, close the wounds."

She turned back to the bloody neck. Elaine couldn't see the injuries anymore. The blood covered them, but she could still feel the bite marks under her hands. Randwulf lay very still under her touch. She turned her invisible touch deeper into his body. She found his life fluttering. He was dying. Why?

She stared at the blood spreading into the snow. "I'm killing him," she said softly.

"Yes," Silvanus said.

Eighteen

"YOU MUST CLOSE THE WOUNDS, NOW," REPEATED Silvanus.

Elaine pulled her fingers together almost like making a fist. The skin smoothed behind her movement. She drew her thumbs over the flesh, leveling the last few imperfections.

"Let me see what you've done, Elaine." Silvanus's voice was careful, gentle, the way you'd talk to a frightened child.

"He's fine," she said.

Thordin encircled her wrists and lifted her hands from the man's neck. The blood ran onto his hands. He knelt, holding Elaine's hands.

"You can let go of me, Thordin."

He looked at Silvanus. The elf had wiped away the blood and was examining Randwulf's neck. "It's perfect." He looked up as if just realizing that Thordin was holding on. "Release her, it is her first major healing. She got carried away. It happens."

Thordin released her. He wiped the blood onto clean snow until his hands were clean.

Elaine knelt, holding her bloody hands in front of her. Blood trickled down her wrists into her sleeves and cooled quickly in the cold air. She rubbed her fingertips together. The sensation of congealing blood squeezing between her fingers was . . . interesting. She rubbed her hands together, slowly, studying the feel of it.

"Stop it, stop it!"

She looked up, startled. Jonathan was standing over her, face mottled with anger.

"You are corrupt."

"Jonathan, it is often difficult to control such powers at first. She will do better with practice."

"Practice? She nearly killed the boy."

Silvanus nodded. "But she didn't kill him."

"I saw her face. We all did. She enjoyed it. Look at her, smearing blood on her hands." His face mirrored the disgust in his voice.

Elaine lowered her bloody hands to her lap. Tears tightened her throat. It was hard after all these years. Once, only days ago, Jonathan's opinion had meant more to her than anyone's, even Blaine's. Her brother could be foolish, leading with his heart rather than his head. She'd depended on Jonathan to help her think clearly, to see all sides of a subject. Now she knew there were some sides the great mage-finder didn't want to understand. And one of them, sadly, was her own.

"She has done nothing wrong, Master Ambrose," the wizard said. He was still kneeling on the ground near the elf. The smile was gone from his face. His blue eyes looked harsh and distant as a winter sky.

"I did not say she had."

"Your face said more than your words."

Jonathan turned away, anger making his movements abrupt. Tereza had come up sometime during the healing. Elaine hadn't seen her come. Tereza touched his shoulder, but he pulled away from her. "I cannot change what I am. I cannot."

"Jonathan, please . . ."

Elaine stood up, leaving both the wizard and her brother's comforting touches behind. "Why do you protest, Tereza? You fear me, too. I saw it in your eyes."

"Elaine, we love you," Tereza said.

"But you still fear me." Tears threatened to close her throat tight. No, no more crying. Blast it all, she was an adult. She didn't need their approval. She wanted it, but didn't need it.

"I know you would never hurt us," Tereza said.

"Do you? Do you really?" She searched the older woman's face, trying to judge the words. Elaine couldn't read her thoughts at that moment and didn't try to. Not out of fear of what she would find out, but out of politeness. If it was rude to eavesdrop, it had to be doubly rude to read another's thoughts without permission.

"The evil is not in the girl," the elf said.

Tereza looked down at him. "We don't think she's evil."

"That's a lie," Elaine said. The tears trailed silently down her cheeks. Tereza's mind had opened to her like a window. She thought that Elaine's burgeoning powers had harmed the man. Tereza knew Elaine hadn't meant to do it, but she had so little control. Images swam in Tereza's mind of the night in the shed over the corpse of the murdered man.

Elaine looked at Jonathan. She riffled his mind like the pages of a book. Distrust, hatred, fear, prejudice. He loved Elaine, but his loathing of all things magic was deeply ingrained. How could he just abandon a lifetime of habit? A habit that had kept him alive and whole.

"I did not harm Randwulf, not on purpose. I have never harmed anyone. I would never harm anyone. I don't even know how to use magic to harm someone." With each word she spoke, she felt the hopelessness of it. They did not believe her. They no longer trusted her. They thought she had tried to kill Randwulf, deliberately. Both of them, it had been their first thought.

"When we go . . . back"—she had almost said home—"from Cortton, I'll leave."

"No," Tereza said. She stepped forward, reaching for Elaine.

Elaine held up her hands as if to ward off a blow. "I can read your thoughts. I know what you think of me."

Tereza grabbed her into a fierce hug. "I cannot control my thoughts, Elaine, but do not leave, not like this. Jonathan and I will learn to. . . . It will be all right."

Elaine pushed her to arm's length. "Jonathan and you will learn to what? Tolerate me? Not hate what I'm becoming? Not fear me?" She shook her head and stepped back, out of reach. She turned to the wizard. "If it's all right with you, Gersalius, we could go back to your home. I could live there while you teach me. If that's all right."

She realized for the first time that she should have asked the wizard in private. What if he said no? What if he didn't want her either? She shook her head, fighting not to cry again.

Gersalius stood up, taking her hand in his. "You are most welcome in my house, Elaine Clairn, always."

Blaine gripped her shoulder. "Will you have me, as well, Gersalius?"

The wizard raised an eyebrow. "You have some natural calling to animals and plants, but you are no mage."

"I don't come to learn magic. I come to keep you company."

"You are welcome in my home." He glanced at Jonathan and Tereza. "Remember this, that it was not magic that drove them away, but prejudice."

Tereza turned away and walked very fast toward the tents. Jonathan just stood there. He didn't seem to know what to say or even what to do. Elaine had never seen him at such a loss.

"You have commitments, Blaine," Jonathan said at last. Elaine knew what he meant. The brotherhood. She had asked to join, but Jonathan had talked her out of it. She had no knowledge of weaponry, no real way of defending herself. Her visions, though useful, left her sick and bedridden for hours or days. But that had changed.

"If Thordin wants another partner, he can pair with Konrad," Blaine said.

"Konrad's all right, but I don't want another partner," Thordin said. The fighter stood up, half between the three of them, as if he could stop what was about to happen.

"I'm sorry, Thordin," Blaine said.

"And who will be your new partner?" Jonathan asked.

"I will be," Elaine said.

Jonathan turned to her, frowning. "We've discussed this before, Elaine. You are not suited . . ."

"I had a vision yesterday. I was not bedridden. Gersalius is teaching me to control my powers."

"You still have no way to defend yourself. What if Blaine is not with you? Who will protect you?"

Gersalius gave a small chuckle.

"What is it, wizard?"

"Elaine is powerful, mage-finder. She will be able to take care of herself once she is trained."

"You see, Jonathan, all your objections are gone just like that," Elaine said. There was a large, hot stab of satisfaction at that. She wasn't helpless anymore.

"This is not the time or place to discuss this," Jonathan said. He was right. They were talking nearly openly about a supposed secret organization. But she wanted to finish this conversation. She wanted Jonathan to feel her anger. Elaine wanted him to hear her anger.

The thought was enough. *I will be Blaine's new partner.*

Jonathan paled, his breath coming in a sharp jab of panic. Thordin grabbed his arm to steady him. "What's wrong, Jonathan?"

He shook his head, not trusting himself to speak.

You are hearing my words, Jonathan, nothing more. It won't hurt you. Think something, and I will hear it. Let us finish this between us, here and now.

His skin looked gray. Elaine could feel his stomach knot with fear at her presence in his mind. She didn't care anymore. "Answer me, Jonathan," she said out loud.

"Are you doing this?" Thordin asked.

"He can read my thoughts as I can read his, that is all. It doesn't hurt. It is his own fear that is harming him."

"Elaine, don't do this," Blaine said.

"I have to."

Jonathan swallowed hard, fighting nausea. Finally, he thought, very carefully. *The brotherhood would never accept such as you as one of their agents.*

They have used wizards before.

He shook his head as if he could block out the sound, but he couldn't. Elaine suddenly knew that he couldn't keep her out of his mind, not if she wanted to be there. *They will not use you.*

Blaine will speak for me.

And I will speak against you.

So be it, Jonathan.

He had regained his color and his temper. "I will do everything I can to see that people know you for the corruption you are." He turned stiffly and walked slowly, deliberately away.

"You shouldn't have entered his mind," Gersalius said.

Elaine watched Jonathan's stiff back march away. "No more games, Gersalius. I am what I am. Jonathan could never accept that."

"He might have, in time, but now . . ." he let the thought trail off. His eyes watched her, concerned, worried.

"Now, I've made sure he thinks me evil."

"Yes, why?"

She shook her head, not sure she could explain. "I grew tired of the glances, of having to guess what they thought. Oh, I don't know what made me do it, but it's done. He'll never forgive me." Stupidly, tears stung her eyes. It had been her choice; why was she crying about it?

"You have indeed burned your proverbial bridges," Gersalius said. He smiled and clapped her shoulder. "You'll find my home less grand than your old one, but it will serve until you are master over your magic."

She turned to Blaine. "I'm sorry."

He gave a halfhearted smile. "I have never seen you lose your temper before. It was impressive, but why Jonathan? Why today?"

"You can stay with them. There's no need in both of us losing our home."

He shook his head, face grim. "No, you are my family. If you are no longer welcome, neither am I."

"Konrad has refused to partner with anyone since his wife died," Thordin said. "You might need another sword at your back."

Elaine looked at him, surprised. "You'd come with us?"

He shrugged. "Jonathan's upset now, but if anything happened to the two of you, he'd never forgive himself. I'd never forgive me, either. Better to go along and make sure you two are safe."

Blaine gave him a rough hug. "You old softie, you."

Thordin just grinned.

"Gersalius, is it all right if Thordin comes, too?" Elaine asked.

"Well, I admit I hadn't planned on expanding my household quite this much." At the look on the twins' faces, he smiled. "But who am I to refuse a stout sword arm to protect my back?"

Thordin slapped him on the back hard enough to send him staggering. "You're a good man, for a wizard."

Gersalius gave a half-cough. "Well, with such ringing endorsement, we'll be just one happy family."

At that, Elaine's smile faded. They had been a family, but no longer. Why had she forced Jonathan like that? It was unlike her. She shook her head. Was it the magic? Was Jonathan right, and the magic was controlling her? What if Jonathan was right and she was being corrupted? What if she was corrupting everyone around her? She had just succeeded in breaking up one of the most successful cells that the brotherhood had ever had. A house divided upon itself cannot stand. Elaine couldn't remember who had said that. She hoped that whoever it was was wrong.

Ninteen

Twilight lay in thick purple clouds across the sky. The snow that had threatened all day began to drift down in huge, fluffy flakes, like the down of some gigantic goose. The village of Cortton lay in a small valley. Lights glimmered from windows here and there. Chimney smoke rose into the fading light to mingle with the purplish clouds.

Jonathan tried once again to explain to Silvanus and his party what lay ahead of them. The elf was mounted just behind him, sharing his horse. Jonathan turned in the saddle and found the elf's disconcerting eyes inches from his own. "There is a plague in the village below. You might live longer if you went on to the next town. Another day will see you to Tekla."

"If there is a plague, where else should a healer be?" Silvanus said. He made a gesture with his half-grown arm.

"I cannot argue that a true healer would be very helpful, but I want you to understand what may lie ahead."

"I appreciate your concern, Jonathan, but we have faced evil before. We have even faced the walking dead before and lived to tell the tale."

Jonathan stared into that strange face and tried to read the expression. Silvanus seemed so confident. The mage-finder remembered being confident once, secure in his own beliefs, but that was before. He glanced back, eyes searching for Elaine. Her yellow hair glowed in the dying light. She rode behind Blaine, having generously offered her horse to the large, mustached man. Her hair glowed against the white of Blaine's hood, and Elaine seemed to feel his eyes upon her, for she turned to look at him.

Jonathan looked away before their eyes could meet. He didn't want her inside his mind again. The thought made him shudder as if something had slithered over his foot in the dark. She'd had no right to invade him like that. It was evil. Yet, he wanted to mend things between them, but didn't know how.

Short of her magic's disappearing overnight, Jonathan wasn't sure things between them could ever heal. He hadn't anticipated Blaine's taking her side, but should have. He'd been blind not to expect that. But Thordin? That had been a complete surprise. Their cell of the brotherhood had more successes than any other—more monsters slain, evil wizards prosecuted, charlatans unmasked. They were a good team. The fact that Elaine's magic had broken them up was proof enough that her witchcraft was a corrupting influence.

He stared down at the lights. Putting to rest the dead of Cortton would be their last task as a family. He was the head of this family. The leader of all who obeyed the brotherhood in his house. So why could he not find a way out of this moral dilemma? It was like watching a wagon barreling down a narrow path. He knew it was going to go careening off into space to smash to the rocks below, but could not stop it, not by wishing or screaming. It was an accident happening slowly before his eyes, and he could do nothing to stop it.

He could not solve his own problems, but he could help this village. Jonathan would have rather faced a dozen zombies than strife in his own household. Perhaps he might yet defeat both.

"Do you still worry over the girl?" Silvanus asked.

Jonathan wanted to say no, but nodded.

"Averil is often strong willed. We quarrel, but we make up. They never stop being our children, no matter how angry we get."

"This not a fight over an inappropriate suitor," Jonathan said. "She invaded my mind without my permission. She showed that she would abuse her power."

"She is what . . . eighteen of your years? She is young. You are the one with the patience and wisdom of years. It is your task to heal this fight, not hers."

"Is that the way you deal with Averil?"

"Yes." That one word sounded tired, as if the good advice was harder to swallow than to dish out.

Jonathan glanced back. Elaine was looking at him. He held her gaze for a moment, then looked away. Did her eyes seek him as his did her? Did she long to mend this quarrel? If so, why had she done it? He could have ignored much, but not this outright invasion. She had to know that. It was almost as if she had done it deliberately.

"I cannot mend this," he said, at last.

"Will not," the elf said.

Jonathan nodded. "Will not." He kicked the horse forward. It began winding down the path.

"Pride is a cold thing, my friend."

"It is not pride."

The elf's voice came close to his ear, like his own conscience. "Then what is it, if not pride?"

It was fear, but Jonathan didn't know how to explain that to the elf. Silvanus's dead wife had been a witch, a human mage. If the elf could love, bed, and father a child with a magic-user, he would not understand Jonathan's fear.

"Please, Jonathan, you have been so kind to us. I will listen with an open mind. You can use my ear to bounce ideas from, until you find a way to approach Elaine."

It sounded so reasonable. Jonathan didn't feel in the least reasonable. How to explain his fear to someone who did not share it in the least?

The sun died in a flash of golden blood in the purple clouds. As they rode down the hillside, the light slipped away from them. Konrad rode ahead, his figure growing dimmer, blending with the coming dark. Konrad was the only one of them who wasn't riding double. He and the paladin. The paladin was simply too large to share. Konrad simply hadn't offered.

"My parents were slain by magic." Jonathan said, at last.

"As was my wife," Silvanus said.

Jonathan shook his head. How to explain? "No, they were not just killed. They were degraded, tormented."

"Tell me, my friend."

But he did not want to. This grief was too intimate. Even after nearly forty years, the wound was still raw. His mother had been a gypsy like Tereza. Perhaps that was why from the first her dark hair and rich voice had captivated him. Do we not all spend our lives trying to get back to happier days? Of course, if that was all Jonathan had wanted, he wouldn't have joined the brotherhood. He wouldn't have become a mage-finder. He would have taken Tereza and found some quiet corner and hidden away. But he hadn't, perhaps because he believed that the evil would find him.

Those who did not seek out evil to slay it, would be sought out by evil. Better to face it, hunt it down, than to be caught unawares.

He had been ten the year the wizard rode into the yard of their homestead. His father was a sheep farmer. His mother, with her delicate hands and rich, contralto voice, was a noted bard. If she had traveled, she might have become a meistersinger, but she was not ambitious. It was a very gypsy trait to have great talent and not worry about whether it was used to best advantage. Happiness was more important.

They had a small inn where travelers could come and stay. Mother sang in the evenings. Father was often away during the day, tending the flocks, but every sheep had to be in by nightfall. The wolves could destroy an entire flock in a single night.

The wizard was a tall, painfully thin man, as if he never got enough to eat, but Jonathan remembered watching him eat great quantities of his mother's food. He never grew fatter, and fascinated Jonathan and his younger brother, Gamail.

The wizard, Timon, stayed for a week. The two boys hadn't even realized he was a wizard until the day the woman rode into the yard. She was small, dainty, with a fall of hair down her back the color of autumn-bronzed leaves. She came looking for an old foe, Timon, and challenged him to a duel.

Jonathan's mother tried to stop it by stepping between them.

The red-haired witch raised her hands to the sky. "Get out of my way, woman. My quarrel is with him."

"This is my home. If you must duel, duel elsewhere. That is all I ask."

"If Timon will go with me, that is acceptable."

The tall, thin man just shook his head. "If I am going to be executed, I will not go willingly."

"Please, Timon," Mother said, "go outside the homestead."

He shook his head again. "I am about to die, and you complain about your house. A house can be rebuilt."

"Timon, my lady, please."

Timon scowled. "Leave us, woman." He made a flat gesture with his hand, out from his body.

Mother fell to the ground. Jonathan and Gamail ran toward her.

"No, stay back." She shouted the words in her wonderful voice. The sound carried into the house. Guests and servants came to the windows and the door, and the cook dashed out and took the two boys by the hands, then pulled them back toward the house.

No one helped Mother. No one helped.

Mother tried to crawl away in the dirt on her hands and knees, but the red-haired witch pointed one hand. A bolt of sizzling green light roared outward, engulfed her. Mother screamed. They could see her through the green light as if through colored glass. Her body began to melt, falling down and down, impossibly small. Her clothes formed an empty puddle on the ground when the light died away.

Jonathan tried to run to her, to help her, but the cook clung to his wrist as if her life depended on it. Her fingernails dug into his skin. From that day on, he would carry a perfect imprint of her fingernails there.

Timon walked forward, carefully, never taking his attention from the red-haired witch. He poked the cloth with his foot. Something small moved under the cloth. Something impossibly small.

Timon stooped and jerked the cloth up. A cat stood huddled on the ground. The cat hissed at him, hair raised on end. It scratched him. He jerked back, tumbling to the ground. The cat ran toward the house, darting inside.

Jonathan didn't realize the cat was his mother. He couldn't hold such an absurdity in his mind, not at ten years old.

The red-haired witch laughed, finger pointed at the fallen wizard. No blaze of light burst forth. Jonathan saw nothing, but Timon screamed. There was a swimming in the air; a nothingness seemed to wrap round him. It squeezed him, that nothingness. It pressed tighter and tighter, until his screams died for lack of air. No air, no screams. He burst in a splash of red and darker fluids. The body fell to the ground.

"Timon was always easily distracted," the witch said. She turned her horse and rode away.

Jonathan wanted to yell after her. What he would have yelled, he did not know.

His father came home that night. He made a sort of quest of trying to find a wizard to cure mother, to change her back, but it was no use. No one had the power, so in the end, Father set out to find the red-haired witch. He did, and she killed him. Mother was run over by a cart like any common house cat.

Seven years later, Jonathan Ambrose had slain his first wizard.

The elf was very quiet behind him. Silvanus did not ask him to share his confidence again. It was rare to find someone who respected silences, though the few elves Jonathan had met before had all seemed more than able to keep their own counsel. Perhaps it was an elven trait to understand silences. Few humans did.

Tereza knew of his past, and that was all. It was enough.

Cortton lay in darkness. Lamps shone at second-story windows. Light gleamed between the cracks of shutters on the ground floors. Jonathan had never seen such a waste of lamp oil. It was almost as if they thought the light alone would keep them safe. Childish. But it was hard to give up that love of light, the hope that light alone can banish monsters.

The main street was wide enough for a wagon to drive through. Snow had been shoveled to either side and piled in man-high drifts by the doors. The frozen earth was rock hard under their horses' hooves.

They could have ridden two abreast, but Konrad did not wait. He led the way down the dark street not looking back to see if anyone followed. Jonathan wondered if Konrad would even notice if they all stopped and let him go alone. He had been going alone since Beatrice died. He still did his job, so Jonathan had nothing specific to complain about, but the spirit in which he worked was soured.

If Tereza had been killed, Jonathan was not sure he would be doing as well as the younger man.

Konrad pulled his horse up sharply. A narrower street bisected the main road. There was something about the way he sat his horse, a tenseness that made Jonathan kick his own horse forward.

"What's wrong?" Silvanus asked.

"I'm not sure," Jonathan said. They drew up beside Konrad, who was staring to the right. He seemed mesmerized by something down that black narrow passage, more an alley than a street. The dark ribbon of road was overshadowed by the eaves of the buildings on either side, so the black of night was the color of coal, and just as penetrable.

"What did you see, Konrad?" Jonathan asked.

"I'm not sure. I saw something move." His hand was on his

sword hilt. Jonathan could feel the tension radiating from the man, like the cold air itself.

Jonathan peered into the blackness, straining until white spots danced in the darkness before his eyes. "I see nothing."

"Nor I," Silvanus said.

Tereza rode up beside them. Averil sat behind her. "Why are we stopped?" Tereza asked.

"Konrad thought he saw something down that alley."

"I did see something," Konrad said.

"Whatever it was, it seems to have gone. Let us ride on to the inn," Jonathan said. He kicked his horse forward. Tereza followed him. Konrad stayed behind, staring into the darkness.

Jonathan glanced back to find that everyone else was following. Only Konrad remained, stubbornly staring into the alley. He could have seen a stray cat or dog hunting for a warm place on this bitter night. But then again . . . Jonathan found himself searching the darkness.

Another narrow street crossed the road. Jonathan stared down both sides of the new street, and saw only thick blackness winding away from them.

A sign hung half into the road. A gust of wind roared down the street like an icy chimney. The sign creaked. The sign showed a white bird winging skyward, pierced by an arrow. Painted blood traced the bird's chest. In small letters the sign read: The Bloody Dove.

Not a cheerful name, but Jonathan had seen worse. His least favorite had been the Lustful Fiend Inn. Its sign had been positively offensive.

"Jonathan," Tereza said. Her voice had a note of quiet panic that made the hair on Jonathan's neck try to march down his spine.

He turned back to her, but she was looking past him, down the wide street. Elaine's face, behind Tereza, was wide-eyed with fear.

It was like a thousand nightmares. Jonathan turned slowly round to face the street. A half-dozen shapes were shambling toward them, man-sized, but moving like drunken puppets. Jonathan had seen enough walking dead to know what they were.

"Zombies," he said softly.

The sound of horse hooves made him glance behind. Konrad was riding toward them at a fast pace. He was motioning for Blaine and Elaine to move. Blaine hesitated for a heartbeat. It was enough. Deadmen poured out of the alley that separated them from Jonathan and the rest.

Konrad pulled his horse up. It reared, screaming as the dead things clawed at it. Konrad's axe slashed downward frantically, but he could not break through. He was forced to back away, trying to control his screaming horse. Blaine had drawn his own sword, but was hampered with Elaine so close behind him. He used his other arm to slide her down to the ground, behind him, away from the zombies, then kicked his horse forward into the shambling horde.

Jonathan watched it all in dawning horror. Elaine's yellow hair vanishing behind the screen of zombies. Had Blaine forgotten there was another alley behind this one, an alley near where Elaine stood, alone and weaponless?

He started to turn the horse to help them. Tereza called, "We've got problems of our own, Jonathan." She had regained control of her voice; it was almost matter-of-fact.

He wheeled the horse back. Silvanus clung desperately with his one arm.

The shambling dead were still coming slowly down the street, but there was something crouched in the mouth of the alley. It looked like a man, but scuttled from shadow to shadow as if even the cold, distant moonlight hurt it.

Tereza had her sword out, trying to keep the creature in sight. A zombie stumbled from the alley, clawing at her horse. The horse reared; Averil screamed, clinging to Tereza's arm, crippling her sword. The man-thing leapt. There was a shimmer of pallid skin, and it hit Tereza and Averil, knocking them both to the ground. More dead closed in, and Jonathan lost sight of them.

He urged his horse forward to help them. A zombie stumbled into the horse. Hands clawed at Jonathan's leg. He kicked at it. The thing staggered backward a few steps. Something that had once been a woman grabbed Silvanus around the waist.

The elf's one arm jerked into Jonathan's stomach, making him gasp. A zombie with most of its face rotted away grabbed the horse's head. The animal tried to rear, but the zombie had been a big man. Its weight kept the horse down. The dead closed in, pressing the shuddering horse back against the inn door. Jonathan kicked the door. "Open! Open!"

Silvanus was pulled from the horse; only his arm around Jonathan's waist saved him from being lost completely. Jonathan grabbed a handful of the elf's tunic, the other hand tight-gripped on the saddle horn, legs digging into the horse's side, holding them against the pull of the dead.

Thordin and Randwulf were there, swinging blades, nearly maiming each other. Blood fell on the snowy street. Dead flesh gave way, but dead hands still reached for them. The horse shuddered, but did not rear. Thordin had trained the mount himself, and that training saved them now. If it had reared, they would have been lost, as Tereza and Averil had been.

Silvanus's fingers slipped. His hand was torn away inch by inch. The elf's fingers bruised Jonathan's skin through the clothing. Jonathan dug his hand into the elf's clothing.

The big zombie clawed the horse's eyes. The mount pressed against the door, pinning Jonathan's leg. Jonathan screamed, "Open the door!"

A blinding burst of light shot the length of the street. The zombies cowered, hands before faces. Silvanus sat upon the road, fingers still laced in Jonathan's clothing. The elf, weary in the brief respite, leaned his forehead against the horse's flank.

Gersalius sat on his horse, hands enveloped in white flame. "Hurry, I cannot hold them long." His voice echoed among the buildings, louder than it should have been.

Tereza had hoisted Averil over her shoulder like a bag of flour, then put their backs to the opposite wall. She pushed through the zombies, using her body to shove them aside. Her sword was naked in her hand, but the zombies seemed uninterested in fighting.

Thordin urged his horse toward the inn. Randwulf poked at the zombies with his boot. The dead simply turned away, barely noticing.

Fredric spurred his mount through the zombies. The horse pushed aside the dead as if wading through water.

"Elaine!" Blaine's frantic cry brought everyone's attention to him. He was wheeling his horse in a frantic circle. "Elaine!"

Konrad rode a few steps into the dark beyond the dead. He called, "Elaine!"

The light was fading around Gersalius's hands, like a white-hot ember dying. "A few minutes is all I can give you. Whatever you're going to do, do it soon."

The zombies were looking at them now. The dead eyes stared at the living, not eager, but patient, as if they knew all they had to do was wait.

Jonathan slid from his horse, banging on the inn door. "I am Jonathan Ambrose, mage-finder. You sent Tallyrand for me." No sound, no movement of the heavy door.

Gersalius had urged his horse forward, using his knees. The light was the barest of flickers now. "My magic has done all it can. It's your turn, mage-finder."

The dead were moving slowly, drawing closer. The rotting hands lifted, plucking at the air, held back only by the invisible wall of Gersalius's spell.

Jonathan turned back to the door, pounding on it. It felt a foot thick. Even with an axe, they'd never get through in time, but it was the only idea he had.

"Konrad, we need your axe."

"Elaine is missing," he called back. The dead had begun to surround his horse, isolating him.

"We will all die if we don't get through this door," Jonathan said. That spoken realization made his throat tighten. He could barely breathe round the helplessness of it. He could not let them all die to save Elaine. Not all, for the sake of one.

Konrad spurred his horse through. The dead did not give way. They pressed their bodies against the horse and Konrad's legs. They did not reach for him, not yet, but it was coming.

"No, we can't leave her," Blaine said. He kicked his horse into the alley nearest where he had set her down.

"Blaine, no!" Tereza yelled.

Konrad hesitated, as if thinking of following the boy. "Konrad, we need you," Jonathan called.

The warrior shoved his way through the dead, sliding from his horse near the others. "If they die out there, it will be your doing."

"We are all going to die if we don't get through this door."

Konrad pushed him aside. "Step back! Give me room!"

They moved back. The last flicker of light faded from Gersalius's hands. A great sigh rose from the throats of the dead. Konrad raised his axe. The zombies shuffled forward, rotting hands reaching. The door opened.

Jonathan could see nothing but the opening. Did it matter who had opened it? No. He pushed Konrad through the door. Silvanus and Tereza spilled inside. Thordin tried to ride his horse through. Randwulf sliced at the reaching hands. A zombie leapt upon Randwulf, spearing itself on the sword and not caring. Hands dug at his eyes.

Fredric's great sword swung outward, and the zombie's head flew onto the street. The headless body kept scratching at Randwulf's face. Fingernails raised furrows down his cheeks.

Thordin grabbed the corpse by its collar and yanked. The zombie fell into the crowd of dead. The reaching hands tore at the unprotected flesh, shoving pieces in their gaping mouths. They tore the zombie apart, eating it. The night filled with the sound of snapping bone, the wet sound of flesh being eaten.

"Inside, now!" Jonathan said.

Thordin rode his horse through the door. Fredric made a last slash at the feasting corpses, then urged his mount inside, as well. Jonathan gave a desperate glance down the street; nothing moved but the dead.

His horse reared, jerking reins from his hands. A zombie had fastened teeth into its thigh. The thing that had jumped Tereza now leapt on the horse's back, sinking teeth too sharp to be human into its neck.

Hands grabbed Jonathan and pulled him inside the doorway. The dead surged forward, reaching for him. Jonathan lay on the floor where he had been pushed. Fredric, Thordin, and a stranger were shoving the door closed. Arms shoved through the opening. A face half-rotted away showed through the partially open door, wedging its chest within.

"Can't close it," Thordin said.

Konrad hacked at the chest. The flesh carved, but the corpse continued to struggle, trying to crawl its way into the building. Randwulf joined him, slashing at the arms. An arm fell to the floor, flopping like a landed fish.

A woman ran forward, pouring oil over the arm. A boy at her side set a torch to the thing. The flesh burned, sending off a foul smoke that stung the eyes and filled the mouth with an acrid, unpleasant taste.

The woman splashed oil on the dead that threatened to spill through the door. The boy hesitated, and Jonathan grabbed the torch, shoving it against the zombies. Flame whooshed to life; smoke rolled. The dead mouth shrieked as it burned, and the desiccated flesh burned with unnatural speed.

Another man was there, suddenly, and the three men forced the door closed, snapping through brittle bone and charred flesh. The wood banged to, and the stranger threw the bolts. The three men leaned against the door, panting.

The stranger stood, sweeping a plumed hat from his head in a low, theatrical bow. "I am Harkon Lukas. So glad to meet you at last, Master Ambrose."

Jonathan managed an awkward bow. Two servants were

beating out the last of the flames around the door, where the oil had spilled. The wood was solid, shut and secure. And on the other side of it, Blaine and Elaine were trapped out in the dark with an army of the dead.

twenty

ELAINE STOOD WITH HER BACK PRESSED TO THE WALL and Blaine's horse in front of her, a solid force between her and the dead. His sword glimmered in the moonlight, slashing at the walking corpses. The dead closed in, clawing at the horse and its rider. Blaine wove a pattern of destruction, cutting rotting faces, slicing hands. A finger flew onto the ground beside Elaine. The thing wiggled like a worm, struggling toward her skirts.

She didn't scream, fearing it would distract Blaine and cost him his life, but instead kicked the severed finger away from her. It rolled into the mouth of the alley behind them, but began to inch toward her again. A zombie came around the back of Blaine's horse. Its dull eyes stared straight at Elaine.

Two more dead clutched Blaine, and he frantically slashed their hands. Even if she called to him, he could not get to her. He was surrounded and barely holding his own, alone, on foot, and weaponless.

Bone peeked through the rotten skin, glimmering ghostlike. The zombie opened its mouth, and liquid dark and thick as pudding slid down its chin.

Elaine glanced away, swallowing hard. If she threw up now, all would be lost. She began easing her way toward the alley, her back sliding along the wall. At least she was safe from behind. Something pecked at her foot. She gave a startled yelp, and glanced down. The finger was trying to crawl up her leg. Elaine screamed and kicked it away, and it rolled under the horse's hooves and was crushed.

Elaine turned all her attention back to the zombie that stalked her. What could she do without a weapon against an entire zombie?

Her left hand found the corner of the wall, the mouth of the alley. The only thing she had that the dead did not was speed. She darted a glance down the alley. It stretched empty as far as she could see. The zombie lunged at her, and Elaine slipped round the corner into the narrow alley. She ran. One glance behind showed the zombie had broken into a lopsided canter after her.

She ran, her heavy cloak spilling out behind her. She burst out of the mouth of the alley and was jerked to the ground. A woman stood over her, hands digging into Elaine's cloak. At first Elaine thought it was a woman, but then she took in the thin white nightdress and the frozen expression on the face. It was better preserved, but still dead.

Elaine glanced back. The first zombie was almost upon her. She jerked loose the ties at her throat and scrambled to her feet, leaving the female zombie holding the empty cloak.

It was easier to run without the cloak, and she was too scared to feel the cold. She was on another main street, not quite as wide as the first but wide enough that she could see it was empty. She hiked up her skirts and rushed away.

The two zombies behind her gave chase. The male was slow,

but the woman ran almost as well as Elaine. Her body did not look dead as it raced over the snowy street. Elaine slipped on a patch of ice, skidding into a wall. She crawled to her feet, scrambling away before she could stand upright.

A glimmer of light caught her eye, lamplight behind the shutters. She tripped on the steps leading up to the door, catching herself on the palms of her hands. The pain was sharp and immediate. She screamed and pounded stinging hands against the door.

"Help me!"

A sound made her glance behind. Three more zombies were walking toward her from the other end of the street. They were well rotted, one missing an arm. The two running zombies were still coming. The woman was almost upon her. Elaine had a second to decide: run or stay. If she stayed and the door did not open, she was dead.

She scrambled off the steps and ran past the three shambling dead. The woman was just behind her, slippered feet pattering on the street.

Two more dead stumbled from a side street to block her path. The tallest one looked quicker, more alive. She couldn't just run past her. Elaine ran into the first alley she came to, not thinking, trying just to run. It was a mistake. The alley was blocked by a wall. A dead end—a phrase that might prove all too literal.

Elaine started to run back out, but the woman blocked her way. Elaine backed slowly away from the dead woman. She stumbled on the garbage in the alley but did not fall. Her fingers traced down one wall to steady herself, and her feet slid backward, searching for footing. She was afraid to glance down, or behind, afraid to lift her gaze from the thing coming down the alley toward her.

The woman looked almost alive, except for that awful stillness, like a painting with all the colors and shapes of life but somehow still lifeless. Flowers had been embroidered into her white gown. Someone had taken great care with the burial clothes, loving care.

"Can you speak?" Elaine asked.

The zombie just kept walking, slowly, deliberately, face empty of anything Elaine could understand. "Speak to me, please. If you can, say something."

The zombie hesitated, then slowly shook her head.

"You understand me," Elaine said. The relief in her voice was painful to hear.

The zombie shook her head again, as if saying no. Did she understand, or was she just moving, reacting to some memory of life? Elaine didn't know and probably never would.

Her back smacked into a wall. She gasped, glancing behind to find the wall that blocked the alley. Her hands spread out upon the bricks. There was nowhere left to run.

"Please, if you can understand me, stop. Please, don't." Elaine wasn't even sure what she was begging her not to do. Not to touch her. No, not to kill her. Not to touch her with cold, dead flesh. Not to hurt her.

The woman opened her mouth, as if trying to speak. Some stray bit of moonlight illuminated her face. The tongue that lolled between her teeth was green with rot. A sound like the mewling of a kitten oozed from her mouth.

Elaine screamed, "Blaine!" But no one was coming to help her, not this time. Gersalius's words came back to her, that she would be able to protect herself, but how?

None of the spells he had shown Elaine would help her now. All the magic she knew was useless in the face of the dead. The other zombies had limped into the alley. They stayed a respectful distance behind the woman, but they were there. Why didn't the woman attack?

"What are you waiting for?"

The woman looked at her and again made the awful mewling sound. Was she trying to talk? Was that it? Was it the fact that Elaine was speaking with her, not just running, or fighting, but talking? Was that what was making her hesitate?

"Do you want to talk?"

The woman shook her head but opened her mouth and tried to speak once more. She coughed violently, as if her lungs were unused to drawing air for breath. A line of dark fluid trickled down her chin from the cough. She wiped it away with the back of one gray-skinned hand.

The woman cared enough to not want the dark fluid on her face. She was not just a walking shell, not a simple zombie. "Do you want to tell me something?"

A shake of her head.

"Do you want to show me something?"

The woman nodded, almost eagerly.

Elaine swallowed a lump that was threatening to choke her. "Show me, please."

The dead woman beckoned and began walking back down the alley toward the other zombies. Was it a trick to get Elaine close to them? She didn't think so. She was trapped. If they wanted to kill her, they could have. There was no reason to try and trick her.

"I'm afraid of the others," Elaine said.

The woman merely motioned her to follow, as if she either didn't hear or didn't understand. The other zombies backed away from the woman, seemingly frightened of her. What could frighten the dead? Elaine was not at all sure she wanted to know, yet what choice did she have? The zombie wanted to show her something. It might be the only reason she was still alive. If she stopped following, would the dead woman kill her? Elaine thought it likely.

The other zombies had spilled out into the main street. They huddled on either side of the alley mouth. The woman stood just beyond them, waiting.

Elaine hesitated, staring at the zombies crouched to either side. If she walked between them, they could simply reach out and grab her. She did not want to pass that close to them, not voluntarily.

The female zombie motioned impatiently. It was the most abrupt movement she'd made so far. If she grew angry, would she leave Elaine to the others?

Elaine took a deep breath and darted out of the alley. The one-armed zombie made a grab for her skirts. She squealed and had the oddest feeling the zombie was laughing at her. Of course, zombies didn't have a sense of humor. Elaine glanced into the sparkling eyes of the corpse. The eyes were alive in a way that the body was not. Those sparkling eyes trapped in the rotting body frightened her more than anything else. It was almost as if a living person were trapped inside.

Elaine shook her head. That wasn't possible.

The zombie woman turned and walked down the street. Elaine hurried after her with a last glance at the others. They waited, huddling together. When the woman was almost to the corner, they got up and began to follow.

The dead woman never looked back. Had she forgotten about Elaine? Why did the other dead obey the woman? Elaine had read in Jonathan's books that zombies were just walking corpses. They would take orders from a wizard who raised them, but not from another zombie.

The woman entered a narrow, winding street. The upper stories of the houses nearly met above the street, plunging them into a darkness that was nearly complete. The woman's white dress was a glimmering shape moving just ahead. That uncertain whiteness moving always away, never turning back, never hesitating, as in the ghost stories Elaine had read. Was that what she followed? Could the woman be a ghost? Did ghosts rot? Elaine didn't think so, but she was unsure of so many things.

Walking quietly through the dark streets, she hugged her arms against the cold. She wished for her cloak lying somewhere back in the winter night. Had Blaine missed her by now? She knew he hadn't been badly hurt, for she'd had no hint of a vision. Of course, she'd never been right next to him in a fight.

A rock skittered behind her. She turned and found the back street full of zombies. All sizes and shapes, filling the narrow way like a stopper in a bottle. Elaine hurried after the distant white figure. She fought the urge to run, fearing they might give chase. They weren't hurting her, just following. For now.

The street began to climb a hill. The woman waited at the top. She was bathed in moonlight. For a moment Elaine thought the zombie glowed with light, but as she drew closer, she realized it was the contrast to the dark sky and street. The zombie stood in a clearing away from any building. The moonlight seemed almost unnaturally bright after the narrow roofed-in darkness.

The dead woman stood beside a high, spiked fence. It was formed of black, iron bars. Elaine came to stand beside the fence. It was a graveyard, where tombstones dotted the ground like the broken teeth of giants.

She looked at the woman. "Why have you brought me here?"

The woman pointed to the fence and what lay beyond. "It is a graveyard—I see that. Did you want to show me where you came from?"

The zombie shook her head, still pointing out into the cemetery.

"Do you want me to go inside the fence?"

Again the head shake.

"I don't understand what you're trying to tell me," Elaine said.

There were scuffling sounds behind them. Elaine turned. The dead were lined up behind her like an audience. A little boy of no more than seven stood closest. Elaine almost asked him what he was doing there, but as he turned his head a bit of bone stuck out of his cheek.

Elaine backed into the fence, one hand holding the cold metal tight, as if only the metal were real. If she could just find something to hold on to, maybe the rest would go away and not be real at all. It was the way Elaine dealt with bad dreams. When you woke, you found something real and normal to hold, to touch, and the dream was just a dream.

Something crawled up the slope toward them. At first Elaine's eyes wouldn't make sense of it. It was alive; it moved, but . . . suddenly she could see it, and wished she hadn't.

It was a badly decayed corpse. Its legs were gone, and only the stub of one arm remained to push it up the hill. The flesh was rotted to a mottled color. The naked latticework of the ribs scraped on the cold ground like metal on a plate.

Elaine was all out of screams for the night. It was just one more horror to add to the list.

A figure in a hooded cloak stepped out of the shadows near the buildings. He walked in a long arc around the zombies, approaching Elaine. The dead watched him with sullen eyes. "Are you all right?"

The voice was a man's voice, normal, pleasant, wondrous. "Yes."

He held out a gloved hand. "Come, I'll take you to a place of safety. My spell won't hold them long."

"Spell?" Elaine said.

"A small charm, nothing more. It won't last much longer. I heard your screams and came looking for you." He still held out his hand, waiting.

Elaine moved to take it. The dead woman reached for her, too. Elaine jerked back and half-ran to the man's waiting hand. His fingers were solid and real in his grasp.

He led her away from the graveyard, glancing back at the waiting dead. "We must hurry. I've never tried the charm on so many at once."

"Are you a wizard?" Elaine didn't think he was; he didn't feel like a wizard.

"Oh, no. I traveled to a local witch to get a charm so I could walk the streets. The town elders sent for some mage-finder, but I say fight magic with magic."

Elaine didn't know what to say to that, so she said nothing. Jonathan had taught her that magic was never an option, but much had changed in the last few days. She was no longer sure if Jonathan had ever been right about anything.

He led her back into the narrow streets. They seemed even darker after the moonlit hill. She stumbled, and only his hand kept her from falling.

"Are you sure you are unhurt?" His eyes caught what little light there was, glinting. They were some dark color. His face was a square-jawed paleness in the dark.

"I just tripped. I'm fine."

He smiled. "Then come. We need to get inside before they come after us."

"I knocked on a door. I know someone was inside. I saw a light. They wouldn't help me."

"Didn't open the door, eh?" he said.

"No."

"They lock the doors and shutters and hide after nightfall. They won't open the doors to anyone. You can scream and cry, and no one will help you."

"But you helped me."

He turned back to her. Elaine thought he smiled again. "I got tired of listening to people scream for help, and no one going to them. So I go to them."

"Thank you."

"Here we are." He stopped at one of the bright-painted doors, one like a dozen others. He released her hand and took a key from his belt pouch. He unlocked the door and motioned her in. She stopped just within. There was no light, and it was darker inside than out. When he closed the door, Elaine couldn't see her hand before her face. It was dark as a cave. There was a musty smell like an unused attic.

She heard the key turn in the lock. "It's the only way to keep the dead out," he said. "Don't move, and I'll light a candle. Wouldn't want to rescue you from the hill only to have you trip and break your neck in the dark." There was a hint of cold laughter in his voice.

Elaine stood frozen in the dark. His cloak brushed her leg as he moved past her. He seemed to have no trouble seeing, but perhaps he was just familiar with the room.

The musty smell seemed to be growing stronger.

There was a hiss and the scent of sulfur. The sputtering flame seemed bright as a star in the darkness. He touched it to the first candle in a candelabrum that sat on a small table. The candle caught, and he shook the match out, placing it carefully on a small tray. He lifted the candle from its holder and used it to light the two remaining ones. The light was warm and gentle, and the flames reflected in the gilt mirror on the wall.

"What's your name?" he asked.

"Elaine Clairn. What's yours?"

He looked up then, face turned so the mirror only caught a sliver of his face. He pivoted toward her, smiling. The candle flames set deep flickering shadows inside his hood. For a moment, there was nothing but the glitter of his eyes reflecting the fire.

"The dead have no names, Elaine Clairn."

"What did you say?"

He pushed his hood back. His face was narrow, with a strong jaw. Long, dark hair spilled out over his shoulders, and his thin nose had a faint dip in the middle as if someone had hit him long ago, and it had not healed right.

Elaine took a step forward, staring. No one had hit him in the face. The nose was crumbling, falling in upon itself.

He gave a wide smile, and his lips cracked, blood trickling down his chin. "I am falling apart, Elaine Clairn, and you will save me."

"How?" Her voice was a whisper.

"Your blood, Elaine. I will drink your blood."

twenty-one

ELAINE BACKED UP INTO THE DOOR. SHE TRIED TO turn the handle, but it was locked. She'd heard him lock it, had stood there like an idiot while he locked her inside.

The urge to just turn around and beat at the door, to panic, was very real. It would feel good for a few moments to scream and rant, but it would be the last thing she ever did. Elaine could not give in to fear. She had to think.

The zombie took off one glove. His skin was stretched paper-thin over the bones. He touched the blood on his chin with two bare fingers. He raised the fingers to his lips and sucked them, slurping the blood off like candy.

Elaine did her best to ignore him. The hallway stretched beyond the candlelight. Two doors stood opposite each other just behind the zombie, and then the hallway gave a sharp turn. If she could get past the zombie, there were places to run to. A door, a window, something. Anything was better than being taken like this, trapped against the door.

The door banged as someone hit it from the outside. Elaine jumped, giving a small scream.

"Elaine, Elaine, open up. It's Blaine."

Elaine glanced at the door, hands pressed on its wooden surface. "Blaine, I'm locked in."

"Locked in sounds good to me. The zombies already ate my horse. I don't want to be next."

Elaine slammed her palm on the wood. "There's a zombie in here. He locked me in."

The zombie in question said, "Who is this Blaine person?"

Elaine pressed her back to the door. "My brother."

The zombie smiled again, licking the blood as it flowed from his cracked lips. "He can listen to your screams while you die. How wonderfully awful."

"Blaine!"

The door shuddered as he beat on it with fists and sword hilt. "The door's too solid. I'll find another way in."

"There is no other way," the zombie said, "I've boarded up the windows, locked all the doors. He is trapped outside with the others, and you are trapped inside with me." He made a small movement with his hand, touching his chest.

There was a sound outside, as if a body had slid into the door. "Blaine, are you out there? Blaine?"

The zombie laughed. "The others will take care of your brother, Elaine Clairn, have no fear."

Elaine pressed her back into the door. "Blaine! Blaine!"

Something heavy slithered along the door, shaking it in its frame. Something bigger than Blaine. The handle turned and rattled frantically.

"Blaine!"

"He's gone, Elaine Clairn, gone before you." The dead man walked toward her slowly, pacing like a cat. "But don't worry. Your time is almost upon you."

He brought the candelabrum with him, carried in his gloved hand. The naked hand he held out before him. The fingers from which he'd licked blood now traced her cheek. The skin felt dry as parchment, not real at all.

He brought the candles down to waist level, his head bowing toward her as if he meant to kiss her. Elaine shoved her hand into the flame. The flame danced on her palm, as it did during a vision. It did not hurt; it did not burn; it only flickered and danced over her skin.

The zombie drew back, just a fraction. "What are you, Elaine? A wizard? I've never tasted wizard's blood before."

Elaine put the tiny flame in front of his face so he could see it better. She took a deep breath and blew the flame into his face. She willed it to catch, to burn, to grow—and it did.

The zombie shrieked, turning in the hallway, beating at his burning head with his hands. He dropped the candelabrum to the floor. One candle went out. Elaine grabbed the other and ran down the hall, shielding the flame with her free hand.

Just around the corner, stairs led upward. She hesitated. Should she go farther into the hall or up?

"I will kill you, Elaine Clairn. I will suck the marrow from your bones."

Elaine ran up the stairs. The flame bobbled, shrinking down to a bluish dot. She stopped running, letting the flame revive. Being lost in utter blackness with a zombie was too horrible. The flame reared up, tracing a delicate bell of light around her. Something heavy slipped at the bottom of the stairs.

She looked down. The zombie's face was at the very edge of her circle of light. The rotting nose was gone. His face had burned down to pinkish ligaments stretched over bone. What had once been a handsome man was now a rotting skeleton, as if the fire had revealed his nature.

"I would have made it as pleasant as possible for you, Elaine, but not now. Now you will suffer as I suffer. And drinking your blood will heal me. Not even fire can harm me for long." He moved up a step, holding on to the banister with his gloved hand. He moved as if he hurt, no matter how brave his words.

Elaine backed up two steps. The zombie dropped to his knees and began to crawl up the stairs like a monkey, hand over foot, faster and faster. Elaine ran.

A hand grabbed her at the top of the stairs. The candle dropped from her shocked grasp and rolled along the floor and died. She screamed, slapping at the hands, struggling to break free. The hands dropped her to the floor. She lay in a darkness so perfect she could have touched her own eyes and not seen her fingers.

She could not see, but could hear. Feet and hands scrambled up the stairs, bumping and skittering. Whatever had grabbed her stood at the head of the stairs. It loomed over her but made no move to touch her or do anything else.

The zombie galloped to the head of the stairs. Its breathing filled the darkness. There was a sound like the very air had been sliced, then a soft meaty thunk. A sound like rain, and warm liquid fell onto Elaine's face. Something rolled, bouncing into the far wall.

Sparks flared into the dark like falling stars. A small lantern woke to life. Kneeling in that warm circle of light was Blaine.

She stared at him for a few moments, stared at his long, yellow hair, his white cloak spilling around him, absorbing the flame as if it were made of gold.

Tears burned her eyes, blurring the light. She wiped her fingers on the wetness on her face and knew it was blood. The zombie's head had rolled along the carpet. The headless body lay at the top of the stairs, leaking black black blood onto the floor.

Blaine knelt to kneel beside her. "Are you all right, Elaine?"

She nodded, not trusting her voice. She sat up and hugged him. They held each other, as if only the two of them existed. For that moment there was nothing but each other, nothing outside their circle of light.

Elaine raised her head to stare into his face. "How did you get in?"

"The attic window. It's covered by wooden slats for air to get through. I guess he thought if you couldn't see through it, you couldn't crawl through it."

"I doubt he thought anyone would be climbing roofs in the dead of winter."

Blaine grinned. "Maybe not."

The zombie twitched, a hand convulsing on the floor. Blaine helped her to her feet. "You think you can climb the roof in skirts?"

The dead man was trying to get his arms under his chest, trying to rise.

"Yes, I can climb."

Blaine led her down the hallway, lantern raised for light, and they approached a small door set in a shattered frame. "The door was locked when I came through, but wasn't nearly as well made as the front door."

The stairs were narrow and twisted. Cold air met them at the top, a swirl of snowflakes, and a cold patch of moonlight. That gaping window was one of the most wonderful things Elaine had ever seen.

Blaine knelt by his fallen backpack. He blew out the lantern, wrapping it carefully before stowing it in the pack. Elaine stood in the cold moonlight and strained to hear anything. There was no sound of pursuit, not yet.

Blaine gave her the pack. "Hand it out to me when I reach for it."

She clutched the pack to her chest and nodded. Blaine grabbed the windowsill and lifted himself. When he was even with the sill, he pushed upward with his arms, locking his elbows. He slid through the window headfirst; only his fingers showed, gripping the sill. One hand vanished, then his face appeared in the window.

He balanced his chest and one hand on the sill, and reached his other hand through. She passed the pack to him, and he slipped one strap over his shoulder, then reached back for her.

Elaine gripped his hand tightly. He flexed his arm, lifting her up. She could feel his wrist trembling with the strain, but he never hesitated. When she was even with the window, she grabbed the sill with one hand, helping him lift her to the window. With one hand, he pulled her through, the other hand tight on the sill.

He tucked her against him. Elaine looked down into emptiness. The roof went almost straight down to the street below. Snow fell, swirling into the blackness. Her boots scrambled at the icy roof. Only Blaine's arms kept her from falling.

"Can you climb up above the window?"

She tried to swallow her heart back into her throat. She couldn't breathe, staring down into the swirling darkness.

"Don't look down, Elaine," Blaine said. "Look at me."

She raised her gaze to his face. He was close enough that she could see the whites of his eyes, the pulse pounding in his throat. He wasn't much happier up here than she was. Due to an unfortunate incident involving a dragon, both twins were afraid of heights.

"Can you climb up onto the eaves?" His voice was calmer than his wide eyes.

She looked up. There was a little projection over the attic window, just big enough for her to sit on if she were very careful.

"Yes."

"Do it. I can't hold us both much longer." His voice was still calm, but there was an edge of strain to it.

Elaine reached for the eaves. The clay tiles were so cold it hurt to touch them, but she was glad she had no gloves on. She needed every bit of gripping ability she had.

She let go of Blaine, putting both hands on the slick tile, trusting him to hold her legs, to not let her fall. If he lost his grip now, they were both dead.

She stiffly clutched the roof. "I need one leg free, but don't let go."

He loosened his hold on her legs. "I won't let go."

She put one foot on the windowsill. Now was the scary part. For her to put both feet on the sill, Blaine had to let go. She stood for a moment, hands digging into the tile, feet solid on the sill. She heard Blaine sigh when he had only his own weight to support.

Elaine stood on tiptoe, hands scrambling for a hold. When her fingers felt as secure as they were likely to, she braced her feet and crawled upward. She felt Blaine's hand shove her from behind, and she ended up straddling the eave's roof. There she sat, relearning how to breathe.

She heard Blaine begin to ascend behind her, and knew she'd have to move. There wasn't room for both of them. She looked up at the icy, snow-patched tiles and sighed. She had to move, but she wasn't going to enjoy it.

She crawled to her feet, hands gripping the tile, lifting her an inch at a time. She could see Blaine's fingers at the edge of the eaves. He gave a muffled yell, and one hand vanished. He hung by the other.

Elaine went to her knees, reaching for him. She couldn't hold him alone as he had held her. Even as she moved to do it, she knew they would both fall, and she was content with that, if the only other choice was to watch him go alone.

The headless zombie had seized Blaine's legs, and its body hung half out the window. Elaine lay flat on the eaves, giving her brother her arm. He didn't take it, trying to grab the roof again but failing.

"Take my arm, Blaine, please."

His eyes said everything. "No," was all he said aloud.

She clutched his sleeve and pulled. The zombie clawed up Blaine's body; the weight tipped. His fingers slid off the tiles. She dug her hands into his clothing, screaming, "Take my hand!"

The zombie fell out the window, still clinging to Blaine's legs. Blaine hung for a moment. She tightened her hold, flattening her body along the roof, fingers digging into the cloth.

Blaine fell, and the cloth ripped. As he dropped away into darkness, he mouthed her name, "Elaine."

"Blaine!" She lay on the roof, the cloth of his tunic tight-gripped in her hands. She watched the snow tumble into the darkness and strained to see him. But there was only black night and the fall of snow.

twenty-two

TEREZA LAY VERY STILL UNDER THE BLANKETS. HER raven hair, rich and full as fur, spread out on the pillow. Her face seemed more lovely and less harsh in deep sleep, and this was a very deep sleep. Her left arm was bandaged tight to her chest. The wound had bled and bled until Jonathan began to fear it would take her life.

Averil had been so badly hurt that the doctor said she might die before morning. Her throat had been bitten by one of the dead.

The doctor had given Tereza an herbal drink to help her sleep, to keep her from going out into the night in search of the twins. Only rest, the doctor said, only rest and time would heal her.

Jonathan sat by the bed, her hand resting in his. Even in drugged sleep, she held lightly to him. The lamplight wavered, smearing in a wash of gold. The tears finally fell in silent streaks down his cheeks. Were the twins dead? Could they survive for hours in the night with the dead?

No. Jonathan knew the answer was no.

He bowed his head over Tereza's hand. He'd called Elaine corrupt, evil, and he still believed her supposed healing was evil, or at least unnatural. But he would have given a great deal not to have quarreled, not to have the last memory of her tainted. The thought that she had died thinking he hated her, perhaps hating him in return, was almost more than he could bear.

Tereza would live. The doctor would not promise that she would ever have full use of her arm again, though. Tereza didn't know yet. He wasn't going to tell her until he had to. He was a coward.

There was a soft knock at the door. Jonathan thought about not answering, pretending he was asleep. The knock came again. He sighed, then said, "What is it?"

The door opened slowly. Thordin stood half in the frame. His gaze went to Tereza's pale form. He looked at Jonathan.

"She's resting."

Thordin took a deep breath and let it out slowly. "The townsfolk are gathered. The town council wishes to speak to us tonight." He stepped into the room, closing the door gently behind him. He leaned against it, arms crossed over his chest. "I didn't explain that Blaine and Elaine were more than helpers to the mage-finder. I . . . didn't know if you wanted them to know."

He shook his head. "No, our grief is our own. Blaine was of the brotherhood. He knew the risks. It is Elaine. . . ." His voice failed him, and he turned his head away so Thordin could not see the tears.

"It is no one's fault, Jonathan."

"Isn't it?" he said. He turned back to Thordin, anger and tears mixing in his eyes. Self-hatred threatened to choke him. "If I had left her behind with the wizard, let her learn her magic in peace, she would be alive."

"We don't know they are dead, Jonathan."

"Elaine was unarmed, Thordin."

"Blaine went to find her. He is a good fighter."

"We would all have been killed if Lukas had not opened the door. He saved us all."

"Someone else might have opened a door to the twins."

"Thordin, it is night, and the dead walk the streets. No one will risk himself for strangers."

"There are always good people, Jonathan, wherever we go," Thordin said.

Jonathan shook his head. "No, Thordin, no false hope. We must face the truth."

"You are burying them before they are dead, Jonathan. You are simply giving up," Thordin said. "It is not like you to give up without a fight."

"Perhaps I have learned that you can fight long and valiantly and still die a bad death."

"You speak of Calum Songmaster," Thordin said.

Jonathan nodded. "Elaine asked if Silvanus could heal Calum. It never occurred to me to ask for Calum's sake. She thought of it."

"Elaine has a good heart," Thordin said.

Jonathan nodded again. He scrubbed his free hand across his face, smearing the tear tracks more than hiding them. "You said something about the town council."

"They want to see you tonight. They are badly frightened and want the reassurance of the great mage-finder."

"We entered the town and lost four people in less than an hour. They still think I can help them?"

"Your reputation is strong, Jonathan. They believe in you."

"I am not some magical talisman that can chase away the evil just by being here," Jonathan said. His voice was harsh.

"They probably do expect something that easy, that dramatic, but even small hope from you will be enough tonight, if you're up to it."

Jonathan stared at him. He wanted to be angry that Thordin would even ask, but looking into his friend's blunt face, his anger faded. He was simply tired, so tired that all he wanted was to crawl in beside Tereza and sleep, sleep, cling to his wife as if just by touching her he could keep her safe.

He raised her hand to his lips, bestowing a gentle kiss on her fingers. He stood and laid her hand under the covers, tucking them beneath her chin. He ran his fingers through her hair, then turned to Thordin.

"Let us go comfort the town council," he said.

Thordin smiled. "We always do a lot of hand-holding in this job."

Jonathan just nodded. He glanced back at Tereza as Thordin shut the door. She looked very pale in the lamplight. She had lost so much blood, but not as much as Averil. He glanced at the door across the hall.

Silvanus stood vigil over his daughter. If she survived until dawn, the doctor thought Averil would live. If she survived.

They had been told there was a plague of the dead, but there were hundreds of zombies in the streets, more than could have died this winter. Cortton was not that large a village. Where had all the dead sprung from? This was a question he intended to ask the council.

The town council consisted of the innkeeper, the meistersinger, and the undertaker. The innkeeper, Belinna, was the woman who had thrown oil on the zombies. She was tall and wide, but not fat. Fat implied softness, indulgence. Her brawn was solid, what some would call big boned. Her hair was tied in a long plait down her back. The boy that had held the torch was her eldest son. He stood by her side now—tall, slender, dark, but his harsh, watching eyes were mirrored in Belinna's.

The meistersinger, Simon LeBec, had been a well-known bard in his younger days. Jonathan had heard him sing once, perhaps thirty years ago. He had been the handsome darling of all the ladies then. His hair was white as snow now, his face lined. Only his eyes remained the same—piercing blue.

Jonathan did not try to remind LeBec that they had met thirty years ago. He had not been known as a mage-finder then. He had been simply Jonathan Ambrose, a wandering adventurer who happened to specialize in slaying wizards. He hadn't had the law behind him then, and was almost an outlaw. Jonathan remembered the surety of purpose he had, like a shield that could not be pierced. No doubts.

He stood, staring at their worried faces, watching the strain fade just a little simply because he was there. It was obscene that they had such confidence in him.

The undertaker, Marland Ashe, was a tall, thin man. His milk-pale skin and violet-blue eyes were typical of the natives in this area of Kartakass. The combination was startling, lovely, but some disease had pock-marked his cheeks until the skin was rough as gravel. The spoiled skin seemed odd below those large, beautiful eyes.

The three of them sat behind a long table in the common room of the inn. There were only a few servants. Jonathan and his companions were the only guests. Visitors did not come to a cursed village. If they happened in by accident, they hurried away before nightfall. If they happened to come after dark . . . well, Jonathan had seen what happened then. They died.

"What is it you want of me tonight, councilors?" His voice was polite. Jonathan was surprised that he sounded so businesslike, almost pleasant. His voice was such a lie. It gave no hint of the anguish inside his heart and head.

"We need to know what you plan to do to help us," LeBec said. The meistersinger's face was calm enough, his folded hands very still on the table before him. Too still. The effort he was making to appear calm showed in his shoulders, arms, even the still hands.

Jonathan fought an urge to laugh in his face. What could they do? They had ridden into town and been nearly wiped out. They had been unprepared for what met them.

"Your messenger told us that a third of your town had died from some evil plague. He further told us that they had risen as undead and walked the streets. There are hundreds of dead out there. Where did they all come from?"

The meistersinger glanced at the undertaker. Ashe spoke, "The village graveyard has been emptied. Cortton was once a much larger village, a town. The graveyard held more dead than the town holds living."

"If we had been told there were hundreds of dead here, we wouldn't have ridden into Cortton after dark."

The innkeeper shifted in her seat. "We did not think it mattered. You are the mage-finder. You defeated the vermin plague of Deccan. Surely there were more of them than there are of our dead."

"You shouldn't believe everything the bards tell you," Jonathan said.

LeBec looked down at the table, studying his hands. He glanced up at Jonathan's face and held his gaze. "I know that some of my brethren exaggerate, but not that much. We truly thought you would be safe, riding straight to the inn."

"Did you really? Then why did no one open the door? The women that lie upstairs might have been saved their injuries if the door had opened sooner."

None of them could meet his eyes. Anger flared through him in a rush that almost burned along his skin. He opened his mouth to say what he thought of them all, but a voice interrupted.

"They were afraid, mage-finder."

Jonathan turned to see Harkon Lukas leaning against the wall. His arms were crossed carelessly over his chest, and a mocking smile curled his lips. He was dressed in a wine-dark burgundy tunic, and pants trimmed in black velvet. His burgundy hat boasted no less than three black plumes. His monocle caught the lamplight, winking at them.

"And I resent the defaming statements against my profession. I assure you I sing only the truth."

"You saved our lives tonight. For that I am grateful."

Lukas pushed away from the wall, striding toward them. He waved the gratitude away. "It seemed silly to let the savior of the village die in the street."

"We could hear the dead outside the door," Belinna said. "We feared they would force their way in and kill us all. All who have died since the plague began have risen to haunt the night. A clean death I would have risked." She touched her son's arm. "But this walking death . . ." She shook her head. "It is a different thing to risk."

Jonathan could not argue with that. "I thought only those

that died of plague rose from the dead."

She shook her head. "All."

"That is odd. If the plague was a spell, only plague victims should rise from the dead."

"What does it mean that all dead walk?" LeBec asked.

"Perhaps the plague is not a spell, or not all of it."

"I don't understand what you are implying," LeBec said.

Jonathan shook his head. He wasn't sure he could explain it yet. It was merely the seed of an idea, not ready to see the light of day yet. Certainly not ready to be explained to a group of nervous strangers.

"I wish to gather more evidence before I speak." It was a standard stalling tactic. The three councilors nodded and murmured, as if he had said something clever.

"Of course," LeBec said, "we understand. Accusations of black magic are not lightly made."

Jonathan said nothing. He had found that a stern face and silence often did better than words. Especially if you had nothing to say.

"Do you think you have the answer to Cortton's little problem so soon?" Harkon Lukas stood in front of Jonathan, hands on slender hips. He was a tall, strong-looking man, but there was something feminine about him, a grace that was closer to a dancer's movements than a bard's. There was a sparkle in his dark eyes that said he suspected Jonathan of bluffing.

Jonathan almost smiled, but managed to swallow it. He gave a solemn nod of his head. "I have some suspicions."

"Care to share them?"

Jonathan shook his head, silent. He couldn't keep the smile hidden. Only Harkon Lukas saw it. The bard cocked his head to one side, staring at Jonathan. An expression passed over his face that Jonathan could not read.

"Remind me never to play cards with you, mage-finder. You have the proverbial poker face."

"I don't have much time for playing games."

"Pity. Games are so diverting."

"Do you really think so?" Jonathan asked. His thoughts were on Tereza and the missing children. "I find games a waste of precious time."

"Ah, yes, you have people lost outside. Time is precious to them. How many hours until dawn? Can they survive on the streets that long?"

Jonathan turned away from him. He couldn't face the bard's mocking face. He didn't think the man was being purposefully cruel, but it amounted to the same thing.

"Harkon," LeBec said, "you are being thoughtless."

His face crumbled into sorrow, his graceful hand touching his heart. "Oh, I am so sorry. I am not merely thoughtless, but cruel. I am already thinking of the song I shall write when they come safely back, having survived the night running from a horde of the dead." He smiled. "They will tell me of their brave exploits when they come through that door."

Jonathan studied the bard's face. He couldn't tell if he were being teased or if the man just had a peculiar sense of humor. Was he trying to comfort Jonathan with such childish tales? The twins were not coming through that door or any other, not alive.

"I am sure if they return they will be most happy to regale you with their night."

"Especially Blaine," Thordin said. He'd been quietly leaning against the opposite wall. Now he walked to the center of the room to stand near Jonathan. "Blaine loves a good brag."

Jonathan nodded. "Yes, he does."

"Then I will give him the chance to brag to a bard, something all of Kartakass longs to do."

"Do they?" Jonathan said. "I do not. I stand by my earlier statement. Bards collect the facts but never quite get them right. I have heard stories of my own exploits where only my name remained unchanged."

"Simon, I believe he accuses us of being liars." He stared at Jonathan, taking two strides to bring them nearly touching. His quick, dark eyes flitted here and there over Jonathan's face as if he would memorize every line of it.

"Enough, Harkon. Leave our guests be. They have people they worry about."

"And well they should," Harkon said. He spoke directly to Jonathan's face from inches away. "I am writing a song about the dead of Cortton, mage-finder. The dead of Cortton are not just murderous, they are hungry."

Jonathan could not speak. It was Thordin who asked, "What do you mean, bard?"

Harkon Lukas never glanced away; he stared straight into Jonathan's eyes. "The dead feast upon the living. That is how they kill, with naked hands and teeth."

Thordin pushed Lukas backward. The bard stumbled, but did not fall.

"Either you are a fool, or you are taunting us," Thordin said. "If it is the latter, we can settle it with cold steel. There is room enough to fight right here."

The bard gave a surprised bark of laughter. "A duel? You challenge me to a duel?"

"Unless you admit to being a loose-tongued fool, yes, I challenge you."

Jonathan knew he should stop this, but he couldn't. He'd seen the bite wound in Averil's neck, Tereza's arm. The thought of that happening to Elaine and Blaine, of them being torn apart piece by bloody piece, mouthful by screaming mouthful . . . the image was thick and red and worse than anything else he could have imagined.

Harkon Lukas laughed again. "I am a fool, sir warrior, a loose-tongued fool. An occupational hazard, I fear." His laughter echoed off the stone walls, rising to the high-beamed ceiling. Jonathan fought the urge to hit him, to stop that cheerful sound. His mind was full of horrors that the bard had put there. He shouldn't be laughing.

"If you cannot hold a civil tongue, then leave us," Jonathan said.

The laughter trickled down and faded. That strange, unreadable look was back on Lukas's face. "My deepest apologies." He gave a low, sweeping bow, hat plumes gliding over the floor. It was the same bow he'd used to usher them through the door.

Jonathan watched the bard give his theatrical apology and didn't believe a word of it. He had meant to upset them. Jonathan wasn't sure why, but he knew it was true. Regardless of motive, Jonathan hated Harkon Lukas. It was one thing to believe the twins dead, but eaten alive . . . The thought made the hours until dawn a creeping, agonizing thing. He had Harkon Lukas to thank for that. Jonathan intended to see that the bard got his just rewards. If it was within the mage-finder's powers to make one bard's life miserable, Jonathan would do it.

It was petty, and he hugged the thought to him like a prayer. He would torment Harkon Lukas for tormenting him now. It was cold comfort, but the mage-finder was willing to take any comfort at all on this long, eternally long night.

twenty-three

Harkon Lukas paced up the stairs like an angry cat. He swatted his hat against his leg as he climbed, beating it in time to his frustration.

Ambrose knew. He knew. Harkon was not sure how much he knew, but he was not the innocent Harkon had thought him. He had invited them here to taunt them. He could have simply captured Konrad Burn, but no, he, Harkon Lukas, had to play games. His own arrogance amazed him. Had he really thought the brotherhood's most visible member was a complete fool?

Harkon nodded to himself. Yes, he had thought just that. He had never been terribly impressed with this brotherhood before. But Ambrose's eyes had held a taunting knowledge. Had Ambrose come here to join in the game? Not an innocent lured to cure some magical plague, but a brother aware that the true heart of all evil in Kartakass was in this town. Surely if the mage-finder had known that he, Harkon Lukas, was the heart of evil, there would be more of the brotherhood in Cortton. There would be a great hunt, and he would be the prey.

No, Ambrose suspected, but he was not sure. But how close was the mage-finder to being sure? Harkon still could hardly believe he had had to save them. He had had to open the inn door. The foolish villagers would have let their potential saviors die. He had thought that saving them would put him in their good graces, but the look in Ambrose's eyes said clearly that he didn't trust the bard as far as the next room.

Harkon liked a suspicious man, or at least respected the trait. But now, he could have done without it.

Konrad Burn stepped out of the righthand room. He smelled of herbs and salves. He glanced up, nodding at Lukas.

Harkon stopped at the head of the stairs to ask, "How is the young woman?"

Konrad closed the door firmly behind him and walked to Harkon, putting distance between himself and the room. He appeared not to want to be overheard; the news would be grave.

"She is not well." Konrad moved past him to go downstairs.

Harkon grabbed his upper arm. He liked holding the strong, muscled flesh. It was a good arm, and he would enjoying having it as his own. "Is it blood loss, or is the wound so terrible?"

Konrad looked down at the bard's hand. He stepped back, forcing Harkon to either release his hold or be obvious about it. It was not yet time to be so possessive. He released the man.

"She's lost a great deal of blood."

"But the doctor seemed to think she would survive if the blood loss did not kill her. You think otherwise?"

"I am sure your doctor is a good man, but I've seen more battle injuries than he has."

"You think she will die?"

Konrad frowned at him, his green eyes filling with anger. "I think that is not a question for idle curiosity, bard."

Harkon gave a small bow, graceful but not quite as sweeping

as before. "You are quite right, Master Burn. I am a bard, and idle curiosity is a hazard of my profession." Still half bent over, he looked up at Konrad. "Of course if I am to sing of this deed, to immortalize her bravery, I need to know the facts." He straightened and found himself distressingly taller than Konrad Burn. He was a tall man and didn't like giving it up, but nothing was perfect.

Harkon forced himself to smile. "So perhaps my curiosity is not completely idle."

Konrad shook his head. "I do not believe you intend to write some great epic. I think you are just a vulture eager to hear of other people's sorrows."

Konrad pushed past him.

"Ah, yes, you have your own more personal loss to mourn, do you not?"

Konrad stopped on the stairs, back straightening. He turned slowly to look upward at the smiling bard. The rage on his face was murderous. It made Harkon's smile widen.

"My loss, my grief is my own business. It is certainly none of yours."

"Forgive me, please. I speak without thinking. It is a terrible fault of mine."

Konrad came up two steps, then stopped. His hand that gripped the banister trembled, white-knuckled. He wanted to rush up the stairs and attack the bard.

Harkon toyed with saying that one last thing that would push the man over the edge of his anger. He had to force himself to stand still, not to widen his smile farther. Even that might have been enough to bring Konrad up those last few steps. It would have been delicious, ironic, but he might have been forced to hurt his future body. That would be self-defeating. He let it go. The hardest thing was to keep the knowledge from his eyes, the surety that he could kill this man if he wanted to.

The pride and confidence in Burn's face, his stance, said clearly that even that one look would have been enough to cause a fight. His future body had quite a temper.

"A loose tongue can get a person killed," Konrad said.

Harkon fought to keep his face pleasant and blank. The man wanted to fight. His grief had translated into anger, and he wanted a target for that anger.

Harkon hoped to witness when that rage found its target, but he could not afford to be that target. He might have to keep a closer eye on Konrad. If the man got himself killed before Harkon could switch bodies, that would spoil all his plans.

"I most humbly beg your pardon, Master Burn. Please believe me when I say you have my deepest sympathies."

"You speak of things that you know nothing about, bard. I won't believe they are dead, not yet."

"I am sure you are right to be hopeful. Some kind soul might have opened a door, as I opened the door for you."

Konrad suddenly looked embarrassed. He took a deep breath and let it out slowly. "I have not thanked you for saving our lives."

Harkon waved it away. "Master Ambrose thanked me for you all."

Konrad shook his head. "No, we would all be dead now if not for your bravery." The words seemed to stick in his throat.

Harkon narrowed his eyes, studying the man. Did he know something as well? Were all his carefully laid plans known by his adversaries? Had Calum Songmaster had a change of heart? Had Harkon been betrayed? If Calum would betray his bosom friends, why not betray Harkon? Because he, too, wanted a new body. Harkon had thought that the offer of escape would insure Calum's loyalty, but there was dislike in Konrad's face. He had saved the man's life. Why would he dislike him?

"Truly, it was nothing."

"Modesty does not sit well on you, bard."

Harkon had to smile. "It is not my natural habit."

"How long have you been in Cortton?"

The change of subject caught Harkon off guard. He smiled to hide it. "I came only recently, a day ago."

"The innkeeper says you were here for some weeks, then left after the dead began to walk. You knew what the town was like, how dangerous it was. Why did you come back?"

"I am a bard. I sing of great deeds, or great tragedies. I could spend my life singing other people's ballads, but the best songs, the ones that make a reputation, are those you write yourself."

"So you came back for a song," Konrad said.

"Yes."

"Is that worth risking your life?"

"Yes."

Konrad shook his head. "You sell your life cheaply, Lukas." He turned and clattered down the stairs.

Harkon watched him go, thoughtful. He had planned to make this a great game, to destroy everyone Konrad loved before he took him. It was part of the reason for the undead plague. Now, perhaps he should simply take the man and leave the others to clean up the mess he had made. Yet, if Ambrose suspected Harkon of being what he truly was, he could not leave Ambrose alive.

They had to die, all of them, as he had originally planned. Perhaps just quicker. It wouldn't be as much fun, but then, occasionally business had to come before pleasure.

twenty-four

Blaine lay on the snowy street. His long yellow hair spilled out around his face like pale water. His cloak was bunched underneath his body, the white fur black with soaked blood. One leg had been bent at a painful angle, trapped under his body. Blood had poured from his mouth and nose, painting the lower half of his face black.

Elaine knelt by his lifeless body. The key to the door had been on the attic floor. It had glinted up at her from the patch of moonlight. The dead man had dropped it while killing Blaine. How she would have gotten outside without the key, Elaine didn't know.

Now, she sat by his body, watching his blood leak into the fur of his cloak. A line of blood trickled from the fur to snake through the snow like a dark river trailing the finger of a god. Elaine screamed and tore at the snow, scattering it. The blood trickled down to pool in the frozen street. There was nothing she could do to stop it.

Or maybe there was something. She had seen Silvanus raise the dead, felt him do it. Could she do it now?

Elaine reached out and touched his face. The skin was still warm. He was barely dead, so close to being alive. Could she bring him back? Jonathan had told stories of sorcerers that raised zombies. If she did it wrong, would Blaine come back as a walking corpse? That was worse than death, but Elaine had to try. She would wonder forever if she didn't.

She gazed at Blaine's wide, staring eyes, looking at the sky but seeing nothing. Snowflakes fell on his upturned face. They melted on his eyelashes, making tiny dots of moisture on his cheeks, like tears.

Elaine took a deep breath and tried to gather what she had learned from Silvanus, tried to imagine how to raise her brother back to life. It wasn't like healing a wound, was it?

A sound behind her made her whirl, half-falling into the snow. Two zombies stood at the mouth of the nearest cross street. One wove back and forth as if drunk. It took a step forward and legs collapsed. When it tried to stand, one leg slid out of its tunic and lay twitching on the ground. The zombie balanced on the remaining leg as if this had happened before.

A puff of snow fell from the opposite roof. She looked up and found a man-shape silhouetted against the moonlight. It leapt downward, almost seeming to float, hands and legs wide as if for balance. It landed with a thump on the snow and scuttled backward into the deeper shadows that hugged the houses.

The thing seemed almost to glow with a white leprous light, the tint of night-growing fungi. It crouched in the shadows. It looked like a naked man, but wasn't. It raised its face and looked at her. Its eyes glowed like black fire, sparking with an eternal flame that had nothing to do with moonlight.

It opened its mouth and hissed.

Elaine rose slowly to her feet. At the end of the street, the dead were gathering, but just as the other zombies had given way before the man that had killed Blaine, so they waited on this crouching thing.

Elaine gripped the key in her hand. Would it let her get to the door? She glanced down at Blaine. He was dead. He'd died to save her. She couldn't leave him like this. She couldn't.

The thing gave a bounding leap and landed on the other side of Blaine's body. Elaine froze, staring down at it. It had been a man once, a man of medium height with brown hair. An ordinary man. It wasn't ordinary anymore; it was bestial.

It grabbed Blaine's arm. Elaine stomped her foot at it as you would at a bad dog. It growled low in its throat and leapt straight at her. She had time to put her arms up to protect her face and neck, but then it was on top of her. Teeth tore into her sleeve, worrying it like a dog with a bone. Elaine screamed.

There was a last tug at her sleeve, and the thing sat back. She could feel its weight shift as it settled on its haunches. The weight pinned her legs, but nothing else happened.

Elaine lay there, waiting for the teeth to tear into her flesh, but they didn't. Minutes passed with her lying on the frozen ground. Snow fell in soft, downy flakes, and that was all. Finally, she lowered her arms just enough to peek at the monster.

She found herself staring into a pair of black eyes. Those eyes looked at her not as a man but as an intelligent dog would. It was not the blank stare of the undead, or at least no sort of undead she knew of. She almost asked it what it wanted, as she had the woman, but there was no one behind those eyes to answer the question. At least, not in words.

But it wanted something or it would have killed her by now. The zombie that had killed Blaine had wanted her blood. What did this one want?

It crept off of her, slowly, moving down her legs hand over hand. It scuttled backward to Blaine's body, grabbed his tunic, and began to lift the corpse over its shoulder.

She sat up, hand reaching outward. "No."

It growled at her, low and deep. Lips curled back from teeth too sharp to be human.

Elaine froze, unsure what to do. It was warning her off. It wanted Blaine's body, but that it could not have. If she could find Silvanus, he could tell her how to raise Blaine to life. If she lost the body, Blaine was truly gone.

"You can't have him." She forced her voice to be gentle, soft, as if she talked to a wild animal. "Please, don't take him."

It gave a growling shout. The dead at the end of the street began shuffling toward them. Whatever power had held them at bay was gone. The creature had called them.

It flung Blaine over its shoulder in one quick movement. Elaine crawled forward, hand outstretched, not sure what she was reaching for, the body, or the monster.

"Please, don't."

It rose to a crouch. Blaine's hands trailed the ground, his hair a golden swash over the creature's back.

Elaine stood reaching for him. The creature sprang forward, moving in a series of leaps that carried it down the street in great bounds.

"Blaine, please, no." She ran after them, but couldn't catch up. A sound brought her whirling to face the street. The dead were a solid wall limping toward the her. They were only a few steps away from the door. If she was cut off from it, they would drink her blood. She didn't want to die, not like that.

Elaine ran for the door. The zombies hesitated, confused by

the fact that she was running toward them, not away. She pushed open the portal, and the dead surged forward. They understood what a door meant.

Elaine slammed it in its frame, shoving the key in the lock. The handle turned. She leaned into the wood and turned the key. The lock shut home. The knob twisted frantically; the wood shuddered as the dead pushed against it, pounding on it.

Elaine leaned back, feeling the strength of the mob thrumming the wood behind her body. She slid down the length of the door to sit, huddled. Tears streaked her face. The first sob escaped her lips. She buried her face on her knees, arms over her head, hugging her body tight and tighter. The dead stormed outside the house, beating on the nailed shutters, trying to get in. Elaine gave herself over to her grief, letting it drown the sounds of the dead outside and wishing it could drown the emptiness within.

twenty-five

JONATHAN STOOD AT THE OPEN WINDOW IN TEREZA'S room. Dawn had come at last. It spread in a soft wash over the village. The sky was white and heavy with snow, and fresh white flakes had filled the street below, deep and thick with footprints. The dead had wandered the streets until perhaps an hour before dawn. Jonathan had listened to them squabbling in the dark. What did the dead have to quarrel over? Why did they stay here in a town prepared for them?

There were hundreds of zombies, a veritable army of the dead. They could move outward into the countryside and raid everything in their path. Here in Cortton the town hid in its upper stories, the livestock below. The livestock living inside had originally been protected against wolves. No wolves now came near Cortton. Even they feared the dead.

Who had done this? Why had they done it? No matter how evil the perpetrator, there had always been a plan—some logic, no matter how twisted. A great deal of magical energy had been used here, but for what purpose? Jonathan could find nothing that the zombies had gained for anyone.

The town had been a center of commerce, but no farmer would

come near it now. Traveling merchants would not enter the main street. The meistersinger's reassurance of daylight safety hadn't helped. After what he had seen in the night, Jonathan could not blame anyone for avoiding the town.

A breeze had come with the dawn, an icy finger of wind that trailed down Jonathan's spine as if he stood bare before the window. He shivered, and could not seem to stop.

"Jonathan," Tereza's voice, hoarse, faint, but there. He turned with a smile. She held one hand out to him. The hand trembled, but the smile on her lips was firm.

He knelt beside the bed, taking her hand in both of his hands. He pressed her fingers to his lips. "How do you feel this fine morning, my wife?"

Her smile widened. "Better than last night."

He spoke with his lips against the back of her hand. "Is there anything I can get you? Are you hungry?"

"Did Blaine or Elaine come back last night?"

It was the one question he did not want to answer, but he could not lie to her face. He'd never been able to lie to those dark eyes. "No, they did not."

She struggled to sit up but fell back against the pillows. "We must go after them. We must . . . help them."

"Tereza, either they found shelter last night, or they do not need our help."

"No, Jonathan. I don't believe they are dead."

"Tereza, please. . . ."

She tried to sit up again but fell back, gasping this time. Her skin paled, and a beading of sweat broke on her skin.

"Tereza, you are too hurt to go anywhere."

She turned her face to the wall, pulling her hand from his

grasp. "No, Jonathan. I won't give up."

"There are hundreds of undead in the streets at night. Hundreds. I watched them from this window. There is no survival out of doors in Cortton after dark."

She turned her head, tears glittering in her eyes. "Then find their bodies."

He looked down at the floor, unwilling to meet her eyes. He was a coward. He did not want to tell her there would be no bodies to find.

"What is it? What are you keeping from me?"

He looked up. Something like a smile twisted his lips, but there was no joy to it. "I could never lie to you, could I?"

"No, and don't start trying now. What is it?"

"The town council demanded to speak with me last night. They said all who died in Cortton rose to walk the night."

"Those that died of the plague," she said.

"No, my love, all who die in Cortton rise as undead." He watched the horror spread across her face, the realization of what that meant for their "children."

"No, Jonathan, not that. I might be able to bear their being dead, but not that. Please, Jonathan, not that."

He held her good hand and cradled her head in his arms. He held her while she cried, but did not cry himself. He had insisted Elaine come. If she had been safely at home, Blaine would not have had to go in search of her. It was his fault, his doing. Jonathan would not let himself cry. He didn't deserve it.

A scream cut the morning, a wordless wail that held all the pain in the world. The sound froze Jonathan, heart pounding in his chest. Feet clattered up the stairs. The sound seemed to release him. He stood, moving gently from the circle of Tereza's arms.

"What was that?" she asked.

He shook his head, but he feared he knew. He opened the door and found a crowd of people filling the opposite doorway.

Jonathan pushed through the people until he stood in the doorway. Fredric had dropped to his knees, head bowed. Randwulf stood to one side of the bed. His young face raw with grief. Silvanus sat in the narrow bed, holding Averil's limp body. He rocked her as he would a child, but her arms flopped with every movement like those of a broken doll.

Silvanus was saying something, over and over, too soft for Jonathan to hear. Konrad stood at the window, staring out at the morning light. His hands were clasped so hard behind his back, the veins corded in his forearms.

The white-haired doctor stood in the middle of the room. For a man that had seen a great deal of death, he seemed at a loss.

Jonathan took a deep breath and stepped into the room. He went to Konrad. "What happened?"

Konrad shot him a quick, harsh glance out of the corners of his green eyes. "She lost too much blood. Then the wound became inflamed. The fever burned her alive. No herb or potion that I had helped her."

"What of her own potions that she brought with her?"

"She used the last on her father."

Jonathan glanced at the bed. Everyone seemed stunned, unable or unwilling to do anything. He stepped forward, past the stupefied doctor. He could hear what Silvanus was muttering now.

"I couldn't save her. I couldn't save her. I couldn't save her. I couldn't save her." It was a piteous litany. His voice squeezed tight with grief and guilt. Yes, Jonathan recognized the taste of guilt. It was too strong in his own mouth not to know it in others.

He placed a gentle hand on the elf's shoulder. Silvanus did not notice. He rocked his dead daughter in his arms as if her limp body were the center of the world. And for that one moment, perhaps it was.

Jonathan squeezed the elf's shoulder. "Silvanus?" He made the name a question.

The elf gave a sobbing cough and looked up at him. Those golden eyes swam with tears. The tears looked like mercury sliding down his cheeks, as silver as the elf's hair was gold. Elves cried silver tears. The sight of it startled Jonathan down to the soles of his feet, tingling. The sight was astonishing, the grief unbearable.

"Silvanus . . ." Words failed him. What could he say? I'm sorry wasn't enough. I grieve with you was a lie. He hadn't known Averil, not really. He'd have traded her life for Elaine's in a moment. "There are no words, but I am deeply sorry for your loss."

"I tried to raise her from the dead. All these years it came easily to me. But this time, when I would have given my whole soul for the power, it did not come. Why?"

Some questions had no answers, or at least none that we wanted to hear. "I don't know, Silvanus. I don't know."

He hugged her to his chest, his one good arm tight against her back. The missing arm was longer, and the stump helped hold her in place. The sight of the growing stump made Jonathan's stomach clench. Nausea burned at the back of his throat. He took a deep breath through his nose and swallowed. He would not let his own fears make this hideous scene worse.

"We have to tend the dead before dark," the doctor said. His voice sounded ordinary enough. Jonathan wondered why he himself felt so startled. He had seen many scenes of grief before.

Silvanus shook his head, rocking faster. Averil's hand slapped the bedframe with a meaty thunk. Every few moments; thunk—thunk—thunk. That one sound seemed worse than all the others.

Randwulf rushed forward, grabbing both the elf and his dead daughter in his arms. Hugging them both. He held them close and the awful sound stopped.

Randwulf's head was bent over Silvanus's shoulder. There was a large bump at the top of the boy's spine. Jonathan couldn't remember it being there before, when he saw Elaine heal the old wound.

He shook his head. Now was not the time.

"We have sent for the undertaker," the doctor said.

Silvanus's head snapped up, rage sparkling through the tears. "No, not yet."

"We must have her out of doors by dark," the doctor said.

"Why?" Silvanus asked.

Jonathan made a movement to attract the doctor's attention. He gave a small shake of his head. The doctor frowned, not seeming to understand.

Jonathan walked over and put a hand on his shoulder, directing him toward the door. "I think we should give Silvanus a few moments alone with his grief."

"But we can't have a dead body inside. . . ."

"I know that," Jonathan said softly, "but it is an hour past sunup. We have time."

The doctor shook his head, eyes wide with what Jonathan now recognized as fear. "The undertaker is on his way. We must . . ."

Jonathan practically shoved the doctor through the door, pushing the crowd aside. When they were in the hallway, he spoke, low and urgent, "They do not know that all dead in this cursed village rise to walk the night. And you will not be the one to tell them."

The doctor's mouth made a little **O** of surprise. "It is my duty to protect this town."

"And a fine job you're doing. Now get out."

The doctor sputtered, protesting. "I am the doctor here. You are to find the source of this evil, but I am to protect the living."

Thordin had come up. He stood at Jonathan's side, simply staring at the doctor. There was really nothing in the look that Jonathan found frightening. It was just Thordin, but the doctor paled.

"I think you had better leave," Thordin said in a low, careful voice.

The doctor's eyes widened, then without another word, he fled down the stairs.

"You must be a great deal more frightening than I think you are," Jonathan said.

Thordin shrugged. "The doctor scares easy."

"That he does," Jonathan said. "It might be interesting to find out why."

They stared at each other for a few heartbeats. It was enough, no words needed. Thordin went to follow the doctor or perhaps to question him, Jonathan didn't care which. Who better to corrupt the dead and dying than a doctor? The village had only one. Who would question him?

He heard Tereza calling his name faintly through the other door. He opened the door with a smile that was all lies. Averil's death was one more reminder of their own loss.

"The girl's dead, isn't she?" Tereza asked.

Jonathan nodded, leaving the door half open behind him. "I may be needed in the other room. Silvanus does not know . . ." He let the thought trail off.

"That all dead rise again as zombies," she finished.

He sat on the edge of the bed, taking her offered hand.

"We must try and find their bodies, Jonathan. We can use fire to destroy them so they won't rise."

Jonathan could not meet her eyes.

"Husband, look at me," she said.

He raised his head and met her dark gaze. "You were always braver than I."

"I am more practical. That isn't the same thing at all, Jonathan. The thought of . . . of watching them burn. A new zombie looks living. It would be like burning them alive."

"They won't be alive, Tereza."

"We must do it for the sakes of their souls, but . . ."

"You are too ill to move from this bed. I will do what is necessary."

She squeezed his hand. "Averil must be treated the same way."

"What I can't understand is why the villagers haven't been burning the bodies, themselves."

"They may not know that fire destroys the body completely," she said.

"The undertaker should have known. Any keeper of the dead in Kartakass has to be aware of how to keep the dead from rising."

"Perhaps it is the old dead that fill the streets."

Jonathan shook his head. "I will find out today. Before another night falls, I will have answers."

"So quickly?"

"We have lost a great deal in one night. I will not lose anyone else. We will find who is behind this."

"You have some ideas. I can see it in your face."

"Yes, I have some suspects."

"Who?"

He glanced back at the open door. "Later. Let me see how Silvanus fares. I promise to come back and tell you all my theories. You know that I do my best thinking while explaining things to you."

She gave a small smile. "I know."

He kissed her cheek and left, closing the door behind him.

Konrad had shooed the idle gawkers away. He stood guard over the door, hands on chest, and wore a forbidding expression. Suddenly, his face changed, a look of astonishment crumbled it into lines of shock. He was staring at something over Jonathan's shoulder, something coming up the stairs.

Jonathan turned. Elaine was ascending. He felt his own mouth drop open with surprise. She looked as she always looked. Clothes covered in dirt and blood, but it was her.

She was a few steps from the top when Konrad broke and ran for her. He lifted her bodily up the last steps, whirling her around in the narrow hallway. He put her down, and they were both laughing. Konrad was laughing. It was the first joy Jonathan had seen in him since his wife died.

Konrad set her on the floor and hugged her again. "Elaine, Elaine, Elaine." He seemed unwilling to let her go.

Jonathan stood there with tears running down his face, mingling with his beard. Her blue eyes glanced at him. He held his arms wide, and she ran to him. He hugged her to his chest, burying his face in the top of her hair. Her arms held him as if she would never let him go.

"I am so sorry for all I said, Elaine."

"It doesn't matter." She pushed away from him, enough to look up into his face. There was something in her eyes, some knowledge that left Jonathan frightened. He was suddenly cold all over as if he'd been dropped in icy water.

"Where's Blaine?" His voice was choked and soft. He knew the answer. It was there in her eyes.

"Gone," she said. One word, not even the right word. Gone, not dead. Mustn't say that word aloud. Gone.

"Are you sure?" Konrad was with them, hand on Elaine's back. "Are you sure?"

She nodded, burying her face against Jonathan's chest. She did not cry, as dry inside as a seashell left on a high shelf to gather dust and dream of lost paradises.

He had believed them both dead, or said he did, but Jonathan realized now it was a lie. He hadn't really believed. It was true for one of them, and he couldn't think. One question came to his mind. "How?" he asked. Somehow that seemed important.

She took a deep shuddering breath and stepped away from him. She stood in the center of the hallway, hands close against her body, tight as if afraid to touch anything. "He was trying to save me. He died saving me." She raised her face and looked at them. The hatred in her eyes pierced him to his soul. Self-hatred was the hardest wound to heal.

"We were trying to climb onto a roof to get away from the dead. He fell." She held out her hands to the empty air. "I tried to save him. I offered him my hand, but he wouldn't take it. Why wouldn't he take it?"

Konrad stepped toward her, gently, as he would approach a wounded animal. "If he had taken your hand, would you both have fallen?"

She looked at him, eyes stricken. She nodded, then hid her face in her hands and said, muffled, "Yes, yes, yes."

Konrad touched her shoulder. She flinched, but did not step away. He encircled her in his arms, and she let him.

"Tereza needs to see you, Elaine," Jonathan said. His voice still sounded distant, as if someone else were speaking.

She looked at him, pain so plain in her face that it was like a physical force. "Must I keep telling it over and over again?"

"Let her see you are safe, then I will tell her."

Elaine took a deep breath, leaning into Konrad's body, seeming to take strength from his touch. Even through his numbness, Jonathan looked at the two of them and saw something he hadn't before—a couple. He shook his head. Time enough for that.

He opened the door, forcing a smile on his lips. "Tereza, Elaine is safe."

Konrad led her through the door, arm still protectively around her shoulders. Tereza's cry of, "Elaine" and her reaching hand were pure joy.

Jonathan stood back and let his wife have her reunion, her moment of relief and happiness, before it occurred to her that someone was missing. He watched the happy tears and waited.

twenty-six

"SO, BLAINE IS DEAD," TEREZA SAID. SHE WAS THE FIRST one to utter that most final of all words. Jonathan had been thinking them, probably everyone had, but it was Tereza who had the courage to speak.

"Why would the creature carry off his body?" Konrad asked. "And why didn't it kill Elaine?"

Elaine was sitting in the room's only chair. Jonathan sat on the edge of the bed. Konrad leaned against the wall. He was frowning. After the initial surprise at finding Elaine alive, he had gone back to his more typical behavior: frowns, suspicion.

"I don't know why I'm alive," Elaine said. "It could have killed me or let the others do it."

"You're sure the other dead obey some of the better-preserved zombies," Jonathan asked.

She nodded. "I saw it three times, with three different undead. The normal zombies obey the others."

"Why did the female zombie take Elaine to see the cemetery?" Tereza asked.

Jonathan stood and paced to the far wall. He turned and looked at them all.

"You know something," Tereza said.

"Why? Why would anyone raise the dead, kill off a third of a village? Why?"

"Whoever it is is mad," Konrad said.

Jonathan shook his head. "Even madness has a logic, just a peculiar logic."

"Do you know why?" Elaine asked.

"Perhaps."

"Jonathan, no games, just tell us," Tereza said.

He nodded. "What if he is trying to make a better zombie?"

Three pairs of eyes stared at him. Tereza gave a snort of laughter. "Jonathan, why would anyone kill so many people just for that?"

"Remember what Konrad said, that it is madness. Perhaps to a madman, perfecting his undead is worth the cost."

Elaine shook her head. "No, there has to be more to it than that."

"Why, Elaine?" Jonathan asked.

She looked up at him, face solemn. "Because Blaine died. It has to be more than making a better zombie. That's . . . " She stopped, then said, "A ridiculous thing to die over."

"It is the blackest of arts to raise the undead, Elaine. Blaine died to save this village. He died to save you. Those are good reasons."

She stared at her lap and said softly, "There are no good reasons to die."

He knelt beside her, taking her hands in his. Her skin was cold to the touch. "Elaine, you know what we are, what we strive for. It is a worthy goal to destroy evil. It is worth dying for."

The look she gave him was so bleak he flinched. "Blaine was

worth more to me than this cursed village. I beat on a door. I screamed for help, and no one helped me. Not a single door opened. They don't deserve our help."

"Elaine, Elaine, we do not help them for their sakes. We help them because it is the right thing to do. We do the right thing, even when others do not."

"I say, let them die."

He was so astonished at the cold hate in her voice that he didn't know what to say.

"I say we find out who is raising this army and kill him instead," Konrad said. He knelt on the other side of Elaine. His face softened, almost the old Konrad looking up at her, a gentleness in his eyes that surprised Jonathan.

Elaine stared into his face. Jonathan wasn't sure what she saw in his eyes, but it seemed to satisfy her. "Yes, we'll find who did this, all of it, and kill him."

"We are agents of justice, not mere revenge," Jonathan said.

Elaine and Konrad looked at him, and their expressions were almost identical. They said quite clearly that he was a fool. He had become accustomed to the bitterness in Konrad, but it was chilling in Elaine's lovely face.

"We have the same goals," Tereza said suddenly. Her voice startled Jonathan; why, he wasn't sure. "We all want this evil to end. We all want the person or persons behind it stopped."

"We are not vigilantes," Jonathan said. "If we can bring the sorcerer to prison for trial, we will do so."

Konrad and Elaine exchanged glances. Jonathan knew in that instant that they would kill the sorcerer if they had the chance. He did not find it surprising, coming from Konrad. He believed the fighter could kill in cold blood, but Elaine, little

Elaine—could she kill for the sake of vengeance?

He looked at her bleak, pain-filled eyes and believed she could. Some piece of her heart had died when Blaine died.

If Jonathan allowed her to kill in cold blood, that piece would never live again. He would stop her, if he could. But he hadn't been doing a good job keeping his people safe of late.

There was a soft knock at the door, but it opened before anyone could speak. Gersalius stood in the doorway. "I felt your thoughts, your grief. I am so sorry." From the wizard the empty words seemed to mean something.

Elaine nodded. "Thank you."

"If you are well enough, I would show you a spell I have found."

She looked up at that. "What do you mean, found?"

"There is a spell on almost everything in this village. It is subtle, like a trip spell, but it is there. I thought Jonathan might trust my news better if you saw it and explained it to him." The wizard didn't seem offended by that bit of truth.

Elaine glanced at Jonathan, either for permission or confirmation.

Jonathan nodded. "Go with him. Learn what you can and report back."

She touched his face, fingers gentle. "So there is room in the brotherhood for a wizard, after all?"

He glanced back at Gersalius, startled that she had spoken in front of him. "He can read my thoughts, Jonathan. It's hard to keep secrets that way."

"My word of honor that all secrets accidently overheard are safe with me," the wizard said.

Jonathan looked back at Elaine. Her face was calm. She had

faith in the wizard. Jonathan had faith in Elaine. "Very well, go with him. Report back as soon as you can."

"Night will be falling in a few hours," she said.

"Yes," he said, "and we must have answers before then."

Elaine looked down at her lap. "I can heal Tereza's arm." She looked up at him, glancing toward Tereza.

Jonathan exchanged a look with Tereza. He loved Elaine, but he would not let her heal again. It was magic, and it was evil. He believed that. He still believed that. But it was Tereza's arm.

"Thank you, Elaine, but no," Tereza said. She made her voice gentle, as inoffensive as possible.

Elaine took a deep breath. "I am not evil."

"Child, I know that," Tereza said.

"Let us agree to disagree on this one matter," Jonathan said. With his eyes he tried to ask her, please, please let this not stand between us. He had thought her lost for all time. She was back, and he did not want to lose her again, not so soon.

Elaine nodded. "Very well, I think you are both being foolish, but it is your right." She leaned forward and kissed Tereza on the cheek. She brushed her lips on Jonathan's beard, giving it a tug as she had as a child.

"We will not let this stand between us," she said.

Jonathan smiled. "No, we will not."

She gave her hand to Konrad, and he raised it to his cheek, not kissing it, but it was an intimate gesture.

Elaine stood and followed the wizard from the room. Jonathan watched her go, watched Konrad watch her. In the midst of every disaster were the seeds of hope. He knew that, but it was good to be reminded.

twenty-seven

GERSALIUS LED ELAINE OUT INTO THE STREET. THEY had found her another cloak. It was brown and stiff, but warm enough. It wasn't until she was outside that she realized she hadn't taken time to clean off the blood. Gersalius had offered her breakfast, but she had refused; though she felt light and empty, it wasn't food she needed. What she needed was to see Blaine's face, hear his voice, feel the touch of his hand. She needed his death to not be true.

Konrad had hugged her. The softness in his face that she had always longed to see was finally there. What would Blaine have thought? Would he have been happy for her? Or would he have been jealous? She would have given up Konrad's newfound love, if that was what it was, to have Blaine back.

Konrad returned her feelings, at last, and it was ashes in her heart. She walked down the snow-covered street. The cold air touched her face. There was a hood on the borrowed cloak, but Elaine left it down. She wanted to feel the cold on her face. Her hair fell unbound around her shoulders. She hadn't even thought to tie it back. It was so like Blaine's hair. She would see a shadow of him in every mirror for the rest of her life.

Gersalius led her to the town square. There was a fountain in the middle of the paved area, and the water within it had frozen to solid white ice. The ice coated even the figure in the center, making it unrecognizable, though a thin trickle of water still played through the ice. The soft sound of water moved oddly through the silent courtyard, echoing off the two-story buildings that hedged the paving.

"It was a large town once. This is the center of an ambitious town," Gersalius said.

Elaine stood by the frozen fountain and let her breath out in a white cloud. Huge fluffy clouds hung low in the sky, pale gray, as if they held not snow but rain. But it was far too cold for rain.

The gray clouds cast everything in a sameness. The day was as dull and downtrodden as her mood. "Why did you bring me here?"

Gersalius turned to her. His smile died as he looked at her. "I know that right now you won't believe this, but it will hurt less as time goes by."

She shook her head. "Why are we here?"

"This is the heart of the town. It wasn't the first thing built, but it was the center of all their hopes. A fountain in a courtyard, very cosmopolitan. This is the heart of the village, and here is where the spell was laid."

Elaine looked around. "I don't see anything."

"Look at the fountain, Elaine. Open that inner sight and truly look at it."

It seemed like such an effort that she wanted to say no, I can't.

"If we can trace this spell back to its owner, we will find the person responsible for all this misery," Gersalius said. "Then you can have your revenge."

Vengeance, was that enough? No, nothing would ever be enough. But revenge was better than despair.

Elaine took a deep breath of the frigid air and closed her eyes. She held the breath, willing herself to be calm, to quiet the maelstrom in her mind. She opened her eyes slowly. The fountain ran with colors, as if someone had melted wax in the water before it froze.

Elaine brushed her hands over the ice. A line of sickly green, red the color of burned skin, the purple-blue of bruises; one line was iridescent, with many colors. Elaine couldn't decipher it at first, until she remember a drowned man she'd seen once. The last line was the color of a drowned man's skin, mottled and putrefying.

The thin line of free water that still coursed through the ice picked up the colors like a river picking up the dirt of different fields. The water ran black as it pooled in icy pockets, deep enough to dip a small bucket into, deep enough to drink from.

There was a thickness on the water's surface that held all the colors like an oil slick, but sparkling with some inner light that had nothing to do with the weak winter sunlight.

"He poisoned the water," she said, at last.

Gersalius nodded. "Indeed."

"Is it poison or magic? It gleams like a spell."

"Both," he said.

Elaine shook her head. "If it is in the water, then why does everybody rise from the dead, even strangers?"

"Most strangers don't die as quickly as Averil and Blaine. Most have time to drink the water before they die."

She turned to him. "Blaine won't rise as a zombie."

"No," Gersalius said.

"Will Averil?"

"I fear she was given water to bring down her fever."

Her relief that Blaine would rest now forever was spoiled by the thought of Silvanus's having to watch his daughter become a shambling corpse.

"Then why take Blaine's body if he won't rise?" she asked.

"Perhaps exactly because it won't rise on its own."

"I don't understand."

"If only people who have not drunk of the water lie quiet in their graves, then the townsfolk may discover that it is the water."

"Oh, so they took his body to prevent that." Elaine thought of something. "Then whoever is behind all this controls at least some of the zombies. He had the bestial zombie steal Blaine's body."

Gersalius nodded. "Good girl. You are right. Now, let us trace this spell back to its lair."

"I see only the ice and the colors. How do we trace it farther?"

"Open more than your eyes to your magic, Elaine. Think of it as opening a window a little more."

She frowned at him. "I am using my magic. I don't understand about windows and opening them farther."

"You are impatient, Elaine. That will not help things. If anything, it will make it harder for you. Magic does not come at the call of a whip, but of a whisper."

She wanted to cross her arms over her chest and be angry, wholeheartedly angry, but she realized it wasn't the wizard she was angry at. It was her grief twisting inside her, spoiling all with its touch.

Elaine took a deep breath and let it out. With the breath some of the tension left her. She would not let even her grief stand in her way. She would find the maker of this spell and destroy him. It was cold comfort, but it was all the comfort she had.

"All right, I'll try to open your window." She could hear the scorn in her own voice. The wizard had done nothing but be her friend, but in that moment, she hated the whole world. It was hard to work around that, but she tried.

Elaine reached into that cavern deep inside herself. The center of her own magic. She brushed it lightly, scooping some of the blue-violet light into invisible hands. Healing and wizardry had that light in common. She opened her eyes and spread her right hand over the fountain.

"No, Elaine," Gersalius said, but it was too late.

Blue-violet light spilled from her fingers, bounced along the ice, melting here and there. There were small explosions where her lights touched the inner poisons. Bursts of ice bouncing skyward.

The light poured into the black water. It bubbled and boiled as if some great heat were under it. The ice looked as if a monster had been eating at it.

"Send it outward, Elaine. Seek the power that you have touched. Find its home."

She gathered a pool of light into her hand, scooping it from nothing. The light pulsed and glowed, painting her face with violet radiance. She flung the light outward, casting it into the air like a hawk.

The light fell in sparks, bouncing along the ground. Then those sparks rose into the air and raced down the street, like manic violet fireflies.

"After them," Gersalius said. "You have cleansed the fountain, but destroyed the spell in the process. We won't be able to trace it a second time." He lifted up his robes and ran. Elaine followed, skirts caught up in one hand, boots digging into the snow.

The sparks raced like miniature comets in the air, diving around corners. Somewhere near the edge of town, Gersalius leaned against a building and motioned her on, too winded to speak.

She glanced back only a moment, then ran. Her own pulse thundered in her ears. Exhaustion miasma ate at her vision in little dots and squiggles. There was a stitch in her side that felt as if it would tear through her stomach if she did not stop. But short of passing out, Elaine wasn't stopping. Gersalius had said they wouldn't be able to trace it a second time. If she lost sight of the sparks now, it would be her fault. She would have failed Blaine again. Even in vengeance she was failing him.

Elaine fell to her knees at the bottom of a hill. Buildings lined the base of the rise, and a graveyard topped it. She had been here before. The violet sparks whizzed into the trees, lost to sight among the graves.

Elaine stumbled to her feet and climbed the hill on hands and knees, sliding in the snow. The high, spiked cemetery gate, meant to keep wolves out, seemed an insurmountable barrier. She couldn't catch her breath, but through the gravestones she saw a sparkling violet flame.

Elaine leapt up, grabbing a crossbar. She managed to scramble to the top of the fence, feet on the crossbar, hands balancing on the spikes at the top. She threw one leg over, skirts catching on the pointed iron, then toppled, fabric ripping. The cloth trailed in the snow as she forced herself to run toward the glimmering flame.

The violet sparks had coalesced into a flame that burned and wavered through the trees and the grave makers. Please don't go out, please don't go out, she whispered to herself, over and over like a prayer.

Elaine collapsed to her knees in the snow. The flame burned over a grave. It hovered about a foot off the ground, consuming some magical fuel. She saw nothing unusual about the grave. It looked like every other one. She dug in the snow below the flame until her hands ached with cold.

The ground had sunk away as the coffin had collapsed, as the body decayed, and the ground had been dug up and refilled. The soil was still hard frozen, but it was frozen in lumps of bare earth. Grass should have covered the grave long ago.

She scrambled at the grave with her bare hands, digging in the frozen soil. The flame was growing dim, fading. She gave a wordless cry and crawled onto the grave.

"Elaine, Elaine." A voice called her name, but it didn't matter. Hands grabbed her wrists, stopped her from digging. She struggled to break free.

"Elaine, look at me!"

She blinked and found Gersalius holding her wrists, kneeling in the torn snow. The violet flame was gone, and they sat in brilliant sunlight. The clouds were gone, and everything sparkled with a clean brilliance. By that harsh, all-seeing light, Gersalius raised her hands so she could see them.

The nails were broken, blood flowed down her fingers. Her skin was cut and torn from digging in the frozen ground. "Didn't you feel this?"

She didn't trust herself to speak. She just looked at him.

"Elaine, speak to me, child?"

"We must find what is in this grave. The flame stopped on top of it." Her voice sounded normal to her ears. Watching the wizard's face, she wondered what he heard.

"We will dig it up, but I think shovels are in order, and perhaps something to heat the ground." He released her wrists, slowly, watching her face. "Are you all right now?"

She gave a harsh laugh. "All right? I will never be all right again. Don't you understand that? Blaine is dead." She choked on the word. "Dead, and I can't bring him back."

"That may not be true," Gersalius said. He looked very intently at her face as he spoke.

"What might not be true?"

"If we can find the body, you may be able to raise him from the dead, as Silvanus did earlier."

"The body is cold by now."

"If you are powerful enough, that does not matter," Gersalius said.

"You mean if we find Blaine's body, I can bring him back?" She grabbed his arm, as if touching him would make it true. "Are you sure?"

"I have seen men raised that have been dead for days."

"Then we must find his body, we must."

"We will, child." Gersalius patted her hand and loosened her grip on his arm. "Let us see who abides in this tomb." He crawled forward, brushing snow from the grave maker.

"Melodia Ashe, beloved wife, lost in death, missed for eternity. Does the name mean anything to you?"

"No," Elaine said.

"Nor to me, but perhaps it will to the townsfolk." He stood, bracing against the tombstone. "Old knees are not meant for running pell-mell up winter streets." He smiled gently at her. "Come, Elaine, let us go back to the inn and get shovels and strong backs to hack this ground."

She didn't want to leave it. "I'll stay here, to guard it."

"Elaine, no one will tamper with it while we are gone. They could no more dig through this frozen soil than we." He held his hand out to her. "So come, let's go back. The sooner we go, the sooner this riddle is solved."

Elaine took his hand reluctantly. She didn't want to leave, as if kneeling on this old grave brought her closer to Blaine. Leaving seemed like deserting him one more time.

"Please, child, these old bones are cold."

She took his hand and let him raise her to her feet. He led her through the graves, holding her fingers as if she were a child. The warmth of his touch began to warm her skin, so that by the time they reached the gate her sores ached. She'd torn a fingernail completely away, and it was a sharp, aching pain. Her hands hurt, but she almost welcomed it.

If she concentrated on the pain, she couldn't think of anything else. If she could find Blaine's body, she would bring him back. He wasn't really dead. She would bring him back. She would not fail him again.

twenty-eight

THEY ENTERED THE INN TO THE SOUNDS OF RINGING steel and shouting. Elaine ran for the stairs. "Caution might be wiser, child," Gersalius shouted at her back. Elaine ignored him. Everyone she had left was up there. She wouldn't lose anyone else.

Her ripped skirt tripped her on the stairs, and she fell heavily, striking her knee. The pain immobilized her leg, freezing her in place. Voices, shouts, a great bellowing roar of a voice. She'd never heard his battle cry, but it sounded like Fredric. The paladin wouldn't be lightly roused.

Elaine crawled upward, dragging her stunned leg behind her. On hands and knees, she neared the top step. The hallway was a mass of people, struggling. A tall man fought with shield and sword from the doorway where Averil had been. Elaine couldn't see who he fought, but she could hear it.

"Back, damned villains, back I say, or I will slay you all." It was Fredric's voice.

Elaine used the banister to climb to her feet. She stood there for a moment, testing her leg. There was a spot of fresh blood on the step where she'd fallen. She didn't bother looking for the wound. It could wait. The leg would support her now. She limped up the last few steps, leaning heavily on the banister.

Gersalius was behind her. "What is all the fuss?"

She shook her head, staggering down the hall toward the fight. Jonathan's voice came from the open door; he sounded calm enough. "Silvanus, all dead in Cortton rise as zombies. All who die here. You don't want that for your daughter."

Fredric stood in the doorway, his great two-handed sword weaving back and fourth. The armed man who faced him said, "Here, good sir, I am doing my duty as sheriff of this town. I don't want to hurt you. We've all lost someone to this plague. We don't wish to make your grief worse, but we must have the body."

"You will have Averil over my dead body," Fredric said.

"That is a possibility, sir, but I would rather not."

Fredric laughed, a great roaring sound that held enough scorn to draw blood. "It will be you lying dead on the floor, sheriff. And you know that."

Elaine was close enough now to see a line of sweat on the sheriff's forehead. The knowledge of his own death was in his eyes, but he would not back down. His pride meant more than death.

"If you kill me, I want them to burn my body. I don't want to come back as some dead thing. You don't want that for your friend, either—to watch her rot before your eyes night after night. Let us have the body, and she'll just be dead. Dead is better, good sir, much better."

Fredric hesitated. The tip of his sword wavering. Doubt showed on his face.

Silvanus spoke from the room. "They cannot have her."

The sword came back up. "You heard him."

"Silvanus, she is gone, let her go." It was Jonathan's voice.

"You should have sent Elaine to us. She can raise Averil. I know she can."

"She cannot. Thordin says that is magic for a great healer. She has barely begun to learn," Jonathan said.

Elaine pushed through the crowd until she stood beside the sheriff. He glanced at her for a second, then back to Fredric. All his attention was on the big warrior.

"I am Elaine Clairn. I believe Silvanus is waiting for me."

"Elaine," Fredric said, "these fools want to burn Averil's body."

"Will that make it impossible to raise her from the dead?" Elaine asked.

"Elaine," Silvanus called, "come in past these fools."

The sheriff and Fredric eyed each other. Neither seemed to want to move. "Let me in, sheriff. Either I can do what Silvanus wants, or I cannot. But until I try, you won't get this body." He still hesitated. "Night is coming," she said softly.

He moved back, sword and shield held in place. "Go in, but we won't wait forever."

Fredric moved back just enough to allow her inside. Gersalius waited at the door. Elaine glanced back, but the wizard said, "I will gather a digging party and get started on our little project."

"I should be there."

"I can do everything you can do and more. Only you can do this, Elaine Clairn. Only you."

She nodded. He was right, as usual.

The room was crowded. Silvanus huddled with Averil's body on the bed; Randwulf stood at the foot of the bed; Jonathan stood near the window; Fredric guarded the door. One more person, and she couldn't have walked through the room.

Elaine sat on the corner of the pallet. "How do I do it?"

Silvanus moved off the bed, laying Averil gently on the wrinkled covers. Someone had closed her eyes so she looked almost asleep, but there was a looseness to her body that nothing but death could bring. Sleep, or even unconsciousness, could not imitate it.

Silvanus knelt beside the bed. "Place your hands on her body, either over the wound that killed her or over the center of her life, where you feel her life-force was most strong."

Elaine dropped to her knees, wincing. There was a smear of blood on the bed covers.

"You are hurt," he said.

"It is nothing."

He raised her skirt to look, and she let him. It was a deep gash that bled freely. "You can heal this first. Otherwise, it might damage your concentration."

Somehow, Elaine didn't think so. She shook her head. "No, I'll use the pain. It will help me."

He looked at her strangely, but nodded. "As you like. Every healer is different. If you start at her wound, you may begin by healing that, then the other."

"How do you heal death?" Elaine asked.

"You heal the injuries that killed her, and the body will function again. It will hold life again." He shrugged. "I know of no better way to explain. Either you will understand or you will not."

Elaine knew what the "will not" meant to them: it meant Averil dead forever; it meant Blaine dead forever, even if they could find his body. She would do it. She had to do it. She wanted to do it.

"I will leave you to your healing, Elaine," Jonathan said. He moved to the door.

She wanted to call him back but didn't. They had agreed to disagree on this subject. They could be a family as long as Jonathan didn't have to watch her work magic. It seemed a small price.

"Talk to Gersalius. We may have found something," she said.

He nodded, not quite looking at her. Fredric let him out the door, and he was gone.

Elaine tore the bandages from Averil's neck. The flesh was red with infection, greenish round the edges of the bite. Gangrene had already set in. That wasn't right. A wound didn't go bad that quickly. Was it the poison?

She traced the ragged edges of the wound. The skin was hot to the touch. Elaine touched Averil's face. It was cool. Why was the wound hot? It was as if the wound were still alive, and only the body dead.

Elaine pressed her hands back over the wound. It didn't matter. All that mattered was the feel of ruined flesh, the rough hole in her skin. She sank her fingers to the wound, digging in the flesh as she had in the grave dirt. This was a dead body, no one to hurt, no flinching. Elaine could do what she wanted with the body. It would not complain. She could not think of it as a person. It was a neck wound; it was blood loss; it was dead.

She smoothed the deeper injuries, as she had before. The clay of ruptured arterioles, a ragged vein, healed perfectly. Elaine smoothed her fingers over the throat wound until the skin was whole. But still the body was dead. She sat back on her heels, staring, hands still lightly touching.

"I've healed the wound." She let her hands fall back into her lap. "I don't know what else to do."

Silvanus touched her shoulder. "She is empty, you must fill her up again. Fill her up with life again."

"How?"

Silvanus gave a ragged sigh. "I cannot explain this to you, Elaine. Many healers never learn to raise the dead. I do not think it is a matter of ability. I think it is a failing to understand, to visualize death, as just another injury."

"The body is perfect. I cannot heal anything more than I have already. The body is whole."

His fingers dug into her flesh. "Elaine, please. You must see this for yourself. I cannot do this for you." There was something beyond panic in his eyes.

She tasted her pulse in her throat. If she could not save Averil, Blaine was truly dead. But try as she might, she could feel nothing but death. The body was dead, there was nothing to heal.

"Please," Silvanus said.

Elaine tried. She put her hands on the body and searched. She smoothed a scar she found on a kidney, a bit of scar tissue left from some illness. Invisible fingers kneaded and fixed until Averil was better than new—perfect. Still, it was a body. Elaine could not fix what was simply not there. The spark, the soul, whatever word you chose, that which made Averil alive—made her more than just flesh, bone, and nerves—was missing. And Elaine did not know how to put it back.

She realized she was enjoying exploring the body, caressing the internal organs. Enjoying it the way a sculptor did, but no longer as a healer. Elaine was playing with the body, nothing more.

She knelt back; her knee stabbed at her. The pain was raw and fresh. Without looking, Elaine knew it was bleeding again. She explored the pain, not to heal, but to gather. She took the tiny rawness of every scrape on her hands; the greater pain of torn fingernails; the throbbing injury of her knee.

The last thing she gathered was her grief. She found the raw, screaming pain in her heart, her head, her body. She wrapped her loneliness in her hands and mixed it well with the pain. She sent it all into the dead body. She could not give it life. She did not know how, but she could give it pain, rage, sorrow.

The body bucked under her hands, flopping wildly. Elaine fell back to the floor. The body sat up, golden eyes wide and staring.

Silvanus stood, holding his arms out to her. "Averil, Averil." He enfolded her against his chest, hugging her. She was stiff and unresponsive in his arms.

He drew back from her. "Averil, can you speak?"

She opened her mouth wide, wider. The sound that came out was a shriek, wordless, mindless—pain given voice. One scream followed another as fast as she could draw breath.

Silvanus shook her, but she did not see him, did not hear him. "Averil, Averil!" He slapped her. The screams continued. He slapped her hard enough to rock her back against the bed. She screamed lying on the bed, hands curled into fists, body tightened as if with pain.

"What have you done?" Silvanus asked. "What is this?"

"You said to fill her up. I did."

"With what!"

"Pain."

Silvanus dropped to his knees by the bed and the screaming thing that wasn't quite his daughter. "Kill it."

Randwulf said, "What did you say?"

Silvanus screamed, "Kill it, kill it! Oh, gods, kill it!"

Randwulf stood, hands at his side. He had to scream to be heard over wordless shrieks. "No."

Fredric turned from the door, sword point collapsing to the floor. "Silvanus, no."

"Look at it. This is not Averil. This is not human. Kill it, please."

Fredric stood over the bed. Elaine stared from one to the other. She hadn't meant to do anything wrong. She hadn't known what else to do. "I'm sorry, I'm sorry."

The men ignored her. For them the room held only their family. Elaine was not a part of that.

"Fredric," Silvanus reached up and clutched the big warrior's hand. He stood, using Fredric's arm to steady himself. "We will do it together," Silvanus said. His grip on the warrior's wrist tightened. Elaine could see the fingers whiten.

Fredric raised the sword up, with Silvanus's hand on one arm, Randwulf's lighter touch on the other. Tears ran down the young man's face. There were no tears for Silvanus or Fredric.

Elaine crawled backward out of the way. She huddled on the floor, helpless. The only help she could give had been worse than no help at all.

The sword flashed downward, straight through the heart, pinning the fragile body to the bed. The body lay still, blood pumping out of the wound in a thick fountain. It was heart blood, black and rich. If Elaine could have given the body true life, Averil would have lived.

The three men stood over the corpse. Their hands had fallen from the sword hilt. The sword stood upward like an exclamation point, a silver stake through her heart.

Silvanus was the first to turn away. He spoke to the shocked crowd that stood in the doorway. "You may have the body in a few moments. First we need some privacy."

The sheriff himself closed the door without a word.

Silvanus looked down at Elaine. She was huddled on the floor, unsure what to do or where to go. Running away had seemed like cowardice. Staring up into his eyes, she wished she had run.

"Now, Elaine Clairn, we will see to your other healing. Let us find out what other differences there are between your healing and mine."

"What do you mean?" she asked.

"Fredric, show me your arms where Elaine healed you."

Fredric unfastened his sleeves and rolled them up without a word. His face was still blank with shock.

"As I feared," Silvanus said.

Elaine stood, slowly.

Fredric's face was no longer blank. A dawning horror painted his features. She stared down at his bare skin. The bite wounds were gone, the skin smooth, but it was no longer perfect. Something that looked like heavy green scales was growing over his flesh.

Elaine reached out to touch it. No one stopped her. The scales were slick, almost sharp on the ends. They covered the entire area she had healed on his arm.

Randwulf struggled to unlace his own sleeves. His skin was smooth, unblemished. His sigh of relief was loud in the silence.

"Let me see your neck," Silvanus said.

Randwulf's eyes widened. He turned, hands tight at his sides, as if he wanted to reach up and touch his neck, but was afraid to.

Silvanus brushed his hair out of the way, tucked the collar back, and hissed. There was something growing out of the top of his spine. It looked for all the world like a tiny human figure—perfect in every detail, but small enough to fit in Elaine's palm. As they watched, it opened pin-sized eyes and looked at them.

Elaine screamed, backing away.

"What is it?" Randwulf asked, fear raw in his voice.

"A growth," Silvanus said. No one corrected him. No one wanted to say it out loud.

Silvanus stared down at the stump of his arm. He untied the sleeve. "Help me," he said. Fredric cut open the sleeve with his dagger. It was an arm just below the elbow, golden skinned and whole, but its end was black and wormlike. The underside of it was white as a fish's belly, with huge suckers on it.

"What's on the back of my neck?" Randwulf asked. "Tell me."

There was a tiny wailing sound. A thin, high-pitched screaming. Randwulf turned this way and that, trying to see what was behind him. The growth's miniature mouth was open and screaming.

Randwulf started grabbing at it, tearing at it. A minute arm fell to the ground; blood sprayed in a threadlike stream. The arm crawled and flopped. Randwulf was staring at it, mouth wide, screaming silently.

"Cut it off," Silvanus's voice brought them all back from the brink of utter madness. "Cut off the thing," he said to Fredric, pointing to his malformed arm. The paladin slashed at the tentacle. Blood poured onto the floor, green and thick, not human at all.

Randwulf dropped beside the blood, clawing and tearing

at the thing on his neck. The tentacle flopped and slapped at Fredric.

Elaine broke. She flung the door open and ran down the empty hallway. The sheriff waited at the bottom of the steps. He looked up. "Are they ready for us?"

Elaine pushed past him and ran for the outer door. One thought ran through her head: Jonathan was right! Jonathan was right! She was corrupt. She was worse than corrupt.

Elaine ran out into the street, ran into the winter cold and welcomed it. She didn't know where she was going, just away. Away from that room and what she had done. The memory of how good it had felt to do all the healing. Even raising Averil to be a thing of pain had felt good. And some small part of her had wanted to touch the little figure, caress it, enjoy it. To touch the thing growing out of Silvanus's body. She forced herself to be horrified, but in truth she was attracted to all of it. Some part of her would have enjoyed it all, if she had allowed it.

It was that, that more than anything else that sent her running down the street. Part of her wanted to be back in that room playing with the things she had created.

twenty-nine

GERSALIUS STOOD OVER THE GRAVE, FLAME POURING from his hands. They had dumped oil over the dirt so Gersalius's fire would reach far into the melting ground. Beneath the blast of flame, the frozen earth had softened enough that Thordin and Konrad could begin to dig. Each time they reached frozen ground again, the mage sent more fire into the grave.

Jonathan objected to this blatant use of magic, but he was out voted. And there was no time. It was early afternoon. Darkness would fall in a few hours.

Gersalius lowered his hands. Flame licked up through the dirt here and there as the oil burned away. When the fire had died completely, Konrad leapt into the nearly empty grave. He plunged the shovel into the softened earth. The blade grated on something more solid than soil.

"I think we've struck coffin," Konrad said. He dropped to hands and knees in the hole, scraping dirt away with his hands. Thordin lowered himself into the grave and began working at the other end. A coffin did appear, but it was rotted. The wood splintered at Konrad's touch, flaking away in long strips. Thordin brushed the dirt away as carefully as he could. A narrow coffin was revealed.

The foot of the box was completely crushed from rot and the weight of earth. Jonathan peered down into the grave. The sunlight beat down, making the snow sparkle and showed bones and the remains of a patterned dress.

Thordin raised his hand, and Jonathan took it, helping the warrior out of the grave. There wasn't enough room for both of them with the coffin to be opened.

Konrad tried to raise the lid, but the wood shattered in his hands. He finally just started tearing great pieces up and handing them to Thordin, who placed the wood carefully on the ground. The body was mostly bones, with some hair attached to the skull. The dress had been some fine cloth. Fine cloth does not weather well in the damp and mildew of the grave. The cloth was thick with wet-looking mold.

"Why would the undertaker's wife not have risen from the grave?" Thordin asked.

"Better, perhaps, to ask why the spell that raises the dead begins in her grave," Gersalius said.

"Do you know something, wizard?" Jonathan asked.

Gersalius shrugged. "Only guesses, and I see from your face that you may have the same thoughts."

"We need to speak with the undertaker; that I know." Jonathan stared down into the ruined grave. "Where is the sack I had you bring, Thordin?"

"Here." He raised a large burlap sack from the snowy ground.

"Konrad, start handing up the bones."

"Jonathan, we've desecrated the grave enough."

"My theory was that someone was doing all this to make a better zombie. What if that were only part of the reason. What if Ashe wanted to raise his wife from the dead, not as a zombie, but as something more. Elaine told of very lifelike zombies. The townsfolk say that the people who died early are normal zombies, rotting corpses, but the later deaths are better preserved. Ashe is waiting until his spell is perfected; then he will raise his wife."

"But why take her body?" Konrad asked.

"We will use it as a hostage," Jonathan said.

Gersalius smiled. "You can't raise someone from the dead without a body to work on."

Jonathan nodded. "Exactly."

Konrad stared down at the skull with its scraggle of hair. "I can't approve of Ashe's methods, but I understand the desire. Beatrice's death killed me, too." He shook his head as if to clear away a bad dream.

"But Elaine awaits you back at the inn," Gersalius said.

Konrad looked up, startled. Then a slow smile spread across his face. He nodded. "Yes." In that one word, Jonathan heard an end to the long grieving. An end to bitterness.

Konrad began to hand up the bones, freeing them from the molded cloth. Thordin placed them in the sack. The bones made a dry sound as they slithered against one another.

Harkon Lukas sat just down the hill, listening. He had grown cold in the snow. The weak winter sunlight was not quite enough to warm him. They had discovered Ashe's secret much faster than he had wanted them to. He had not counted on the magic-user. Ambrose had such a reputation for hating magic. It had surprised him.

Harkon did not like being surprised. If they questioned Ashe, he might reveal that it was Harkon who had given him the idea for the poison and the spell, Harkon who had whispered in the undertaker's ear that he might raise his wife back to life, Harkon who had broken his mind with talk of rotting corpses and his beloved wife as so much meat for the worms.

He could not afford to have Ashe tell all. He was Harkon Lukas, a bard of some reputation, but not a known force of evil. To have the brotherhood know him for what he was would spoil everything.

He could simply kill Ashe, but he wanted Konrad. Perhaps he could go offer his aid to the undertaker. Yes, that had possibilities. He could be Ashe's ally, and in the process he could betray Ashe, steal Konrad's body, and perhaps be a hero. He laughed silently, shoulders shaking with his inner mirth. Oh, that would be rich, indeed.

He stood and walked quietly down the hillside. He didn't have much time to work his plans. He needed Ashe alive for the trap and dead before he could spill the truth. Needed to appear as Ashe's friend, and his enemy. A neat trick if he could pull it off. And, being Harkon Lukas, he was confident he could.

thirty

ELAINE COLLAPSED AGAINST A WALL. SHE HAD FOUND her way back to the center of town. The fountain's water bubbled and flowed where her magic had melted the ice. A woman dipped a bucket into the freestanding water. A small child, so bundled from the cold Elaine couldn't tell what sex it was, clung to the woman's skirts. She walked carefully across the icy pavement with the full bucket. It was pure water again, the poison burned away, thanks to Elaine's magic.

Of course, the townsfolk were all contaminated. If they died, even of natural causes, they would still rise. There had to be an antidote. Gersalius would know. She leaned into the cold stones of the building and wondered what to do. She could not bear to see Jonathan's face when he learned what she had done, what her so-called healing had done. It was too horrible, and the fact that she was fascinated by it made it worse. She knew that the little man on Randwulf's neck would have branched off, become independent, and she would have kept it, like a pet or . . .

She had wanted it. It had been her creation, and she had wanted to touch it, hold it. She had wanted to hold and caress everything she had made. Every horrible thing. That was a knowledge she hugged to herself, to be shared with no one.

If she asked Gersalius about an antidote, he might read her mind. Would he see the horror in her? Would he read the sickness in her soul? She could not bear it, but neither could she leave the village to its fate.

She hid her face in her hands, shivering in the dying light. Night was coming. If she just stayed out in the streets, the dead would kill her, and she would rise as one of them. Elaine raised her face to the sky, too confused to cry.

A tall man with pale skin and black hair stopped in front of her. "Are you all right?" His voice was kind. She didn't deserve kindness.

"I'm fine."

"I am Ashe, the undertaker. You are Elaine Clairn, are you not?"

She nodded.

"You look cold." He pulled his own cloak off and offered it to her. It smelled of herbs and medicines, and reminded her of Konrad. She took the cloak because she was cold and didn't know what else to do.

"I was told you have been searching for a particular body." He touched her long yellow hair, gently. "One that has hair like this, but a man, your brother."

She stepped away from the wall. The cloak trailed into the snow to puddle around her. "Have you found Blaine's body?"

"Yes, if a body is found in the village, they bring it to me for tending. Would you like to give your last respects? I must burn all bodies before dusk." He glanced up at the darkening sky. "Time is nearing."

"Take me to him," she said.

He placed an arm around her shoulders, one hand lifting the cloak's edge. "Wouldn't want you to trip on the ice."

It was more physical closeness than Elaine was comfortable with, but he was taking her to Blaine. For that, she could put up with a little familiarity.

He hurried her through the darkening streets. The light was failing. A soft blue dusk wrapped the village. He fumbled a key out of his tunic pocket. "The dead will be out soon; we must be inside."

Elaine agreed. He pushed her through the door and locked it behind them. He leaned on the door with a sigh. "Safe, I think."

The room had a richly woven carpet from wall to wall. Brilliant reds, blues, yellows covered the floor in cheerful luxury. The walls were a dark polished wood. Velvet-covered chairs and couches bordered the walls. Lamps gave a warm glow to everything. And in the center of the room on little cloth-draped stands, were coffins.

Each coffin was a different color, a different wood: the near-black of cherry, the thick brown of oak, the paleness of pine. Some had golden handles, some were just painted in gilt. One was white with silver edging—dainty, a child's coffin.

"Don't have much use for these now," he said. "Just wrap the bodies in shrouds and burn them. Only just figured out that fire stops them rising."

He helped her off with the cloak and spread it carelessly on a pale wooden coffin. The cloth looked strangely at home on the wood. "Just upstairs, in my best laying-out room." He took a lamp from a wall sconce and led the way up a broad set of carpeted stairs.

Carved doors bordered the hallway. He stopped before the last door on the left. Again he unlocked the door. "I have found that a locked door can keep the dead in as well as out. I lock all the doors just in case."

Having been on the streets of Cortton after dark, Elaine couldn't argue with the precaution.

Ashe pushed the door inward, raising the lamp high. The pool of golden light fell outward, gleaming in a fall of yellow hair.

Elaine stood breathlessly in the doorway. She could not see his face, but the hair alone was enough. Blaine lay on a cloth-draped table near the far wall. The last rays of sunlight cast only grayness against the windows.

Her breath fogged in the room, and she shivered. It was as cold in this room as outside. The windows were raised to let in the winter night. Cold to preserve the body.

She walked as if in a dream. Even though she had seen Blaine in the street, his death had somehow become unreal. Perhaps this sense of unreality was a kindness. It made the grief less raw. If it simply wasn't real, it couldn't hurt you.

Blaine lay wrapped in rich cloth, hands folded over his chest. His hair had been combed and spread around his face. There was no trace of blood or what had killed him. Ashe was good at his job. In the uncertain light of the lamp, she almost expected Blaine to open his eyes, but she knew he wouldn't. He had never drunk of the contaminated water. He was well and truly dead.

An idea occurred to Elaine. She knew Blaine wouldn't rise from the dead, but how did the undertaker know? The sunlight was almost gone. Why wasn't he burning the body, or locking the door?

Ashe smiled at her. "I was at the inn just after you left. The sheriff told me of how you raised the elf's daughter from the dead."

Elaine shook her head. "It didn't work. She was . . ." She had no word for what Averil had become. Not a zombie, but not alive, not really.

"I know it did not work as you had hoped. I have had that problem for weeks now."

Elaine turned away from her brother's body, giving her full attention to the undertaker. "What do you mean?"

"I lost my wife, as you've lost your brother. You want him alive again, don't you?"

Elaine nodded.

"I want my wife back. I have had some success with other dead, but it is never quite right. You can raise the dead back to life, but it is not quite right. Together, perhaps, we can solve both our problems."

"You poisoned the water. You brought the plague. That's why you hadn't been burning the bodies." Her voice was soft, almost matter-of-fact. It was better than screaming.

"I have been trying to prefect my spell, yes. It was only a few days ago that someone else voiced the idea of burning the dead. I knew it would stop them from rising, but I didn't want that." His face was cheerful in the lamplight, almost self-satisfied. He was mad, completely. Jonathan had been right. He was trying to raise a better zombie. No, that wasn't it. Ashe wanted his wife alive again—not a zombie, but alive.

"I can raise the body, but not the mind. If you've seen the others I've healed, you know what I've done."

He set the lamp on the edge of the table. The light gave a golden aliveness to Blaine's face. "You are very new at healing.

You will get better at it, as I have gotten better working with the dead."

Elaine stared into his smiling face and had no words. What could she say to someone who was crazy? Who had seen the horrors her healing had created and wanted her to continue, to experiment, to get better at it? Ashe seemed to think practice would mean Elaine could heal without deforming the patient. Elaine feared practice would give her control of what deformities she made. She could heal, but at what cost.

There was a sound, almost like an explosion from downstairs. "I think we have company," Ashe said. He didn't sound afraid. He walked toward the door, but did not give Elaine his back. He was crazy, but still didn't trust her completely. He left her the lamp.

"Gaze upon your brother's face while I tend to our company. When I return, you can tell me if you would not spend every ounce of your life-force on bringing him back. I think I know what your answer will be." With that, he closed the door. The key turned in the lock. Elaine was locked in, alone, with her brother's corpse.

thirty-one

Jonathan stepped through the splintered door. Thordin was already in the room, naked sword gleaming in the light of many lamps. Gersalius and Konrad entered behind them. The door had fallen to a combination of Konrad's axe and the wizard's spells.

Jonathan glanced back at the gaping door, and the darkness that sat just outside. "If we can walk through the door, so can the dead. We don't want our retreat cut off," he said.

"Then we'd best hurry," the wizard said. "There is every chance that this Ashe can control the dead his spell has raised."

"You didn't tell us that," Konrad said.

The wizard shrugged, looking a little embarrassed. "I just thought of it."

"The wizard is quite correct," a voice spoke from the far doorway. Ashe stood just inside it, out of sword range. "I can control the dead."

Something crawled into the doorway behind Ashe. It was the undead Tereza had seen that first night, the one that moved with inhuman speed. This was Jonathan's first clear look at it.

Its skin was smooth, but discolored, spotted with patches of odd shapes, like the skin of a snake, mottled and patterned. It opened its mouth and hissed at them.

Ashe touched its head, absentmindedly as though patting a dog. The thing leaned into his legs, apparently enjoying the attention.

"This was the first one that had some mind left, but as you can see, it never progressed. He will always be a loyal animal." The undertaker smiled as he spoke. "Have you missed your little blonde companion?"

Konrad took a step forward, axe raised. "You have Elaine?"

"I found her wandering the streets, quite distraught. She's upstairs with her brother's body. She's quite talented in her own way." He looked at Jonathan when he said the next: "Do you know what she did to your friends at the inn?"

Images flooded Jonathan's mind. He saw again what had been waiting for them at the inn. They had passed it on their way to the undertaker's house, hoping to enlist Fredric and Randwulf's aid. There had been blood everywhere. The stench of burning hair and flesh had been chokingly thick. Randwulf lay on his stomach in the floor, the back of his neck a blackened mass of burned and butchered flesh. Fredric had carved his own arms nearly hollow, trying to cleanse himself of the scales that had burrowed into his flesh.

Averil's body was pinned to the bed, blood everywhere, as if she had died twice.

Silvanus lay on the floor, arm chopped clean and burned on the end. He had grabbed Jonathan's robe and whispered, "She did not do this on purpose. It was an accident."

Jonathan had fled that room to Tereza's arms, only to find her burning with fever. He had left her side not knowing if she even knew he had been there. The wound had gone septic. But after what he had seen in the next room, he was glad Tereza had refused Elaine's healing.

He had led them to Ashe's house through the gathering dusk, determined to end this tonight. There had been no time to seek Elaine, and Jonathan wasn't even sure he wanted to. His worst fears had been confirmed in that small room.

"I think Elaine and I can work together," Ashe said. "Our combined powers should be able to raise the dead in truth."

"Elaine will never help you," Konrad said.

"Oh, I don't know. Lock her in a room to watch her brother's body rot, and she might."

"You're more a monster than any of the dead," Konrad said. He stalked forward, but Thordin grabbed his arm.

"Not yet," he said.

Thordin released Konrad's arm and palmed a small clay jar with a waxed stopper. Jonathan and Gersalius lifted stoppered pitchers from sacks at their belts. They pulled the tops from them. Konrad threw the jar at Ashe, and as the clay shattered, oil splattered over his clothes. Ashe yelled, and the creature leapt.

Thordin fell to the floor with the creature atop him. He dropped his sword—the fighting was too close for that—and scrambled for his belt knife.

Konrad sunk his axe in the thing's back. The spine crunched under his blade. The creature screamed, rearing, and Thordin speared it through the belly with his knife. It screamed again but did not die. Thordin doubled his feet under it and kicked it backward. It landed at Ashe's feet, but scrambled to turn and fight.

The undertaker laughed. "Let's see how you do against more."

The coffin lids slammed back, and the dead crawled out.

Jonathan splashed oil on the dead and the coffins. He heard more liquid spatter behind him and knew Gersalius was doing the same.

Konrad yelled, "Wait! Where's Elaine?"

Jonathan shook his head. He couldn't think of it. He struck fire with flint and steel. Flame sputtered to life.

The creature circled Thordin and Konrad. Ashe turned and ran. Konrad bolted past the creature, leaving Thordin on his own, and gave chase.

Jonathan called, "Konrad, don't." But he was gone, and the oil went up in a whooshing rush. They were suddenly surrounded by flame.

Thordin had pinned the first zombie to the floor. He smashed a jar of oil on it, and the flames crawled over its skin. The thing rolled and screamed as if it hurt. The dead didn't hurt, did they?

The other zombies fell back into the coffins and burned. No screams, no struggles; they died like good zombies should.

Flames ate the rich carpet and licked at the walls. The far doorway was a wall of dancing fire. A backwash of heat chased them toward the shattered door.

"Jonathan," the voice brought him whirling around. Tereza stood just outside the door. The flames showed blood on her face. The varnished panels must have been flammable because they went up in that moment with an intense flame that drove the three of them outside.

Jonathan stepped from the shattered door to his wife, taking her arms. "You're hurt."

She smiled. "It's not my blood."

"You shouldn't have come. We can fight this evil without you."

She glanced at the flames. The room was almost engulfed. Gersalius and Thordin stood to either side. They all looked at the blaze and up to the untouched upper story. Elaine and Konrad were up there, somewhere.

Tereza leaned into her husband's chest, arms wrapping round him. She didn't know. She had fought her way through the streets to find them, and she didn't know Elaine was upstairs.

"We have to do something," Thordin said.

Tereza hugged Jonathan tight. Both arms hugged him. He tried to move her back a step to see her face. Her skin was cool, the fever broken. She nestled against him, arms pressing into his ribs.

"Tereza?" he said it softly.

She spoke with her lips against his neck, cheek nestled in his beard. "Jonathan, I'm so hungry."

Teeth cut into his neck. He screamed and tried to push her away. She clung to him, mouth fastened to his neck, lapping up the blood, digging for flesh.

Thordin pulled her head back by the hair. Gersalius helped peel her off Jonathan. Thordin flung her into the snow-covered street. Tereza stood there, looking just like herself except for the blood on her face.

Gersalius splashed oil on her. She screamed, "Jonathan."

"No!" He took a step forward. Thordin grabbed him.

Gersalius snapped off a flame spell. It arched through the air like a tiny star, then hit the oil with a loud blue rush of heat.

Tereza shrieked, and what she screamed was his name. "Jonathan!"

He collapsed. Only Thordin's arms kept him from falling. The big man lowered him to the ground and sat, cradling him.

She burned. The skin that he had caressed so many times peeled and blackened. The hair went up in a shower of sparks. Through it all, she screamed his name. At the end, Jonathan screamed hers.

She fell forward into the snow, one burning hand still reaching for him.

thirty-two

HARKON LUKAS STOOD IN THE SHADOWS OF THE ROOM, last door to the right. Ashe had come running, with Konrad behind him. It had worked better than Harkon had hoped. Only Konrad had followed. He waited in the shadows, expecting the others.

"Where's Elaine?" Konrad stalked into the room, axe held ready.

"I don't think I'll tell you," Ashe said.

"Tell me where she is, and I won't kill you."

"I don't think you'll kill me at all." He backed away toward where Harkon was hiding. "I think you will be the one who dies." He swept the drapes aside, revealing Harkon.

Lukas had to smile. He did so love a dramatic gesture.

"The bard. What are you doing here?" Konrad said. He stood in a crouch, axe at the ready. He was surprised but still sure what to do. Kill it if it threatens you, no matter who it is.

Ashe was smiling out at Konrad, eager for the show to begin. Harkon stabbed the narrow undertaker through the back. He fell to his knees, a startled expression on his face. His hands groped at the sword point coming out of his chest, then he fell slowly forward, sliding off the sword on his own.

Harkon stepped away from the wall. "We don't have much time. I'll take you to Elaine."

"What were you doing here with the undertaker?"

Oh, he was nicely suspicious. "From the smell of things, we don't have much time. She's locked in. She'll be burned alive."

Doubt passed over Konrad's face.

"I suspected Ashe, but needed proof. When he ran in here, I hid. I was certainly glad to see you."

Konrad lowered his axe but did not put it away. Harkon sheathed his own sword. "We must hurry. Without our help, she'll never escape."

Harkon walked toward him, hands loose at his sides, showing himself unarmed without being obvious about it. "She's just across the hall in the next room." He pointed out the open door.

Konrad turned to look, and Harkon slid a hidden dagger into the man's heart. Konrad gave a wordless cry, and his axe dropped from suddenly nerveless hands.

Harkon lowered the dying man to the floor, holding him close. He grabbed the amulet and tossed it over Konrad's neck.

"Sleep. Sleep forever, my suspicious friend."

Something hit him in the chest, like a club. Harkon stared down to find a knife in his chest. Konrad's hand slipped away from it, and he fell backward, collapsing to the floor.

Harkon grabbed at the knife, trying to stop the blood. It bubbled, hot and wet. He tore it out of his chest with a scream. Blood poured over his hands. Darkness ate at his vision.

Harkon fell forward, on hands and knees. He tried to change into wolf form, but it was too late. He was dying. No, he was dead.

It was his last thought before the darkness ate the light.

Elaine pounded on the door, screaming. Smoke was pouring through the cracks. The door opened inward, and she stumbled backward. Konrad stood there, half-lost in smoke. He grabbed her hand and pulled her into the choking cloud, then into the next room where there was a window with a rope of drapes tied to a heavy chair.

"Climb," he ordered.

Elaine didn't ask questions, there was no time. She grabbed the makeshift rope and climbed down. When she was halfway down the wall, the rope sagged as Konrad climbed on.

"Drop, and I'll catch you, girl." Thordin's voice.

She took a deep breath and let go. Strong arms caught her, tumbling them both to the ground.

Konrad dropped the last few feet, landing on hands and knees in the snow. Elaine ran to him, throwing her arms around him. He hugged her back, face pressed into her shoulder. Smoke billowed out of the window they had escaped from.

With a shuddering roar, the floor collapsed, and flames whooshed to the ceiling. Blaine's body was in there, but clean flame was taking it. It was a better end than the fate of most of Cortton's dead.

Konrad raised his face to hers. He was so close, so close. He kissed her, and she let him. His lips were soft, and his skin smelled of smoke.

The amulet around his neck glinted in the flames. Elaine didn't remember him ever wearing jewelry.

Konrad ran his soot-blackened hands through her hair and laughed. He kissed her again, fierce and hard, as if he would push himself inside her through her mouth. It almost hurt.

Thordin and Gersalius stood over them, watching the house burn. She looked for Jonathan and found him huddled in the snow, beside the burned body of a zombie.

"Jonathan." She called his name, but he didn't move.

Gersalius put a hand on her shoulder. "Tereza came back as one of them. We had to destroy her."

Elaine looked at Jonathan's huddled form. She wanted to run to him, to tell him it would be all right, but in her heart of hearts, she knew it was a lie.

thirty-three

THE IRON GOAT TAVERN WAS CROWDED. THE NEW bard was bringing in a lot of business.

Kelric was a man of medium height but broad shoulders and a narrow waist. He had learned to play the guitar, harp, and harpsichord with larger hands than he had now, but these fingers were long and slender, made subtle by thievery, not practice. He had used that suppleness, re-teaching the fingers to play music rather than lift money from unsuspecting backsides. Kelric Cutpurse had become Kelric Sweetvoice in a matter of months.

He missed his reputation as Calum Songmaster, but at twenty years old, he had years to rebuild his lost fame. Kelric had a higher, cleaner sound to his voice, which Calum quite liked. It was merely a matter of choosing new songs that suited his new voice, a new beginning in every sense of the word.

Harkon Lukas had brought the young Kelric to Calum's bedside. He had placed the amulet on the young man's neck. A few words, and the change had been complete. Calum couldn't even remember a sensation. One moment, he was lying in bed, racked with pain, the next he was standing staring down at an old shriveled man.

It had been so long since he had looked in a mirror that he was shocked. His skin was parchmentlike, wrinkled, hanging in folds from his bones. The skin of his skull had slid downward like half-melted wax. Only his eyes were familiar. Only the eyes were left of what he remembered. Calum Songmaster had died a long time ago. He just hadn't known it.

Those eyes blinked up at him, mouth wide with a silent scream. Kelric had volunteered for this—he truly had—but he hadn't understood. No one could explain the pain. He screamed, wordlessly. The tongue flopped in the toothless mouth, lips so thin there was nothing but the wordless hole.

"I can't, I can't," he screamed. "Take me out, oh, gods, take me out."

"What do you think, Calum? Should we trade bodies back?" Harkon touched the strong, new shoulders, kneaded the new muscles with long fingers.

Calum stared down at the dying body. He looked at the panicked, pain-filled eyes. His eyes. But not anymore, not if he simply said no.

Harkon's lips gave a slow, spreading smile, like those of a well-fed serpent. He stalked to the bed, his gliding walk almost dancelike. He was enjoying himself.

"I will take away this pain, Kelric. I will free you of this terrible burden." He knelt on the bed. "Come Calum, move round so there is eye contact. That is very important."

Calum started to say no, but something in Harkon's face stopped him. He shifted so he could see his old body with a stranger looking out of it.

Only then did he realize it was not just age and illness that made his old face look strange to him. The facial expression was alien, too. It was Kelric's personality staring out.

Harkon knelt, touching the aged face gently. He smiled sweetly, as if tucking the old man into bed for the coming night. Calum half expected Harkon to ask that the man close his eyes, but he did not, instead slowly drawing his belt knife, making a great show of it.

The eyes widened. "No, you promised. . . ."

Calum wondered what Kelric had been promised. What could Harkon have offered for this?

"No, please!" The old man looked at Calum, at his own body standing there. He raised an age-spotted hand out, beseeching, "Help me!"

Harkon lay alongside the aged man. He rubbed the flat of the knife blade along the bedclothes, over the thin chest. "You have failed to grasp something, dear Kelric. He wants to keep your body. He had no intention of ever giving it back."

The pale eyes widened, and the knowledge of the betrayal was plain on his face. His mouth opened, and Calum tensed for the accusations, the recriminations. But the knife slipped upward, touching the soft flesh of the neck. The mouth froze open, eyes wide.

"Get on with it," Calum said with the young voice, his voice.

"And how would we explain slitting his throat?" Harkon jerked a pillow from under the man's head. The man gave a startled sound, and Lukas pressed the pillow over that face. He sheathed the knife with one hand, then bore down with both palms on the pillow. Thin, bony fingers beat at the case, plucked at Harkon's sleeves.

Lukas pressed the pillow down a long time after those frantic hands fell still. He stared into Calum's new eyes, a small smile playing along his lips.

Calum's nightmares had been haunted by that smile.

But then word had come that Harkon Lukas had died in a fire in Cortton. He had died heroically, trying to save the village.

Kelric Sweetvoice gave a bow and left the small stage at the Iron Goat Tavern. The bartender, who was also the owner, slapped his back. "I've never had such crowds. I wish you would you sign a contract with me."

Calum smiled, but shook his head. "I like to be free to go where I please, but I thank you again for the offer."

A second pair of hands clapped him on the back. Calum turned to find Konrad Burn standing before him. He started to greet him as Calum would have, but saved himself, just in time. They were strangers now. This instant recognition was one of the reasons he had gone far away from his old home grounds. Konrad's was the first old face he'd seen.

"You remind me of an old friend, a famous bard named Calum Songmaster. Did you ever hear him sing?"

Calum nearly choked on his drink. He managed to shake his head, not trusting his voice.

"Let me buy you your next drink," Konrad said. "I'd like to request the 'Ballad of Omartrag.' It was one of Calum's favorites."

He found his voice at last. "I don't know it, friend."

Konrad's smile slipped, but he regained his unusual good cheer.

Calum could not help himself, he had to ask. "You seem to be in a good mood, stranger. What's the occasion?"

"I'm engaged."

Calum fought with all the training he had ever had to keep the shock from his voice. "Whom to?"

"You wouldn't know her."

"Give me a name, and perhaps I'll write a song about her."

Konrad laughed; he actually laughed. "Elaine Clairn—perhaps not a poetic name, but she's the most beautiful girl in the world."

"A fiance should always think his woman is the most lovely in the world," Calum said. He wanted to hug Konrad, to tell him how genuinely happy he was that he had found love again. And to find it with little Elaine. . . . Calum wished he could congratulate her, too. But he couldn't. He could never risk seeing them again.

Konrad bought him the drink even though he did not know the ballad. Calum kept slipping glances at this new, laughing Konrad. The change was remarkable.

Calum wanted to say how glad he was that Harkon had died, that Konrad had survived to find happiness at last. But he sang other songs for the patrons, and after a few hours wanted nothing more than to be out of the stifling atmosphere of the tavern. He walked outside into the late spring night, leaving Konrad in the bright laughing crowd.

Calum stood in the small paved courtyard, breathing the faint growing smells of the meadows just outside of town. A sound made him turn.

It was Konrad. He came to stand beside him, gazing down past the city walls. It was so like old times that Calum did not question, did not want to break the silence and be strangers once again.

"Did you really think I died in Cortton?" The voice was Konrad's; the words were not.

Calum turned and found Konrad's face, but the smile on those lips . . .

"Harkon!"

The smile widened. "At your service." He made a low, sweeping bow that looked odd without one of his plumed hats.

Calum swallowed his suddenly pounding pulse. "Are you truly engaged to Elaine?"

"Sadly, no. Konrad has grown strangely distant to our young Miss Clairn."

Some tightness loosened in his stomach. At least he had not brought ruin to Elaine, as well. "Did you enjoy your travels outside Kartakass?"

A scowl fell over those handsome features. "Again, no. I stood at the border of Kartakass for days, but could not cross. I soon discovered that Konrad's body was just an additional form I could take. In a day or so, Harkon Lukas will come out of hiding and take his place among the bards of Kartakass once more. I hope you are enjoying your new body better than I am."

"Well, yes, I am. Kelric is not as strong, but I have another twenty years to practice sword work. Practice makes, well—you know."

"Yes," Harkon said, "I know." He rolled back on the heels of his feet, then forward. Hands clasped behind his back, all good-natured cheer. "I am glad you are enjoying your body. You seem quite pleased with this new lease on life."

"I am."

"Good, very good."

They stood in silence for a moment, but it was no longer companionable. Calum wanted to go back inside the tavern, to be surrounded by song and laughter and life. Standing out in the dark with the creature known as Harkon Lukas was not what he wanted to be doing.

"I'm going back inside. They're expecting another song set."

Harkon turned to him with a smile. His hand came up too fast for Calum to react. The knife caught him just below the ribs, but he did not make that final upward thrust. The pain froze Calum in place, gasping.

"If I cannot have my heart's desire, neither can you." The smile was a slow spreading of lips. It was the same smile he had worn while he suffocated Kelric. The smile that had haunted Calum's nightmares until he heard Harkon was dead.

Calum collapsed to his knees, and Harkon knelt with him, holding the knife in place. "Good-bye, Calum Songmaster." The blade plunged upward, giving a last twist. Harkon's mocking smile chased Calum down into the darkness.

A world of adventure awaits

The Forgotten Realms® world is the biggest, most detailed, most vibrant, and most beloved of the Dungeons & Dragons® campaign settings. Created by best-selling fantasy author Ed Greenwood the Forgotten Realms setting has grown in almost unimaginable ways since the first line was drawn on the now infamous "Ed's Original Maps."

Still the home of many a group of Dungeons & Dragons players, the Forgotten Realms world is brought to life in dozens of novels, including hugely popular best sellers by some of the fantasy genre's most exciting authors. Forgotten Realms novels are fast, furious, action-packed adventure stories in the grand tradition of sword and sorcery fantasy, but that doesn't mean they're all flash and no substance. There's always something to learn and explore in this richly textured world.

To find out more about the Realms go to www.wizards.com and follow the links from Books to Forgotten Realms. There you'll find a detailed reader's guide that will tell you where to start if you've never read a Forgotten Realms novel before, or where to go next if you're a long-time fan!

WELCOME TO THE

WORLD

Created by Keith Baker and developed by Bill Slavicsek and James Wyatt, EBERRON® is the latest setting designed for the DUNGEONS & DRAGONS® Roleplaying game, novels, comic books, and electronic games.

ANCIENT, WIDESPREAD MAGIC

Magic pervades the EBERRON world. Artificers create wonders of engineering and architecture. Wizards and sorcerers use their spells in war and peace. Magic also leaves its mark—the coveted dragonmark—on members of a gifted aristocracy. Some use their gifts to rule wisely and well, but too many rule with ruthless greed, seeking only to expand their own dominance.

INTRIGUE AND MYSTERY

A land ravaged by generations of war. Enemy nations that fought each other to a standstill over countless, bloody battlefields now turn to subtler methods of conflict. While nations scheme and merchants bicker, priceless secrets from the past lie buried and lost in the devastation, waiting to be tracked down by intrepid scholars and rediscovered by audacious adventurers.

SWASHBUCKLING ADVENTURE

The EBERRON setting is no place for the timid. Courage, strength, and quick thinking are needed to survive and prosper in this land of peril and high adventure.